Ben Blackshaw Novels
by
Robert Blake Whitehill

DEADRISE

NITRO EXPRESS

TAP RACK BANG

GERONIMO HOTSHOT

DOG & BITCH ISLAND

BLAST (2019)

Blackshaw Short Fiction

SLUDGE
by
Robert Blake Whitehill
with
Taylor Griffith

PARDON ME
by
Robert Blake Whitehill
with
Erin Blake

DOG & BITCH ISLAND

A Ben Blackshaw Novel

by

Robert Blake Whitehill

TELEMACHUS PRESS

Cover Designed by Carol Castelluccio www.studio042.com/

Cover Art by Buffalo Gouge www.facebook.com/AcrylicNative

Published by Telemachus Press, LLC
www.telemachuspress.com
and
Calaveras Media. LLC
www.calaverasmedia.com

Visit the author website:
www.RobertBlakeWhitehill.com

ISBN: 978-1-948046-01-5 (eBook)
ISBN: 978-1-948046-02-2 (Paperback)

FICTION / Thrillers / Suspense

Version 2018.01.23

PRAISE FOR DOG & BITCH ISLAND

Fast-paced, engaging and addictive from the very beginning. Whitehill's newest installment in the Ben Blackshaw saga reminds us of the enemy within and without.
Cyrus Webb, Media Personality & Top Amazon.com Reviewer,
www.cyruswebb.com

Dog & Bitch Island is an action packed story of intrigue, corruption, and the hunt for a killer. Robert Blake Whitehill's latest entry in the series is a thrilling, clever, and intelligent tale of Ben Blackshaw's unique vision of justice, and right and wrong.
Sandy S. at The Reading Café,
www.thereadingcafe.com

Reading *Dog & Bitch Island* is like being strapped to the front of a runaway train. Whitehill's latest book screams from the first page to the last. With a plot straight out of the real world, you will be out of breath by the end and afraid to pick up the newspaper!
Jeremy DeConcini, Author, Former Special Agent,
www.jeremydennisdeconcini.com

Another high adrenaline scavenger hunt for the recalcitrant Ben Blackshaw. In *Dog & Bitch Island*, Whitehill yet again creates a patchwork of violence and intrigue amongst his characters like a friendship quilt crafted by a sewing circle of the bullet-crazed.
Jack Kolton, Author, Maelstrom Series,
www.jackkolton.com

The Conspiracy King continues his reign in his fifth book, *Dog & Bitch Island*. Ben Blackshaw, who has quickly worked his way into legendary underdog status, investigates the murder of a fellow SEAL and becomes entangled in yet another death-dealing, mysterious cover-up.
R. L. Gemmill, Author, The Demon Conspiracy Series,
www.rlgemmill.com

DOG & BITCH ISLAND delivers another rollicking adventure with Ben and LuAnna Blackshaw and Knocker Ellis Hogan! Whitehill intersperses scenes of stark violence with lyrical descriptions of the Chesapeake. The details Whitehill provides create a verisimilitude that pulls the readers into the story, and keeps them gripping the gunwale through the plot's twists and turns, with a cunning surprise at the gripping conclusion of the Blackshaws' wild ride!
Matty Dalrymple, The Ann Kinnear Suspense Novels and Lizzy Ballard Thrillers, www.mattydalrymple.com

I am soaked, windblown, and thoroughly delighted after reading Whitehill's *Dog & Bitch Island*! Whitehill's crisp writing style makes this another one of the Blackshaw series that's hard to put down. The only reason I did was to empty the water out of my boots!"
Suzanne Crone, writer, *Mirvish Village People, The Spin* (upcoming),
cravethespin.blogspot.ca

Set against the choppy waters of the Chesapeake Bay, and filled with guts and true grit, Whitehill has definitely packed *Dog & Bitch Island* with plenty of intrigue, danger, and adventure. Gear up and climb aboard!
Ted Fauster, Speculative Fiction Author, *The Ross Island Bridge*,
www.tedfauster.com

Whitehill is a shrewd writer, and his characters are smart people. I feel like I know them, although they are unlike anyone in my life. I'd want LuAnna as a friend, but never as an enemy. No one messes with LuAnna. Need I say more?
Gail Priest, Annie Crow Knoll Trilogy,
www.gailpriest.com

In the blink of a mind's-eye, Whitehill's rocket launched narrative blasts through the cranial frame, hurtling the reader aboard a genuine Blackshaw sleigh ride in the hollow point of a .357 magnum. Grab the handrails and hang on for an explosive read and deeply satisfying denouement.

Patrick Skip Bushby, Author,

patrickbushby@author.com

For My Cousin

Walter Robert Whitehill
1952-2017

MACV-SOG, Illinois State Police, Poet, Hero

CONTENTS

Special Acknowledgments

I owe a great debt to my precious family as ever, especially for their forbearance when my attention drifts away from them at the dinner table as I solve a plot problem. I must include profound gratitude to vital members of my extended family, Liza Moore Ledford of Northstar180, my stalwart advisor in the feature film world, as well as Karl Guthrie, my steadfast attorney, and the two most dedicated interns ever, Erin Blake, and Heather Bailey, for their collective wisdom and tireless attention to all things Blackshaw. My sincere thanks also go out to early readers of the manuscript for their pointed and critical encouragement.

I am deeply saddened by the loss of my cousin and friend, Walter Robert Whitehill, who always turned his critical eye upon the Blackshaw books to point out my flaws in both the tactical and emotional truths of soldiery. You will always be missed, sir, just as my books will forever be informed by your hard-won insights.

Dog & Bitch Island is a better book because of all of you.

RBW
1 January 2018
Chestertown, Maryland

DOG & BITCH ISLAND

PART I
MY BODY LIES OVER THE OCEAN

CHAPTER 1

THE BEAUTIFUL SUNRISE on Smith Island in the Chesapeake held no promise of death as far as LuAnna could tell, and certainly no harbinger that she would lend her hand to the deed. She had spent the night consoling a girlfriend after a rough breakup. There was no easy breakup on an island with so few eligible bachelors. In the wee hours, they had baked a traditional nine layer cake together, continuing a chat about the worthlessness of some men until dawn. Now, LuAnna carried half of the cake in one hand as she pushed through the kitchen door of the saltbox she shared with her husband, former Navy SEAL Ben Blackshaw.

It was not a complete surprise that Knocker Ellis Hogan, Blackshaw's friend and former business partner, was already seated at their drop-leaf table. She knew that Ellis's habits, formed first in the army during service in Vietnam, and driven deeper into his DNA later on from working as a waterman, meant he was usually up and about when the rest of the world was still asleep. Ellis and Blackshaw each had a steaming mug of coffee, and the aroma filled their home with a sense of welcome.

More surprising to LuAnna was the fact that the two men were not alone. A lovely Black woman in her late middle years sat at the head of the table, her fingers woven tight before her, knuckles blanched from a pressing worry. Her face was drawn with pain, her breath came shallow. She could have been Ellis's younger sister, with her thin and sinewed frame and her careworn eyes, which were fixed on the pistol resting in the middle of the table.

As Blackshaw studied his wife putting the cake on the counter, he asked, "Is everything okay?"

LuAnna knew he meant her pregnancy, which was well along and without complications. He asked because there had been another pregnancy before, and they had yet to become parents. After his Middle East wartime service, Blackshaw was susceptible to traumatic stress. The miscarriage, and the brutal circumstances that brought it on, had made her husband hypervigilant again; LuAnna could tell he was using every coping tool at his disposal to remain calm.

"I'm fine, Ben." She did not chide him for asking after her health over and over again. There was no sense making him feel bad about feeling bad.

Ellis said, "This is Mrs. Cobbins. Ma'am, this is LuAnna, Ben's wife. It's all right if she knows. LuAnna's good people."

Mrs. Cobbins stood and shook hands with LuAnna, but did not speak.

LuAnna was sure everyone had heard a man's muffled groans coming from the parlor, but neither Blackshaw nor Ellis reacted. Mrs. Cobbins's eyes flared from their natural sadness to an ancient anger. A moment later, LuAnna wondered if she had really seen any change at all in the other woman. Mrs. Cobbins wore the face of long-suffering heartbreak once again.

"Who wants to try this cake?" LuAnna asked. She got desultory replies in the affirmative. Everyone must have been hoping to push past these strange pleasantries, but was unsure how to go about it. She pulled a long knife from the wood block and sliced four pieces onto plates in hopes their thin yellow layers and fudgy icing would irresistibly move things along. LuAnna sat with the plates and some forks, and distributed paper napkins from the dispenser they kept on the table. "Oh, will the fellow in the other room be wanting any?"

No one answered. They all took up the forks but only picked at the cake. Rather than take offence that her delicious offering was so tepidly received, LuAnna tried another tack, and poked her fork toward the pistol on the table before them. "Nice gun. Ruger SR45?"

"It's the gun used to kill my boy," said Mrs. Cobbins.

Gears meshed in LuAnna's recollection. She said, "You're Delia Cobbins. Your son is Sh'iah Cobbins."

"*Was*," said the bereft mother without a trace of self-pity.

"I'm so sorry for your loss," LuAnna said. "It's terrible what that man did."

"He felt afraid. He stood his ground," said Mrs. Cobbins. "Stood his ground against my boy. You know he was a Down child?"

"Yes," said LuAnna. "Fortis Entwistle is a very bad man." In truth, LuAnna was not so much sorry as she was furious that a boy could be gunned down and the killer would suffer nothing more than a few missed days at work. It utterly galled LuAnna that Entwistle's shiftless, fear-stunted life had actually enjoyed an injection of notoriety, Alt-Right radio talk show bookings, and an offer of a book deal from a small, fascist-leaning press.

"That's not what the judge said," replied Mrs. Cobbins. "Entwistle stood his ground—against a boy walking away."

There was a louder outburst from the living room, as though a man was screaming beneath a truckload of blankets.

LuAnna asked, "What exactly is happening here?"

Ellis glanced at Mrs. Cobbins. She shrugged a kind of silent approval of Ellis doing the honors answering LuAnna.

He said, "Seems after Travis was murdered, and after the judge ruled how he did, the gun that Entwistle used to kill the boy was returned to Entwistle."

"That gun right there," LuAnna confirmed, leaning toward the weapon.

"Yes," answered Ellis, when it was clear Mrs. Cobbins was not going to speak. "And then Entwistle put that damn thing up on eBay to auction it off. Like folks would want it as a souvenir in defense of the Second Amendment."

Blackshaw said, "For goodness sake, the Second Amendment's not going anywhere."

A hard, dark look crossed LuAnna's face. In a quiet voice, she asked, "Did anyone bid on the gun, Ellis?"

Ellis said, "I did." When he saw LuAnna's pained expression he went on, "Of course, there were a couple other fellows bidding, too. And one had deep pockets."

"But not as deep as yours," said LuAnna.

"Obviously," said Ellis. He had made millions with Blackshaw on two separate clandestine missions, but offshore tax havens and a simpler life-style closer to home kept him from drawing attention from the IRS and other nosey authorities. Yes, Ellis had a few large-ticket luxury items stashed here and there, but they were owned by shell corporations, and his name was nowhere to be found on the paperwork.

"So you bought the gun," said LuAnna, "but not as a souvenir."

"Of course not," said Ellis. "I wanted that thing off the market."

LuAnna narrowed her eyes at Ellis. "But you really wanted it as bait."

"Guilty," said Ellis. "I outbid everybody so I could take possession of the gun in person, and meet Fortis Entwistle face to face. Made that a con-dition of the sale. Said I wanted his autograph. Sonofabitch said *okay*."

There was a gagged shout from the parlor.

LuAnna said, "And that's Fortis Entwistle in our parlor, Ben?"

Blackshaw said, "How'd you guess?"

LuAnna turned to Ellis and said, "You brought him here."

Ben said, "You were out for the evening."

Ellis said, "I offered Mrs. Cobbins an opportunity to meet her son's murderer in less official surroundings. She'd seen him in court, of course."

"Okay. So, what now?" LuAnna asked.

"We were just discussing that," said Blackshaw.

"Mrs. Cobbins," said LuAnna, "Have you spoken with Fortis Entwistle? Has he given you satisfaction for what he did?"

"He said he was scared when he saw my boy coming home at night. I asked why did he follow him? He said my sweet boy looked suspicious."

CHAPTER 2

ELLIS WATCHED LUANNA. He knew she was made of stern stuff, but he was surprised she didn't balk at what he'd done, luring Entwistle. And she did not rail at Blackshaw for bringing the matter to their home. That didn't mean she wasn't angry. She had a tan, but underneath it was a pallor of fury. Motherhood was a sacred subject to LuAnna, and Ellis could tell she had put herself firmly in Mrs. Cobbins's shoes and walked the hellish mile. It was clear she was stricken with pain at the thought of raising a boy from a baby only to have some runt-hearted skell put that child down like a dog to see what killing felt like, to see if it made him feel like more of a man.

LuAnna said, "Mrs. Cobbins, Mr. Entwistle is an evil stain. I ask you again, did he give you satisfaction?"

Mrs. Cobbins's shoulders shook with silent sobs. Tears welled in her eyes. She said, "How could that animal give me satisfaction while he still draws breath?"

Ellis saw LuAnna nod, more to confirm something inside herself than to agree with anyone else present. Then she stood, tossed her honey-blonde hair out of her eyes, and wiped the yellow cake crumbs and chocolate from the long steel blade. Knife in hand, she left the kitchen for the parlor. There was one last muffled shout from the other room, but it ended quickly.

CHAPTER 3

BLACKSHAW HOISTED THE heavy end of the body off the deck; Knocker Ellis hefted the feet. The corpse came down with a thump onto *Miss Dotsy's* washboards.

LuAnna muttered to Ben, "Lift with your legs."

Blackshaw wondered if she merely thought he was getting geezerly enough for such advice, or if she had actually spotted the sharp twinge in his lower back showing up in his face. Though it was many years since Blackshaw had gone through BUD/S Hell Week at Coronado (and yes, subsequent DEVGRU missions had taken their heavy toll on his body) it was a sad state either way, with LuAnna pregnant out-to-there with their first child, and his back paining like an old man's. He noticed that, as ever, neither the exertion nor the grim bite of the job twitched a single muscle in Ellis's deep brown face, and he was north of sixty.

"Did you have to use my good crab pot wire?" Blackshaw asked.

Ellis frowned as he inspected the shiny mesh encasing the corpse head to toe. "Folks at the hardware store would look askance if a waterman bought regular chicken wire instead of the good, twice-galvanized stuff. You raising yard birds?"

Blackshaw shook his head. "Outside a stew pot, I hate the things. The way they look at you. It's like they know."

"And everybody, including folks down to the hardware store, know that too. This stuff was already to hand in your crab shanty." Ellis flicked a disapproving glance at LuAnna. "Not like we were left with much time for niceties either way."

Pressed between the wire mesh and the corpse lay that kitchen knife, the once-bright blood on its edge drying ruddy. There was still gore under LuAnna's fingernails. There was a pistol under the wire, too. *The* pistol.

"If he swells from rot, the wire should cut him, vent the decomp' gasses, and keep him from bobbing up again," LuAnna said.

Blackshaw glared at his bride.

LuAnna stared at the deck. "I saw it in a movie. *Sabotage*. Schwarzenegger's best work, if you ask me."

In case the movie gimmick failed, Blackshaw and Ellis had wired the rear axle of a derelict pickup truck lengthwise along the body for extra weight.

"Now, it's sixty foot deep here," said Ellis. "No oysters, no clams, nor mussels. Nobody's going to tong, dredge, or scrape these parts." He put both hands on the parcel and coiled down to push. As an afterthought he straightened and asked, "Anybody want to say a few words?"

Mrs. Cobbins, the fourth living soul aboard, slowly stood up from her place forward by the cuddy cabin, and inched her way aft against the Chesapeake's swell holding tight to the deadrise's side. As tears worked their way down through wrinkles toward her proud chin, she studied Fortis Entwistle, giving special attention to the eyes already clouding with postmortem cataracts. She hawked up a gobbet of phlegm from deep around her heart and spat in the dead man's face. With a howl of grief and rage, she shoved the body over the side where it disappeared with little splash.

She met their astonished gazes one by one and said, "Thank you. You've been so kind. Thank you."

As Mrs. Cobbins inched her way forward again to her place, Ellis started the engine, and Blackshaw pointed *Miss Dotsy*'s bow back toward Smith Island.

~~~~

Later that afternoon, Ellis took Mrs. Cobbins aboard *Miss Dotsy* to Crisfield on the Eastern Shore. A nephew was to meet her at the city pier, and drive her through the rain back to the rest of her life in Georgia secure in the irredeemable knowledge her son was avenged.

At Blackshaw's saltbox, LuAnna busied herself cleaning up the parlor where she'd used the knife. As if she were making a kind of penance, she wouldn't let Blackshaw help at all. Yet Blackshaw did not blame her in the least for what she had done. He was proud of her, though he wondered if he should be. Once again, the usual moral code by which most people lived seemed to have a deeper encryption understood only by Smith Islanders.

"It was brave of you," Blackshaw said. "You didn't have to. Ellis and I—"

"You were sitting on your butts jawing, and that poor woman was in such terrible pain. It couldn't wait. I couldn't wait. No mother could, nor should." LuAnna scrubbed the floor for a moment more before rocking back on her haunches. "Though it might've been hormones."

Blackshaw laughed until her glance cut the mirth out of everything. He asked, "Do you want to talk about it?"

LuAnna said, "Maybe you should go out and meet Ellis when he comes back. Make sure *Miss Dotsy*'s all tidied up."

"We saw to it already. She's clean as a whistle."

"Go meet him. Double-check."

Blackshaw got the message, threw on a slicker, and stepped outside into the drizzle.

CHAPTER 4

SOMEONE POUNDED ON the saltbox door. LuAnna knew it wasn't Blackshaw; it was their place for goodness sake, and it was his alone before they married. Even when he was in the doghouse, he would never cringe, nor tip-toe, nor skulk, nor God forbid knock. Ellis usually rapped a couple times, then stepped inside without waiting for any kind of by-your-leave. He knew coffee was always on for him. Neighbors with any sense, and that was most of them, usually phoned ahead before stopping by. The Blackshaws were known to be armed and prickly, and LuAnna never did a thing to change that perception.

She dropped the scrub brush in the bucket, used the wall to help her stand, and waddled her belly to the door. She drew her Beretta .25 Jetfire, let it hang in plain sight by her side, and opened up the door.

A pretty White woman in clever city maternity clothes, and a hunky older Black man all betweeded like a Purdey squire, waited on the stoop. The stoop was wide enough, but they stood closer than need be. LuAnna knew a couple when she saw one. From her time with the Natural Resources Police, she could also spot a Fed or two, even without the flip wallets and gold badges they were holding out. They both eyed her pistol which was only fair.

"It's not loaded," LuAnna said.

The woman spoke. "We're Agents Molly Wilde and Pershing—"

"—Lowry. I can read. I didn't hear a helicopter. Don't you fly around in a helicopter? You did last time you came by, so I'm told," LuAnna said.

Lowry said, "The last time, the bird went home with a pumpkin ball slug in it."

"I was poorly then, and can't recall. Was it deer season?"

Wilde said, "No."

"Imagine that," said LuAnna. "I guess for some 'round here, it's always Fed season."

"If you're LuAnna Blackshaw, then you're ex-NRP yourself." Wilde said, obviously trying to gain some ground showing off personal intel.

"*Former* NRP," corrected LuAnna. "Not ex. Retired. And I didn't shoot your whirlybird. Is that why you're here? You got a bill from the body shop? That was some time ago."

LuAnna tried not to smile as the agents stood there getting soaked in the strengthening rain. She knew she should take pity on a fellow mother-to-be, but for a moment it amused her that, like vampires, the agents could not cross the threshold until invited. They were not flapping warrants around, after all. At least not yet.

"We'd appreciate a word with your husband," said Lowry.

LuAnna cast a glance around the yard. "He was here a minute ago."

Wilde asked, "Did he say where he was going? When he'd be back?"

"Smith Island's got maybe four-point-five square miles of land and less and less every day," LuAnna said. "He can't have gone far. I can't stop you if you want to look around."

"May we wait inside?" Lowry asked, water dripping from his trilby's brim. "That's if you expect him soon."

LuAnna stepped back from the door, slipped the Jetfire into its holster, and watched the woman's nose wrinkle from the chemical smell of the cleaning bucket as she came in.

"That's a lot of bleach," Wilde said. "We're interrupting."

"Maid's day off. Coffee?"

"Black," Lowry said. Wilde dittoed.

"No cheese? Have a seat in the parlor there. I'll only be a minute," LuAnna said.

"Your gun's really loaded, isn't it," Wilde said.

LuAnna stopped at the door to the kitchen and looked over her shoulder at the agents. "Of course it is, hon. Where the hell do you think you are?

CHAPTER 5

AGENT MOLLY WILDE studied Blackshaw. The subject of their interview had finally come home. There followed an awkward half-hour sipping coffee and pretending everything was fine. Wilde and Lowry had crossed paths with Blackshaw on two previous cases, but this was the first time she had seen him up close, where he could not drop his information bombs and bolt away. He had even saved Wilde's life once, but he did not stick around for the least praise or thanks, likely because he had broken reams of laws in the doing. Today, at least at first, he seemed grateful that nothing from their strange shared past was coming back to haunt him. Wilde and Lowry bore other bad news this morning. He took it the way you would expect of a soldier. His face went gray, and he spent a few moments picking at the cracked leather arm of what must be his favorite chair in the parlor.

Then Blackshaw asked, "And you found Travis—where?"

Wilde said, "On Dog & Bitch Island."

LuAnna said, "By Ocean City?"

Lowry said, "Yes. Isle of Wight Bay."

"It's all sand. It's tiny," said Blackshaw.

"Bold words from a Smith Islander," Wilde said. Needling was usually not part of her non-hostile interview style, but she couldn't stop herself.

"What was he doing there?" LuAnna asked.

"We're trying to figure that out. Ben, we need to know when you were last in touch with him," Lowry said.

Blackshaw seemed on the verge of replying directly, but then he said, "Travis has family. Why aren't you asking his wife?"

Wilde watched Lowry weigh his reply. She knew he would never say more than necessary, but sometimes tactically he gave a little in order to strategically yield a lot.

"I guess that answers my question," said Lowry after a moment. "Lieutenant Cynter and his wife have been divorced for over five years. There are no children, so there's been no direct contact between them in over four years."

Blackshaw surprised everyone when he said, "No. Trav and I talked on the phone three months ago. First time in a good while, sure, but not one word about him and Polly splitting up. You think you know a person..."

Damn this guy's good, Wilde thought. Blackshaw had risked volunteering a small detail, pointing to a lack of intimate knowledge of the deceased, just to make himself appear less valuable to the investigation. *Brilliant.*

"How long did you serve with him?" Wilde asked.

"Eight months in Iraq. Ten months in Afghanistan."

Wilde followed up. "And the missions?"

"Classified." Blackshaw's expression almost, but didn't quite say Wilde should have known better than to ask.

"Back to your phone call with the Lieutenant," Lowry said. "What *did* you talk about?"

"He said he was home a while, and was sorry we hadn't caught up face to face. And he was going in-country again soon. But not where to. The usual." Blackshaw picked at the chair arm, and seemed baffled and upset when a piece of leather the size of a stamp came off in his fingers. "It happens. I've been out a while, and he was still in. You lose touch. You lose that rhythm. The bond. Even though you've been through hell and back together, since then, he'd been on missions that I hadn't been on, been through difficult things I hadn't, and he can't say what exactly. Not allowed to. You know how it is. Serve together and the hardships bind you. Miss a mission, and it's a great story. Miss years of missions, they drive a wedge between you."

Stonewalling again, thought Wilde. Then she said, "You haven't asked about cause of death."

"Plenty ways to get dead, even stateside" Blackshaw said.

LuAnna added, "You're saying it wasn't a boating accident."

Wilde thought, *She's just as good as her husband, maybe better*. Then Wilde found herself wondering if she and Lowry would ever be as harmoniously synchronized as this couple.

Lowry reached into his coat pocket and removed a small clear evidence bag. A mangled copper colored bullet lay inside it. "It entered his left shoulder through the left strap of his rifle plate carrier, and after tumbling through his heart, stomach and intestines among other things, it lodged against his left pelvic ilium."

Blackshaw did not bat an eye. And he did not touch the evidence bag. "He was shooting seated."

"He was prone," corrected Lowry. "Based on how we found him."

"Beg to differ," Blackshaw said. "That bullet is in too good a shape. If it came in fast and flat, with a lot of energy, it would have deformed a lot more. But it's all pretty, like it came in high and downward at end of its trajectory. He was shot from a good ways off, and he was sitting, leaning forward."

"We found him prone," Lowry insisted.

"How many shooting victims do you find dancing a hornpipe?" Blackshaw challenged. "They're going to be prone, or supine, or left-lateral recumbent, or right-lateral recumbent, or someplace in between. Death is relaxing that way. Most everybody lays down. You said he was wearing a vest on U.S. soil. A training accident?"

"Nope," said Wilde. "But he was armed, and in full tactical gear. Not just the vest. Now what do you think?"

"Don't you have people for this? I think that bullet's a .338 Lapua Magnum Very Low Drag. Effective range between a thousand and seventeen hundred meters. But since it petered out inside him, I'm guessing it was fired from the far end of that range."

"Unless—" Wilde fed.

"Unless it's what I think it is. A beefed up British round," Blackshaw went on. "Shot from an L115A3 Long Range Rifle. Travis is tall. Was. Plenty of meat for that round to tumble through."

"Agreed. So maybe a British sniper weapon. In that case, what kind of range are we talking about?" Lowry asked.

Blackshaw said, "The all-time confirmed record with that setup is two-point-two miles. A Canadian Spec-Ops fellow. Joint Task Force 2."

Wilde sensed Blackshaw was hedging. "Is that the longest kill-shot you know of?"

Blackshaw was almost coy. "The longest confirmed one."

Wilde felt a chill run down her spine. LuAnna must have sensed it too, because she refilled Wilde's coffee cup from the carafe beside her, and said, "You think he was deployed and killed on an operation on American soil, or he was shot someplace else, and his body was moved post mortem to Dog & Bitch."

So much for playing the sassy redneck chick, thought Wilde. LuAnna's former cop instincts were coming through.

Lowry said, "There was evidence he died on the island where he was found. Not very much blood at the scene, because he died quickly, but enough to be conclusive he was struck where he lay. Or sat, if you prefer."

Then Blackshaw surprised them all again. "How'd you two Feebs catch the case? It's murder, and that's local stuff. Who brought it to you?"

Wilde smiled. "Classified."

Blackshaw ignored the barb and shot back, "No it's not. It was Homeland dropped this in your lap. Or a Company spook. There's a G-WOT angle, but it's hinky, or you wouldn't be sitting here chugging our coffee."

Lowry conceded a little more intel. "Yes, you're right. The Global War on Terror is part of this, but even we aren't clear how."

"Don't tell me," said LuAnna. "It's our duty as patriots to un-stupid this mess for you."

"He was your friend, Ben," Lowry said. "A brother in arms. You'd help just to set things right by him."

Wilde was more direct. "Do we need to crack open that business at Dove Point, and your involvement? A lot of VIPs killed. Not a whole lot of answers to this day. Or how about that shit-storm in Arizona a couple months back. Be a pal, Ben. I could still get you a bunk at Leavenworth. Gitmo's not closing up any time soon."

LuAnna stood so fast her chair almost toppled. Leaning close in to Wilde's face she hissed, "You little bitch! You'd be dead if it wasn't for him!"

Bingo. Wilde guessed the former cop might have had her own piece of those cases beyond the little woman waiting for her brave soldier man to come home.

There was a coldness when Blackshaw told Wilde, "Swagger die, I don't know what you mean."

Two sharp raps on the front door. Knocker Ellis stepped into the parlor and sensed the fuse flaring fast toward the powder keg. From previous dealings, he recognized Wilde and Lowry on sight. "Well ain't this some dickery-fuckery. You two lost?"

LuAnna said, "They were just leaving."

"One way or the other," said Blackshaw.

CHAPTER 6

AFTER LAYING IN ample stores aboard *Miss Dotsy*, Blackshaw, Knocker Ellis, and LuAnna cast off from the saltbox pier on Smith Island. From there, they bore down the Chesapeake past Tangier Island toward Cape Charles at the southern tip of the Eastern Shore, and then east to the Atlantic. The boys had tried to talk LuAnna into staying ashore. That had backfired and just made her want to go all the more. They should have known better.

Wilde and Lowry had boogied off Smith Island by the afternoon boat soon after Ellis's arrival at the Blackshaw saltbox. LuAnna hoped those fools would think twice about coming around again. As a former law enforcement officer herself, an outlaw's change of heart the year before had made it hard for her to tolerate her husband's weird, delicate bond with those Feds. Blackshaw had helped focus their investigative resources, sometimes as a volunteer seeking his own intel from those who had it, and sometimes not meaning to. Truth is, whatever good Ben did always meant some law-bending of his own, along with the agents' willingness to look the other way to close a nasty case file. Until now, they'd kept quiet, accepted the assist, and left him alone. By damn, LuAnna thought they owed Ben some peace for all he'd done! Never had Wilde and Lowry tried to strong-arm or threaten her man into seeing his way to do right. What a mistake! He never took an order from the likes of them, no matter how heavy the lifting, no matter how bloody things turned out. And yet here he was, off to the races again aboard *Miss Dotsy*.

LuAnna reflected that Ellis sure was an interesting piece of work. Since coming into his fortune, he kept a sweet Escalade in a garage on Crisfield for his road trips on the main. As if that extravagance wasn't enough, Ellis also held a Bugatti Veyron captive in his Smith Island shed, a two million dollar supercar with less than thirty feet of dirt path on his little private hummock to drive it. For a while he had just liked to rumble and snarl it the few car-lengths from the shed to his mailbox by the water. He'd pick up his bills and Playboy Magazines, then he'd back the beast right up into the shed again, just because he could. But he'd taken things a step farther when he cut that Veyron's roof off, filled the car with dirt, and planted geraniums in it, like money didn't mean a thing.

Now, the Escalade, that would have been so much more quick and plush than taking the long way around to Ocean City by boat. By road, the trip was just an hour's hop across the Delmarva Peninsula instead of two days on the water in *Miss Dotsy*. But Blackshaw was Navy always and forever. A boat was his way. She saw his point. This way there'd be no need to rent some puke-sobbed tub in OC to get out to Dog & Bitch Island, and no questions asked.

LuAnna still regretted her outburst at the FBI agents the day before. Even if she hadn't exactly incriminated Blackshaw in past troubles, she had confirmed she knew a thing or two about the doings herself. For the second time in a day, Blackshaw had assured her she'd done no wrong and caused no harm. He was so sweet and patient it utterly burred her britches, and left her wishing she held tighter reins on her temper and tongue. Making a baby was making her a madwoman. Where was her share of the pregnant lady's angelic glow? The sunbeams of Jesus sure weren't shooting out her susie, that's for damn sure.

They'd rounded Cape Charles, and were bearing north again, leaving Chincoteague Island to starboard when LuAnna had to say something. "They're playing you, Ben. They're playing both of you like an old cheap banjo."

"A cheap one?" Blackshaw said.

"And not new. Second hand. Poorly cared for," LuAnna said.

If Blackshaw stayed quiet after that, Ellis sure didn't. "You don't think we know it? What's he supposed to do when his buddy's dead?"

"It's okay Ellis," Blackshaw said. "For all their questions, they were telling me things I'm glad to know."

LuAnna shot back, "They all but said you did it! Do you know what *person of interest* means? Lucky you didn't break out in manacles right then and there! And me on my knees swabbing up that other bastard's guts when they come knocking. I almost went into labor when I saw those badges. Hello Braxton? Meet Hicks!"

Blackshaw said, "Their coming by was a sign of how bad things are for them."

"It's not always a compliment to be needed," Ellis said.

"You heard them," said Blackshaw, checking *Miss Dotsy*'s course and depth of water. Sandbars had a way of shifting, even in the littoral Atlantic, especially inshore of barrier islands. Though the deadrise drew no more than a whisper, she wasn't a crab scrape, and couldn't float on dew. "It wasn't their case to begin with."

"I've got strong feelings about picking up side jobs in the Army from no-account brass, and I'm sure as hell against it as a civilian." Ellis tried to hide his anger by dipsticking the fuel tank. He was vicious about it, like a man churning butter after hearing his cholesterol was through the roof. She understood his leery view of government jobs. LuAnna knew that Ellis and Ben's father, Dick Blackshaw, had a death sentence hanging over their heads because of off-the-books missions they had accepted in Vietnam.

"Where's the percentage in it?" finished Ellis.

"Sleeping better knowing I've done the right thing," Blackshaw said.

"It's called Ambien, honeyboy," LuAnna said. "You should get some."

"I must have missed something before I came in," said Ellis.

"Trav was likely operating too close to home turf," said Blackshaw.

"*Deployed* kind of operating? He was on the job?" Ellis topped off the gas tank from a jerry can, but his pour was splashy. Usually not a drop touched the deck even in the wickedest Chesapeake chop. A strong steady hand was a point of pride for him in all things fueling and gunning.

"Give or take," Blackshaw said. "Full kit and load-out. And he might've been taken down with an Alpha-3. You didn't see the bullet."

"That's British stuff," said Ellis. The man knew his shooting iron, LuAnna had to give him that.

"Or Dutch. Or Norwegian. Hell, even the Russians bought a few." Blackshaw corrected his course with a gentle lean forward on *Miss Dotsy*'s vertical, starboard side tiller. They had left Wallops Island to port, getting out of the Atlantic, hiding from its longer swells behind Chincoteague Island. Now Assateague shielded them to starboard. When he saw Ellis's face droop into his socks, Blackshaw added, "You didn't have to come along. Neither of you did."

"You're welcome," said Ellis.

"My child will have a living, breathing daddy," LuAnna said. "Not some dead man's picture on the wall. I'm seeing to that personally, no matter what kind of stupid you get up to."

"Your vote of confidence is duly noted and recorded by the clerk. Ellis, we've talked about you and adrenalin. LuAnna, I have no idea why you're here, with that nice shower the ladies were planning for you."

"Shut up, Ben. I'm busy making ears for your baby."

LuAnna was thoughtful for several minutes before she said, "Ben, you know you can tell me anything."

"Yes, I know that," said Blackshaw.

LuAnna watched Ellis squirm as he sensed a private conversation between husband and wife coming on, and him with no place to retreat to on the small boat to give them privacy.

LuAnna continued, "You talk to Ellis all the time about soldier's business."

"He understands those things," Blackshaw explained.

LuAnna was having trouble choosing her words. "I understand a few things myself, Ben. Not from the military, but from when I was a cop. I saw things. Drowned men. Men murdered. And not too long ago, I took a bullet in that mess on Dove Point. Put me in a damn coma while you were strutting around in Arizona. You do remember."

"Reckon so. It broke my heart," Blackshaw said.

Blackshaw's broken heart had drawn him away on walkabout to the desert, rather than to her bedside, but LuAnna picked her battles and let that one go for the moment.

LuAnna went on, "You can talk to me, too, Ben. Not just to Ellis. I've lost. I've bled. It might make you feel better, sure, but I'm saying this more because you're hard to read. I need to know what's going on in your head. In your heart. Talk to me too, Ben."

"Okay," said Blackshaw.

"Just to be clear, I'm not *asking*." LuAnna knew Ellis was easier to talk to but that could change.

Blackshaw steeled himself, and made a stab at this intimacy LuAnna demanded.

He said, "My friend's dead, LuAnna. I don't know what I should do, or where I should be doing it. Standing at his grave and mumbling a prayer, that doesn't seem like the right thing. If I'm to feel any peace, I need to know what happened to him, and why, and who did it. Does that make sense in the way you're asking? I am sad. I am angry. And I hate talking like this."

LuAnna smiled, and kissed Blackshaw on the cheek. Ellis kept his gaze to the horizon.

After LuAnna's plea for deeper candor from her husband, it was soon her turn to feel the awkward twist of honesty. The southerly breeze and northerly course held *Miss Dotsy* in a nausea-inducing cloud of her own exhaust. LuAnna finally gave in to it and parked her cookies over the side, fitting punctuation to her feelings on the whole matter. By reflex, Blackshaw held her hair back as she grunted between bouts of retching, "Could you please tack a little right and give us all some fresh air?"

Blackshaw eased back on the tiller, watching his depth as the Assateague Island shoreline drew closer.

"Thank you I'm sure," said LuAnna, dabbing at her mouth.

Blackshaw spoke after a while, clearly trying to reveal more of his inner workings, demonstrating a willingness to make this experiment despite his natural discomfiture at burdening, or worse, possibly boring others with his inmost thoughts. "I'm glad you're both here. It's a nice cruise. Just looking around. Satisfying my own curiosity isn't throwing in with the Feds—"

"Ponies!" shouted LuAnna, pointing at the Assateague Island shoreline. She knew they were there. They'd been to Pony Penning Day many times to watch the little ones get herded across the water for sale, but LuAnna always had a girl's excitement about them.

Blackshaw and Ellis both followed her gaze. There was a bunch of those famous wild ponies, mares mostly, and a few subordinate stallions late to leave their natal band.

"Put in to shore, Ben." Once again, LuAnna wasn't asking.

"It's not legal to bother them," Ellis said.

The former Natural Resources Police Corporal said, "We shoved a dead man in the bay not twenty-four hours ago, and you're worried about spooking the wildlife?"

"Tide's going out," said Blackshaw. "I don't want *Miss Dotsy* stranded."

"Look at them!" LuAnna said. "That mare. She's top lady. See the flies all around? Her shoulder-shakers are quiet, not even trying to shoo off the bugs. And her head's low. All their heads are."

"It's where the food is," said Ellis.

LuAnna glared at her friend. "Those ponies are not eating. Ben, I'm telling you, put ashore."

CHAPTER 7

KNOCKER ELLIS SET the small CQR day-anchor in the sand above high tide line. The three of them moved slowly down the beach toward the band of ponies. Ellis was careful to let LuAnna go first out of respect for whatever was bothering her so much about those foul tempered beasts. He noticed Blackshaw casting glances back to check *Miss Dotsy*'s lie in the small cove well north of the Chincoteague Road causeway.

LuAnna said, "Travis died two days back, right Ben?"

"So Molly said."

"They dropped this in your lap pretty quick," said LuAnna. "Oh, and I hate it you're on a first name basis with them."

Ellis agreed, but kept his mouth shut. His friends were touchy enough right now without his stoking matters. And he also had to admit that this herd seemed lackluster. Surely wouldn't star in any tourism videos. No nickering, nor tossing manes. No swishing tails. It was like they were staring at the glue factory door wondering who's next.

The breeze shifted around to the northeast, and the three of them registered the eye-watering funk at once.

"Oh damn," said Ellis. "That's not a pony."

"Yeah it is," LuAnna said. "A dead one."

The herd parted like mourners making way for a latecomer paying respects. The hum of blowflies sounded deeper as Ellis moved forward by himself. And there it was, a pony shape on the ground with a living, heaving shroud of insects crawling and tucking in for dinner. There weren't so many bugs that Ellis couldn't see the animal's head looked wrong, and the eyes bulged. He took off his cap and waved it nice and easy. The flies lifted off, their collective hum pitching up to a whine as more and more took flight, but the ponies did not stampede.

"Natural causes?" said Blackshaw, who was a few feet back trying hard not to gag from the stench.

"Not even," said LuAnna.

"One bullet," said Ellis, touching between his own eyes. "Whoever killed Travis Cynter took a practice shot."

The alpha mare's colt nuzzled LuAnna's cheek. LuAnna didn't seem to notice as she stared at the destroyed creature. Might be its pappy lying there.

CHAPTER 8

IT WAS BUCK work for Blackshaw and Ellis to shove *Miss Dotsy* off the Assateague beach and back into the receding tide even though they had been ashore less than an hour. LuAnna managed engine and tiller, and showed no interest in giving up the helm once her boys were back aboard. Blackshaw let her be. She knew what she was doing.

Blackshaw asked Ellis, "Sure it was the same rifle? Hunters use .338 Lapuas, too."

"Not sure at all." Ellis spat a mouthful of toothpaste over the side, anything to clear that reek of death from his head. "It wasn't a Barrett. A .50 cal' BMG would take the head clean off a Cape buffalo. A hunter's .338 round would leave the same smaller entry wound, but wouldn't dig a canoe like that into a pony. Same with a .300 Win Mag, or a .308. Might could be it was that overpressure Limey load from an Alpha-3 like the Feebs brought you. All I can say, sure as hell wasn't colic."

Blackshaw trusted Ellis's working knowledge of kill-sign. His old friend had served several tours in Vietnam on a sniper team with Blackshaw's father, and seen death aplenty and its leavings.

LuAnna spoke from some place far away. "He killed a pony."

Blackshaw was observant, but he was not crazy. He would be the last man to remind his wife that the way she weighed human life opposite the lives of God's other creatures might seem skewed to some.

"Not just any pony. The stallion," Ellis said. "What would a Feeb pro-filer say about that?"

"We're sure the shooter's a *he*," was all Blackshaw said.

The waterman knew what they were all thinking now. His half-sister, Annie Vo, fathered by Dick Blackshaw toward the end of his service in Vietnam, had grown up to be a world class sniper-for-hire. Until recently, she had sometimes teamed with their father, who also lived as a roving mercenary.

"You don't think it was her," said Ellis.

"It's some straight shooting after all, which is Annie Vo's trademark," Blackshaw said. "And Wilde and Lowry came right to my doorstep with this."

LuAnna said, "What do they know about her? It could have been your pappy for that matter. And besides, I don't know one girl who'd hurt a pony, especially if she ever read *Misty of Chincoteague*. For a paid killer, Annie Vo's got her headpiece on. She wouldn't risk a practice shot if she ever thought she needed one, which I doubt. Not at a living thing. Not so close to the—what do you call it—the theatre of operations. She's effective, but not demented nor stupid."

Blackshaw had to agree. With a sick feeling in his gut, he wondered if his father was involved, if not his sister. It wouldn't be the first time more than one Blackshaw got bailed up in the same mess. It was turning out to be a family dysfunction.

"I still say those agents pulled your trigger on this. It's something they don't want any part of, but they're sure comfy-cozy snatching your neck in the noose." LuAnna throttled back and bore east before rounding north into Isle of Wight Bay. "And like that damn woman said, if you don't deliver on this, they could always hang plenty of other things on you."

"You mentioned," groused Blackshaw.

"No, Molly Wilde said it," corrected LuAnna. "Because it's true."

Blackshaw watched as the dunes and grasses of Assateague gave way to the choked streets of Ocean City. So long after Labor Day, at least Isle of Wight Bay was clear of other boaters. With LuAnna clinging fast to the helm, they rounded northeast past Drum Point. Then left Drum Island astern and to port.

"There it is," Ellis said, though they all knew it, and could not take their eyes off it.

Dog & Bitch Island had eroded since the 1930s until it was barely a shoal, a high point in the bay's bottom to which recent dredging spoils were added. Since then, it had become the new favorite destination of Ocean City jet boaters though some kind of pending waterfowl habitat designation threatened to make it off limits to humans. It was off-season now, but Blackshaw admired the American flag still flying from a pole someone had stepped in a small caisson of concrete on the island's central rise.

Then, without warning, Blackshaw felt his breath shallow up and come quicker with that first telltale chill of sweat. For him, it was one thing to visit a fallen comrade's grave. It was another matter entirely to visit where he'd breathed his last.

Ellis asked, "What are you thinking Ben?"

"Trav was a true blue patriot. He didn't happen to die here on this patch of dirt. He was defending it."

CHAPTER 9

KNOCKER ELLIS WATCHED his friends walk with care around the rise, gaining what elevation there was in a spiral with the flag pole at its center. He said, "The lieutenant died here? This is a crime scene?"

"Hardly," LuAnna said.

Blackshaw stopped scanning the ground and looked to his bride.

"You need to watch more TV," said LuAnna. "Where's the yellow tape all over the place? How come nobody's still here working it?"

"It's been two days," was all Ben could think of.

"It was murder," said Ellis. "Still and all, maybe we're wrong about how important this whole business is."

Blackshaw glanced into the sky. "Oh, it's important all right."

LuAnna halted at a place where the grass looked mashed flat. "Could a fellow make a shooting hide here?"

Blackshaw knew it wasn't really a question but he answered anyway. "I reckon, if he brought some cover. Maybe some tan and gray mesh veg'd up nice and easy like his ghillie suit to blur out his profile."

Ellis said, "That spot's not perched up on top of the crest, such as it is, so he wouldn't have skylined himself. The Feebs said time of death was likely after dark, isn't that so?"

Blackshaw glanced skyward again. "That's what they said."

Ellis went on, "Then I think LuAnna's got the smart of it. Right there after dark, and with the proper gear, he'd be invisible 'til you stepped on him. From offshore, hell, he'd be a ghost even before he died, no offense to your friend."

Blackshaw looked across the bay. "Somebody saw him. So what was he watching out that way?"

LuAnna said, "That's charted as Collier Island, but Trav could have been peeping a boat. That amusement park over there's buttoned-up for the season.

"I agree it's strange there's nothing but footprints here from the police, or whoever was looking into this," Ben said.

LuAnna had squatted and was examining the spartina blades. "There's old blood on this cordgrass. Not gloppy. Sprayed fine, like from a high velocity hit. Ben, how come you're all the time looking at the sky?"

"You were worried this was much ado about nothing," said Blackshaw.

"Relieved is more like it," Ellis said. "So you can get to grieving like a normal man without all this cloak and dagger business."

Blackshaw's smile was grim. "I hate to break it to you, friend. A drone's been shadowing us for the last three hours at—I'd reckon—fifteen thousand feet give or take. It's still overhead. Say cheese."

CHAPTER 10

ELLIS GLANCED UPWARD trying to spot the drone, and said, "Cameras, or is there a Hellfire missile up there with our names on it?"

Blackshaw said, "Reckon it's no sense worrying either way. If there's cameras, they're keeping tabs on us. If it's armed, you won't know that 'til you're at the Pearly Gates wondering what hit you."

Despite the threat, LuAnna was still eyeing Travis Cynter's shooting hide, or what was left of it.

Blackshaw said, "I've had enough of this. Let's put in for fuel and head home. If we go now, I can get cleaned up and still make it to Arlington for the service in a couple days."

Ellis had another thought. "Sure you don't want to make a call or two first?"

Blackshaw knew who Ellis meant him to dial.

"Oh my blessing," said LuAnna, plucking something from the sand by a clump of grass. "Take a look at this."

"Don't move, Ellis! Don't go over. Everybody stay still." That was as close to an order as Blackshaw had ever given his friend. "LuAnna, pocket whatever you found, and let's exfil toward *Miss Dotsy* nice and easy. No congregating, nor oohs-and-ahs."

LuAnna kept her movements casual, standing up, and taking a few steps away from Cynter's blind as if giving the little island a final look.

Ellis sauntered toward *Miss Dotsy*, pulled up the day hook, then coiled the line as he ambled to the bow. "Fine time to get paranoid, Ben."

"Better late than never. Wait 'til we're aboard and the engine's going. Let's not make things too easy for Big Brother."

With LuAnna and Ellis weighting the stern, Blackshaw found that the tide had ebbed all the way; *Miss Dotsy* came off the sand with a singlehanded shove. He hopped aboard.

With the Atomic 4 warming to its usual clamor, and the bow pointed at the fuel dock of a small Ocean City marina that still showed signs of life, LuAnna rested her hand on the engine box. When she removed it a moment later, Blackshaw and Ellis saw the silver cufflink she had left there. It danced and spun from the engine's vibrations, and grains of gray Dog & Bitch sand shook free.

"Looks like a ship's wheel," Ellis said. "Think it was Cynter's?"

"With that pink inlay?" said Blackshaw. "Not the man I knew."

"After a long summer, could be anybody's," said Ellis.

"You're both so stupid sometimes," LuAnna said. "Boaters wear bathing suits. That thing was right by where he died. And he was operating forward, not wearing French cuffs."

"Whose point are you trying to make, hon?"

LuAnna took a slow breath. "He wasn't wearing it. He had it with him."

"So he was going to exfil and hit a party," Blackshaw said. Seemed that though LuAnna had known Blackshaw all her life, she still had strange notions of what soldiers did after-action.

"Lordy go to fire, who ties your shoes, Ben?" LuAnna said, "It was a *keepsake*. The cufflinks were a gift, like as not. Sure, a guy might not buy something like that for himself, but a woman would think a ship's wheel is just the thing for a Navy man."

"You wouldn't—"

"Of course not, Ben. Wouldn't dream of getting a pair like this for you. But that's because I've known you a while. It's what a woman of short acquaintance but certain interest would give her new guy. A woman with money. Silver. Handmade. Wouldn't be cheap."

"I'm with Ben," said Ellis. "Pink?"

"Takes balls to wear pink," LuAnna agreed. "But it's not enamel. And not pale rubies. It's sand inlay. And pink sand isn't common."

Ellis had his phone out, and was cranking in a search in the browser. He said, "She's right. Greece and Sardinia got pink beaches. Indonesia, Spain. Bahamas. Two in Bermuda."

LuAnna said, "For goodness sake, just put in *ship's wheel cufflink* and *pink sand* and see what you get."

Ellis thumbed at his phone. "Everybody's making wheel cufflinks on Etsy. But, now there's a picture of this one." He held it out for Blackshaw and LuAnna to see.

"Who makes them," LuAnna asked. "A designer?"

"Some gal named Alexandra Mosher," said Ellis. "And you're right, they're spendy."

"Where's home for her?" Blackshaw said.

"Downtown Hamilton," said Ellis. "Bermuda. But she ships anywhere."

LuAnna totted up the evidence. "You both say there's a good chance the rifle and the bullet that killed Trav were British. And he's got a keepsake, maybe from a trip, likely from a new honey, and she shops at a boutique in Bermuda which is British, in person, or mail order. I vote she got them in person."

"So it's the sand that makes it special," said Ellis.

"I knew you were a romantic somewhere in there," said LuAnna. "And he felt enough for this gal to take them along on some kind of mission."

"That's thin soup," Blackshaw said.

"It's stew compared to what we had a few seconds ago," said Ellis.

Blackshaw picked up the cufflink just before it jittered off the engine box to the deck. "So, where's the other?"

CHAPTER 11

THE SAT-PHONE WAS on speaker. Knocker Ellis could hear Blackshaw punching in the number, though the waterman was crouched inside the door of the cuddy cabin to avoid the prying eyes of the drone loitering high overhead.

Blackshaw waited until the encrypted call went through.

A voice answered, "Rocco's Pizza."

"Do you know who this is?" Blackshaw asked.

The man on the other end said, "I told you, I couldn't be happier that your country is now free, Generalissimo-For-Life Espada. Timing the coup for a hurricane was your brilliant concept from beginning to end. Telling you precisely when the rain bands would be at their heaviest so you could plan accordingly was a small effort on my part, and you've paid me handsomely already, and as I just said a moment ago, an emerald the size of my fist, while doubtless as beautiful as it is priceless, it's too much, especially in an engagement ring for your eldest niece, who you've said is only fourteen, and who might cause a domestic disturbance with my dear wife, Nicole, to whom I am completely devoted."

Blackshaw grinned for the first time in two days. "Mike, you need a new line of work."

"Oh. It's you." Michael Craig was a reclusive giant who worked weather magic in a cave somewhere in the White Mountains of western Maine. He was an infallible genius in predicting weather, and was paid ever more by powerful men and women the world over depending on how far in advance the forecast was needed. NASA and SpaceX double-checked their launch windows against his proprietary software and uncanny intuition. World leaders and despots-in-waiting also purchased his services for planning anything from South Lawn Easter egg rolling contests to military coups. Russians were checking with him regularly for the first date that the Northwest Passage would be navigable for surface ships this year. What most of his clients did not know is that Mike Craig was also a diabolical hacker. No firewall on earth or in high earth orbit could withstand his incursions for more than a picosecond. Blackshaw, who Craig regularly regretted rescuing in Iraq by leading his dicey exfiltration through the blinding smoke of oil well fires, knew all of his friend's myriad skills, and called upon them from time to time.

"Did I do something to piss you off?" Blackshaw asked.

"You're doing it now," Craig said. "What do you want?"

"Can you tell where I am by my signal?"

"Seriously?"

"Dead serious," Blackshaw said.

LuAnna said, "Tell Nicole hi from me!"

After a pause, "She says hi back, LuAnna. Ben, is this about the company over your position?"

"Yes," said Blackshaw.

"But you sound—"

"I sound what, Mike?"

"Poor."

"You know I'm not. You charging me now?"

"I should," Craig said.

"Travis Cynter's dead." Blackshaw hated to twist his friend's arm. When he heard nothing in reply, he said, "You there?"

"I'm here. What do you need exactly?"

"I need about thirty—"

"Sixty," said Ellis.

"Make that sixty minutes in the clear."

Craig began to sound interested. "So you need me to bring the drone down? I could do that. Tell me where."

"No! Can you just mess with the feed? I need confusion," Blackshaw said. "I need them to know there's a problem, but not what's wrong. A crash is too obvious."

"I can make the engine incinerate itself. I can dive it into a building, or ditch it somewhere out at sea. Before that, I can make it do a crazy airshow for you, or fly that baby to Greenland—"

"Mike! Just sixty minutes of what-the-heck. Can you swing that or not?"

"I've got a new thingy that might do the trick."

"I appreciate it. Just give us an hour," Blackshaw said. "Then you can fly it to Greenland."

CHAPTER 12

SENIOR RESIDENT AGENT Molly Wilde peered over Lowry's shoulder at the screen. It always surprised her that the surveillance nodes at Langley were bright, just regular offices with keyboards and flatscreen monitors, not the dim, cinematic, overwrought high-tech lairs resembling the flight deck of a Klingon Bird-of-Prey. Yes, her well-concealed Star Trek enthusiasm had surprised Lowry the first time she had made this comparison out loud.

Wilde was grateful to this day for his measured response. Without judgement, Lowry had uttered his longest sentence in their relationship since declaring his love for her. "The Constitution Class Federation starship, especially NCC-1701, has always been the scene of more dramatic tension precisely because it revealed more emotional truths in the literal and figurative light of the bridge." Wilde's inner nerd had squealed with delight though she kept a poker face. The sex that night had been amazing.

Wilde said, "Lucky there aren't too many boats. You're sure that's Blackshaw's."

"Certain as can be," said Lowry. "We had a satellite on them since yesterday."

"Do you think he knows there's a UAV on him now?"

"In Afghanistan, if a Humvee broke down and help was a long way off, sometimes soldiers couldn't fall asleep until they knew there's a Reaper on station for overwatch. At least, that's what I'm counting on. With

Blackshaw's experience, his suspicions, he'd look up almost out of habit." Lowry barked into a speakerphone. "Pilot, this is Lowry."

A male pilot in a MQ-4C Triton flight control cabana in Jacksonville, Florida replied, "Go ahead, sir."

"Are you still holding at fifteen thousand feet?"

"Affirmative, one-five thousand feet."

Wilde said, "Take it down to ten thousand."

Lowry considered Wilde's suggestion, then asked the pilot, "Would ten thousand feet put the Triton in conflict with OXB traffic?"

The pilot said, "Nice of you to ask. Not with the Ocean City Muni' planes." After a moment's pause, the pilot went on, "But maybe with the Salisbury Class D approaches, especially the RNAV GPS approach to runway two-three. No flight plans filed for right now, and our kite has TCAS II for collision avoidance for the bigger planes, but some poor sport pilot up for a look at the fall foliage might get a face full of our big swinging—"

"Yes I get it," Lowry hastened to say.

Wilde could feel Lowry blushing on her behalf. He needn't have worried. She had three older brothers. Three older, quite disgusting brothers.

The pilot sensed he had overstepped the bounds of good taste liaising with these civilians. He continued, "Is there something wrong with image resolution on your end? We're seeing five-by-five here."

Wilde said, "We want the target to know the Triton is overhead."

Another brief pause. "Negative on ten thousand feet. We're on the floor of our operational envelope for this mission as it is."

Wilde wished she had some override code that would force the pilot to comply. It was telling that Langley had made the Triton available at all— almost forced it on them to track Blackshaw—but it seemed there were limits, and they'd hit one.

"Remain on station, please," Lowry said.

"Affirmative."

Lowry muted the speakerphone.

Wilde said, "What about that stop on Assateague? Did your Company contact happen to mention the dead pony?"

"Seems their investigation was less than thorough. The rush means what?"

Wilde asked, "What's the espionage equivalent of panic?"

"Calling the FBI to roust a civilian," said Lowry. "You were heavy-handed threatening Blackshaw at his home. And perhaps just now, asking to buzz him with a UAV."

"Ten thousand feet's hardly buzzing. Do you really think Blackshaw would have helped out as a favor for old time's sake?"

Lowry said, "Probably not. But passing undue pressure down the chain of command like we did might not get us his best work."

Wilde considered the debt she owed Blackshaw. "He probably won't speak to us again."

"I agree. Maybe, in your way, you meant to piss him off enough cancel any sense of obligation he might've had."

"For not busting him? That's pretty deep, Persh. There isn't enough evidence, either from that Dove Point holocaust, or the thing in Arizona. He must know that."

"Perhaps not. Your threats were convincing. Anyway, if you wanted to run him off, it backfired. He's got his teeth into it now."

"If he'd heard about Cynter's death through the grapevine instead of from us, he wouldn't be on that boat right now."

"Nor would his friend. Or his wife," said Lowry.

"I didn't see that coming. Ellis, sure. But not his wife. Jesus, Persh, she's preggers like me."

Lowry didn't seem to be listening anymore. Staring at the screen, he unmuted the phone and said, "Pilot, I don't see the target. Do you?"

"Stand by one."

Lowry jabbed a thumb at the screen and mouthed, "What the hell?"

Wilde couldn't see the boat anywhere near Dog & Bitch Island.

The pilot came back on the line, "Its last known course put it headed straight for that fuel dock. It's not there now."

"Thank you for sharing," Wilde said. "It's a twenty-something foot boat with three souls aboard going eight knots on a good day. Find it!"

CHAPTER 13

AFTER FUELING THE draketail deadrise, Ellis suggested they put some money down on a slip and leave the boat there.

"We have someplace to be," Blackshaw said.

"Agreed. Take a walk with me," said Ellis.

LuAnna had taken a boot off, and was rubbing her foot. "Exactly how long a walk?"

"Not far." Ellis was smiling.

The dockmaster was grateful to have post-season business, and accepted Ellis's cash for the slip. When he presented his usual paperwork for the slip rental, more cash made that go away.

Ellis guided Blackshaw and LuAnna to another marina adjacent to the one where they'd fueled and left *Miss Dotsy*. This one, with its wide new piers and plentitude of Gardenway carts for hauling stores and gear, catered to the carriage trade. Here, multimillion dollar Clorox bottles sat at their moorings from one end of the year to the other, as if forgotten by their owners who were prisoners of the wheeling and dealing that made such luxury purchases possible.

A watchman at the walkway to the piers glanced at Ellis and opened the gate for him without a word. Blackshaw tried not to look impressed. LuAnna couldn't help herself.

Amid all the towering fiberglass sport fishermen lay a vessel from another age. It looked like an old dreadnought or cutter, less the guns.

Ellis stepped onto her deck and turned to hand LuAnna aboard.

Despite the dusk and overcast, Blackshaw could read the gold-leaf nameboard on the wheelhouse. *"Bystander of Man.* Lordy go to fire, Ellis, what have you done?"

"She's an old Camper and Nicholsons. 1934. I got her for a song."

"That's a damn lie. I've heard you sing."

"She's no boat," cooed LuAnna. "She's a ship!"

"Boats go on ships, so yeah," Ellis said.

From nowhere, three crewmen, all gnarled, wizened, sunburned and squinting from lives at sea, appeared on deck and presented themselves.

"Evening, Captain Hogan," said the oldest man.

"Oh hey, Mr. Curlew. How're you keeping?"

"Well enough thank you sir."

"We got stores and fuel enough to put to sea?"

"Always," came the answer.

"Mr. Auk, coffee for three please, and no cheese," said Ellis. "Mr. Gannet, we're casting off in thirty."

"Aye-aye, sir," said the sailors with a fair stab at unison.

A few moments later, LuAnna was seated in a plush chair in the Bohemian styled main saloon.

Ellis said, "Oh go ahead, girl. You know you want to."

Needing no further encouragement, LuAnna whipped her boots off again, and massaged her toes through her socks.

After Mr. Auk served coffee and retired forward, Blackshaw said, "Reckon she's not too pretty."

Ellis said, "With you flipping half your take my way—"

"A deal's a deal, forgetting you earn every nickel—"

"That I do," Ellis said. "I figured some investments like this might come in handy. But I didn't want to seem all hypocritting, tying her up at Smith Island."

LuAnna said, "Where would you? There's no place deep nor broad enough. So she just sits here."

"Investments," said Blackshaw. "Like that nice Gulfstream jet we rode in a while back."

"Oh that. No, I told you it was a rental," Ellis said.

"Bullshit. Your initials were embroidered on every leather seat. I always wondered where you got to," Blackshaw said.

"The world's my oyster, now that I don't have to size them or shuck them. I got people for that."

LuAnna was always learning things about Ellis. Surprising things. "And those scathely old farts just stay aboard waiting for you to show up?"

"The seabirds are friends from before-times. They had their share of trouble, like me."

"Sounds like Witness Protection," said Blackshaw.

"Sure," Ellis said. "Now they've got new names, and a berth, and a decent job at decent pay."

"They'd fit right in on Smith." LuAnna's eyes brightened. "The coffee's amazing."

Blackshaw stopped with his mug halfway to his lips. "This isn't that Kopi Luwak cat-ass stuff again, is it?"

Ellis belly-laughed. "I wish you could've seen your face, Ben! I'll surely never forget. No, it was fun to try once, but at six hundred bucks a pound, it seemed extravagant. This here's Luzianne, straight from the can, but with a scoop of Medaglia d'Oro to put some knuckles in it."

Blackshaw's first sip was timid, but then he relaxed. "How long to Bermuda?"

"Seven hundred miles at nine knots," said Ellis. "Seventy hours or so."

"We could just fly," said LuAnna.

Blackshaw said, "We need options on getting to shore."

"A passport isn't an option?" LuAnna wasn't letting this go.

"It is, but it's not my favorite."

LuAnna laced her boots back on. "Ridiculous. Why does everything have to be all hugger-mugger?"

"It's for the best."

"Not for me." LuAnna stood. "I'm going home."

Ellis said, "You can't run *Miss Dotsy* for two days straight by yourself. When will you sleep?"

"*Miss Dotsy*! Hell, it'll take me an hour to Uber to Crisfield, and Uncle Conrad can get me back to Smith Island on *Winnie Estelle*. I might still make that baby shower, but it sounds like you'll miss Travis's service."

"It's a better service to find out what happened to him," said Blackshaw. "You sure you won't come to Bermuda?"

LuAnna stood. "Thanks for the java, Ellis." She hugged him. Then she kissed Blackshaw long, hard, and hungry.

CHAPTER 14

FIVE HOURS LATER, Wilde and Lowry had rousted the Ocean City marina owner. Going there was a guess based solely on *Miss Dotsy's* last known heading before it disappeared from the UAV's surveillance screen. Now they were interviewing the owner in the dockmaster's office. Oscar Thraves was overweight, tousled, sleepy, and flustered. Lowry did not care. They had hit paydirt, and needed to sift it quickly if they were to find Blackshaw again.

Thraves protested innocence. "Like I said, a young White guy, an older Black guy, and a pregnant woman. She was White, too. They bought gas. They came right in here. They rented a slip."

"For how long?" Lowry asked.

"I offered them a transient slip, in case they were just stopping for dinner, but they wanted long term."

"For how long?" asked Wilde.

"We don't rent long term for less than a month."

"So they rented for a month." Lowry looked around for a coffeemaker or a Coke machine to get Thraves thinking clearer.

"No. For three months," Thraves said. "And he wanted a bubble line around her. That's extra."

Lowry said, "Bubbles."

"To agitate the water," Thraves said. "It doesn't freeze up then. Ice can damage—"

"Who asked for that?" asked Wilde

"The White guy."

"And who paid?" Lowry wondered how this man ran a business.

"The Black guy."

"How did he pay, Mr. Thraves?" Lowry could tell Wilde was losing her cool as well.

"Cash."

Lowry said, "We'd like to see the rental agreement."

"Sure. I mean, no. You don't have a warrant or anything." Thraves sounded triumphant tossing out this scrap of knowledge that anyone with a television would know.

"No," said Lowry. "But I'm not the only one shy some paperwork, right?"

"No." Thraves looked embarrassed. "But Jeez, if you want to know the owner's name that bad, it's on record with the boat registration, if that's legit. You think they're running drugs or something? Didn't seem the type."

Lowry wondered if a veiled threat would sink into Oscar Thraves's befuddled brain. "Are you aware there's an ongoing murder investigation on Dog & Bitch Island?"

"Dog—?"

"That island, Mr. Thraves!" Wilde had reached Def Con 2. "That island half a mile from where we're sitting right now."

"I didn't do it!" Thraves was going white.

"Obstruction of justice," said Wilde. "The three people in that boat are material witnesses to murder."

"But they're not here! They paid up and left." Thraves seemed to be scratching his thigh through his pants pocket. At least that's what Lowry hoped the man was scratching.

Lowry stepped in again. "Did they leave by cab?"

"They didn't call one from here. I didn't see."

Wilde said, "Take us to the slip now, and we'll try to keep your name out of it."

Thraves rose, and led the way out onto the pier. Two minutes later, they were standing in front of slip number 16.

Thraves said. "Three months in advance, and a bubble line. If that don't beat all."

Lowry and Wilde felt the same way. Slip 16 was empty.

Five minutes later, Lowry and Wilde were driving back to D.C. Wilde said, "That boat disappears off the surveillance screen for an hour, then it's gone."

Lowry said, "The UAV malfunctioned. That's certain."

"How is that certain? It cratered in Greenland. In Greenland! We won't know anything until the Navy gets it back. You can bet the Danes'll take their own sweet time about that."

CHAPTER 15

THE PATIENT OPENED his eyes to gray light from a high window below beautiful crown moldings. There were no bars on that, nor any of the other windows in the room, which seemed odd at first. Then he realized he was unable to move much more than his eyes. He could move his head from side to side, but not very much. The bullet wound there had healed, hadn't it? Yet he was not bound, not restrained in any way. He was not old. He was simply ill, more a prisoner of his own body's frailties than of his captors' wiles.

The Patient watched as a technician in scrubs entered the room in near silence, a military man by his fit youthful demeanor and short haircut. Without a word, he made adjustments to the medical equipment by the bed. He checked the IV pumps and drips, and found them running the proper amounts of fluids into the Patient's left arm. Hydration. The Patient was always so thirsty, parched, but had not taken a sip by mouth as long as he could remember. The white tube in his nose was probably liquid nourishment. He could feel the tube worming down the back of his throat. The urge to gag it up was constant, but he hadn't the strength. There was probably a sedative in the other line in his arm. How else could they keep a man like himself subdued? The world knew his name.

The Patient's right arm was attached via two intravenous tubes to the other piece of equipment, which made familiar sounds, though the machine looked quite new. Nothing but the best for him. Blood was removed from his arm through one line, passed through the machine, and went back into his arm through the second tube.

The technician placed a cloth beneath the Patient's chin, and carefully trimmed his beard. Satisfied with his work, he removed the cloth with the clippings, folded it, and sealed it in a red plastic bag marked INCINERATOR.

Last of all, the young man inspected the Patient's foot, the one missing two toes. That wound had never healed properly. His time in the mountains, with shortages of basic supplies like vitamin C, made old hurts open again and again. Diabetes had complicated things.

The Patient had lost all sense of time, but he still retained a shadowy recollection of his great sense of purpose. The technician poked a moistened swab around inside the Patient's mouth, then left him alone in the room as if he were harmless.

For the hundredth time, the Patient wished he were gone to Paradise. What he could not know: the entire world believed he was already dead.

CHAPTER 16

SENIOR RESIDENT AGENT Molly Wilde got home first. Pershing Lowry had been careful to take a leave of absence from the FBI so there would be no shadow cast either on his romance with Molly (he had been her superior when they were both still at the Calvert, Maryland, office) or upon his conduct at the bureau. Wilde thought her man was honorable to a fault to jeopardize his career for love of her. She need not have worried. Lowry was so highly regarded at the bureau that his superiors wasted no time making him an offer of promotion at the FBI Headquarters in Washington lest he be seduced away to some other government agency, or to a billet in the much better paid private sector. And now he was the Executive Assistant Director for Counterterrorism and Counterintelligence. At times like this, all it meant to Wilde is that their brief, happy days of commuting together were over. Lowry would be home soon, but that could mean in an hour, or long after she'd dozed off reading in bed.

Wilde rifled through the refrigerator, and discovered the ravioli, sausage, and meatballs left over from their Sunday supper. A quick shot in the microwave did not ruin the pasta's texture, but made the sauce sizzle around the edges of the bowl. The kitchen began to smell like her childhood.

She decided against sitting at the big dining room table alone, even though news on the small flatscreen TV would have been some company. She went into the den, and fumbled one-handed in the dark for the several remote controls needed to turn on the cable box, the too-complicated sound system and, finally, the TV. The glow from the plasma screen revealed that the real news of the day was much closer to home.

"Hey girl," said LuAnna from Lowry's recliner.

"What the fuck!"

LuAnn smiled. "You kiss your handsome man with that mouth?"

Wilde's hands were full of hot food; a quick draw of her service weapon was impossible. As it was, LuAnna had that small pistol in her hand again, but instead of pointing it at the floor, like on Smith Island, the business end was casually aimed toward the agent.

LuAnna rocked forward in the chair, but it was plain her pregnancy would make getting on her feet a clown act. "Sit yourself down. Eat. Eight-forty-five. Must've been a long day harassing citizens."

"You are in a world of deepest shit, LuAnna. Get your ass out of my house now."

"Oh I already ate, thanks. But when I said you sit and eat, I well and truly meant it." A small motion of the pistol drove the suggestion home.

Wilde placed the dish on a side table, and lowered herself onto a Haverford chair. "I set the alarm this morning."

"They go on, they go off. Take a bite."

"I've lost my appetite."

"You're eating for two. I think I'm due before you. How far along?"

"I want you to leave."

"I want to remodel my kitchen," said LuAnna. "Doesn't mean it's going to happen."

Wilde was finding it hard to contain her anger, her sense of violation. Of course she'd had hostage negotiation training, but it was different when you were the captive.

She said, "Aside from the kitchen thing, do you have something on your mind?"

"Where are the Cynter crime scene photos?"

"At the office," said Wilde.

"That's a load of bull. Take out your service gun, put it on the floor, and give it an easy kick under my chair."

There was no fighting the facts. Wilde was careful. LuAnna registered every move, every twitch, even though she seemed relaxed.

"Now, unlike your security alarm, that computer's already on. Bring up the photos."

Wilde rose, crossed to the desk, and opened the laptop. Its cooling fan whispered to life. The screen bloomed with a field for a password.

"Oh, and honeygirl—"

Wilde turned. In her other hand, LuAnna held the 1911 Colt .45 that should have been in the desk's top drawer for times like this. Wilde meant to get a biometric pistol safe before her baby was born. Over the last couple of years, toddlers in the U.S. had shot someone on an average of once a week. Safe or no safe, tonight that Colt was not an option.

Wilde keyed her password into the laptop, and went through the other steps by rote to access her files at work. She stepped back when the requested photos opened.

"Autopsy, too," said LuAnna.

"How'd you make your boat disappear?"

"It's sitting right there in OC."

"No it isn't."

"Oh well. Guess she got stolen."

Wilde said, "I meant before you took it to the marina there. It vanished."

"You were peeping us? I swear I don't know what you're talking about."

"Forget it. Where's Blackshaw?"

"That'd be telling, and right now I'm the one asking. Autopsies, please."

Wilde brought up those images as well. The negotiator tool of give a little, get a little had failed. "And personal effects? Clothing? Gear?"

"And weapons. The whole kit-and-caboodle."

Wilde's fingers played over the keyboard and touchpad.

"Now sit down."

Wilde complied.

After an awkward dismount from the recliner, LuAnna waddled over to the computer. Wilde admired how the former cop divided her keen attention between the screen and her unwilling hostess. With the examination

Lowry drew his phone. "Should I call—"

"Don't!" said Wilde glaring at him in fury. "Now who the hell is Siobhan?"

CHAPTER 17

FBI ASSISTANT DIRECTOR Pershing Lowry had never felt the full impact of a hostile interrogation—not even during his rigorous training at Quantico—not until the woman he loved had taken him to task.

With no appointment, Wilde had come to his office after a chilly night that made their home feel more like a tomb.

When Lowry's door was closed, Wilde announced, "This isn't working."

Lowry's heart sank. He knew what she meant, but he had to hear it. "What's not working?"

"Us being together. We're supposed to be a team! We're good! And we can't communicate?"

"Wait, are you breaking up with me?"

"Idiot! Of course not." Wilde shelled a square of Nicorette gum out of its plastic capsule, remembered her pregnancy, and threw gum and wrapper away.

"You don't feel safe? Should we move until this is over? I should have been there. LuAnna Blackshaw wouldn't have been able—"

"Don't you dare play that card with me, Persh. I'm not some damsel. If you'd been there, she'd just have gotten the drop on us both. She's a cop, or was. She's still damn sharp."

Lowry felt the old bewilderment creeping over him. He should know enough to keep silent and let Wilde's storm pass. Then they could talk. Or at least, he would have a better chance of understanding her, instead of being wrong with every word he uttered.

"She could have hurt you," said Lowry. "She had a weapon."

"Of course she could've hurt me if that's what she meant to do. And I could get hit by a bus crossing the street. I don't live my life like that, going from one fear to the next on permanent defense."

That was exactly how Lowry lived now that Wilde was his and she was expecting. He dreaded every phone call away from her presence, in case it brought tragic news. He was clever enough not to mention that fact. Wilde would hear it as controlling, not romantic. Not now. Probably not ever.

He said, "I can put an agent at the house."

"You'll do no such thing. You're the only one who gets to see me scrub-face and wearing sweats. Good God!"

"In a car then," Lowry ventured.

"And in the back yard?" Wilde had been calming down, but she was connecting with deeper emotions again. "She didn't get me in a car on the street. That's a hundred miles away from our den."

"I admire your fearlessness, Molly, but is it practical? Please tell me what can I do, and I will."

Wilde took several slow, deep breaths, as she would have in the Lamaze class she had signed up for, but would never attend. "First, you were right, Persh."

Lowry held still. This was an exciting, if baffling moment. He said nothing.

"I might've come down too hard on the Blackshaws. But it earned me LuAnna's visit."

"Breaking and entering! At gunpoint." As he said that, Lowry groaned inside. He could not stay quiet to save his life.

"You say B&E, I say back-channel." Wilde was smiling. Lowry had no idea why. She went on, "We'd never have shown them evidence that would've been helpful. You were barely willing to show Blackshaw that bullet."

"It was a risk, but it got Blackshaw kinetic on Cynter."

"Sure, but we were playing to the wrong Blackshaw." Wilde was standing, her gestures cut the air. "LuAnna came to our place extremely pissed. Maybe that part was paybacks for bracing her in her home like that."

"If we'd been nicer, she'd have given us Smith Island cake as well as the coffee?"

"I will kill you if you mention cake of any kind for the next three months." Wilde waited until Lowry nodded, message received. "So she was mad, but her cop genes were working as well. She wanted more information. She wanted to see what we had."

"Thank goodness the transcripts and most of the case files weren't accessible," said Lowry, the conscientious administrator.

"No! Wrong, wrong, wrong! That is exactly the problem!" Now Wilde was stabbing her index finger at Lowry's chest. Bad sign. "You know things I don't. I had to have a gun shoved up my nose by an angry pregnant woman to learn about Siobhan, whoever she is."

Lowry felt he could identify with Wilde on the matter of angry pregnant women, but said nothing except, "So you want to tick her off again, so she drops in again, gets some more intel, and gives us a hint or two without meaning to?"

"It's a back-channel line of communication, but the connection's awful. If you were talking to me, I wouldn't need to get intel in from LuAnna's crazy self in this totally ass-backwards way."

"Do you think this Siobhan is important?"

"Can you say categorically she isn't? A newer, but unfinished tattoo of her name. Why start it and not finish it? Did they break up? Did he split town? If he did, then why? Don't you want to meet her? I mean who blabs more than an angry ex? She knows things we don't. Was the name in the ME's report?"

"Yes, it was." Lowry wanted to get up, stretch, get coffee, rub fresh wasabi in his eyes, anything to find some way to take a short, precious break—and yet this conversation was getting ever more interesting. "I think I see your point."

"Maybe. And why was LuAnna asking about—what'd she call it— kickshaws? Little jewels or something. Point is, why does that woman know things I don't? Why do you have clearances to talk to God, and I need a home invasion to get pointed toward my next crumb. We sleep in the same bed, but we live in different silos. We need to blow this open."

Lowry's head ached. "You want to see other people."

"No! The intel silos. Be my Gabriel, Persh. Blow your trumpet. The walls have to come down."

"I think you're conflating Gabriel's trumpet signaling the return of the Messiah, which actually isn't in the Bible, and doesn't appear in literature until 1382, in John Wycliffe's *De Ecclesiæ Dominio*—that, and the book of Joshua, in which the priests signal the attack on Jericho by blowing—" Lowry paused his disquisition when he noticed a twitch around Wilde's left eye. "The Israelites destroyed Jericho to the last man."

"Persh."

"It's a theme in Negro spirituals, too." Lowry wished he could stop mansplaining, as Wilde called it. Her eye twitch was getting worse.

"Forgetting how odd it sounds when a Black man says *Negro*—", she said.

"It's a music classification. I could call it something else."

"Persh, I need to see everything, read everything, be able to talk about everything, ask questions, at least with you."

"I admit it. It would help you to know—"

"No Pershing! It would help you! It would help the case! Why's this your case? How come you're on it? Why you? I can ask that."

Lowry reached into a pocket, removed a memory stick, and held it up. "I was going to give this to you tonight. It's everything. It can't leave your sight, or your possession. But it's for consultants. It's a work-around for when we need expert help fast, but the red tape on getting a full-on security clearance would take too long to process."

"What's that even mean?"

"It's read-only. And it means that you can see it, yes, but it'll delete itself in twenty-four hours from when you first access it."

Wilde looked angrier, more desperate, if that were possible.

Lowry said, "Start with this. I can get you a permanent copy, and I will, but I need to persuade a judge on the merits of formally assigning you to the case."

"A judge!"

"For the clearance to read you in!"

"Formally? I'm not on the case? What the hell have I been doing all this time?"

"Please don't take this the wrong way—" said Lowry.

"Starting like that, I promise I already have."

"You're like a bloodhound. You see things I don't, and in ways I can't. I had to know if this whole Cynter business was important to you. I found out that it is, but I went about it in the worst possible way. I'm sorry, Molly."

Lowry could see Wilde was trying to stay calm so her womb did not become a human crockpot for their baby. She snatched the flashdrive and said, "What's going on, Persh?"

"We have reason to believe the former President of the United States went on television and he lied."

Wilde said, "Happens every day. Is it a girlfriend? A boyfriend?"

"It deals with the one of the administration's major accomplishments."

"So what the f—" Wilde stopped. "See Persh? I'm all out of *fucks* on this one."

"The former president is not aware that he lied. There are global consequences, which, if this lie were discovered, in the parlance of kids today, it would be epic."

"What the hell did he say?"

Lowry braced himself. "I can't tell you."

"Pershing!"

"Molly, this lie originated within the intelligence community."

Lowry could see the gravity of it all sinking deep into Wilde's psyche. He said, "The most important thing is, we need to solve Travis Cynter's homicide."

CHAPTER 18

BYSTANDER OF MAN cruised watch-on-watch toward Bermuda through easy Atlantic swells at first. Blackshaw and Knocker Ellis took their turns at the helm with the old bird men, Curlew, Gannet, and Auk, managing the engines, and the galley, as well as rechecking the contents of the concealed gun locker, and studying the waters around Bermuda.

The British island territory lay farther east than Haiti, but was still on a latitude with South Carolina. Knocker Ellis watched the weather satellites closely, because a large seasonal storm was due to form soon, and some years this monster sat well off the Carolinas murdering ships until spring. The U.S. Coasties at Elizabeth City in North Carolina called the system a bomb. So far, the weather was kindly to the old yacht's timbers. On this third night at sea, there was another problem holding Ellis's attention.

"Mr. Auk, what do you make of that little dot on the radar?"

The old salt said, "It's a curious thing. No Automatic Identification System tag. And it's held five miles west of us for the last eight minutes."

"But where did it come from?" said Ellis.

"Nowhere."

"I don't like it. The return on whatever it is seems too small to be this far offshore without some kind of mothership. Let's go to electric, start a nice jam. Maybe we'll start Moby Dick, too." Ellis picked up the intercom and said in his softest voice. "Mr. Curlew to the bridge please."

Mr. Auk worked several controls on the engineering panel. The rumble of the diesel engines died, and was replaced by a gentle, low frequency hum.

In a moment Blackshaw and Mr. Curlew stepped into the wheelhouse. Blackshaw said, "The engines."

Mr. Curlew smiled, "Never you worry. We had a hell of a time, but we squeezed three electric motors and a bank of batteries into the engine compartment and along her keel in place of some of her ballast."

"Slow us down for silent running please," Ellis said. He toggled more switches, and the already dim lights of the wheelhouse turned red to better their night vision.

Mr. Auk eased three chrome levers back, and the slight hum dropped to nothing.

"Ben, would you mash that button right there next to you?" Ellis asked.

Blackshaw noticed the white button with the scrimshaw silhouette of a whale. Ellis nodded. Blackshaw pressed it. Over the speaker, gentle ticks, like a Geiger counter began to crackle, seeming without pattern.

"I love this stuff," said Ellis. "Now the boat's quiet, and from our hull transducer, we sound like the Caribbean pod of sperm whales. Each pod has its own accent, and slang, did you know that? And we put some jam out on common radar frequencies. Our own radar works on a super long wave, right Mr. Curlew?"

"As rain, Captain Hogan."

"So on the surface, *Bystander of Man* looks less like a boat, more like a big rain cloud," said Ellis. "The edges feather nice and easy, like the real thing."

Mr. Auk said, "That contact is falling astern, sir."

"And there you go," said Ellis. "*To the confusion of our enemies.*"

Blackshaw said, "She doesn't dive outright, does she Captain Nemo?"

"No, but wouldn't that be something?"

Blackshaw knew his friend's expression. Wheels were turning.

The men spent the next three minutes in the pilothouse chatting about the weather, and how the waves seemed to be quartering as well as stacking into steeper walls with horsetails blowing off the crests. But their eyes always scanned from the ports, to the barometer, to the radar.

Though they all saw it, it fell to Mr. Auk to say it. "The target's picked up speed and is on an intercept with our course now. Time to howdy, sixteen minutes give or take."

Ellis said, "Mr. Gannet—"

"Is on the foredeck and ready." Mr. Auk nodded toward the bow.

There next to the anchor winches, the third crewman held what appeared to Blackshaw to be a large glider spanning ten feet, and a small box on a sling looped over his shoulder. A closer look, and Blackshaw realized the glider was a fine model of a young albatross.

At a nod from Ellis, Mr. Gannet hurled the bird into the weather. It rose into the night spume and disappeared in less than a second. Mr. Gannet picked his way aft into the pilothouse, watching a small screen on the transmitter while he worked its small levers.

When Mr. Gannet gained the pilothouse, Blackshaw said, "Shame to toss that rig into this fuzz cod."

Mr. Gannet said, "An old man's arm and a small electric ducted fan launch her well enough, but this weather's perfect. She's programmed to slope soar these big waves just like the real creature." Mr. Gannet held up the box on the lanyard. "This mobile unit's slaved into a shipboard transputer for launch. She can go miles and miles past line-of-sight. We piggy-back the signal off GPS satellites." Mr. Gannet pressed a button on the handheld unit. "And now the bird's autonomous. Intercepting target in seven minutes."

Ellis turned on another screen on the control panel forward of the helm. The screen showed green waves rolling underneath the drone.

He said, "For night work, the bird has Night Vision and dual FLIR fiber optics run to each eye lens for circling surveillance, or we can point them both forward for some mean synthetic depth perception. It even flaps a little now and then."

"Come a long way from a Ward Brother's merganser decoy," said Blackshaw.

"Not as beautiful by half," said Mr. Gannet. "But I'm working on it. Perhaps you'd give me your thoughts?"

"A little late, now that she's launched."

"We've got six more just like her in ship's stores," said Mr. Gannet.

Everyone watched the Albatross-Cam. Endless waves careened under the bird.

"Let's hope it's just some boat in trouble," said Blackshaw.

"If it's not in trouble, it soon could be." For all his calm, for all the pleasure in his stuff and things, Ellis had blood in his eye.

"Any minute now, Captain," said Mr. Gannet.

The men edged closer to the screen watching for something other than the emerald sea.

Blackshaw said, "There's something out there. Maybe we could switch to FLIR."

Mr. Gannet keyed a command into his transmitter. The screen changed from a green palette, to an ashen world of black and white, but with the color values reversed like a photographic negative.

Mr. Gannet said, "If there's any anomaly, she's programmed to circle it."

The endless heaving hues of gray were finally broken when something distinctly manmade came into view.

"A boat," said Ellis.

"A RHIB, with six souls aboard," Blackshaw said. "A lifeboat?"

The faux albatross banked left, and began carving a great circle which held the boat in the middle of the screen with only a gentle sway as the aerial unit adjusted its flight path.

"Digital steady-cam," said Blackshaw.

"Nothing but the best," Ellis answered, taking a step toward the screen. "That fellow in the stern. Looks familiar. Can you zoom in closer?"

"Aye-aye, Captain," said Mr. Gannet.

"Be damned," said Ellis once the adjustment was made. "Big as life! I saw you blow his head off."

"Not enough of it," said Blackshaw. "That's Chalk."

CHAPTER 19

MAYNARD PILCHARD CHALK hated Rady Karkov to a depth well below the capabilities of the mad Russian's elderly Quebec class submarine. Without affection, even the crew referred to the sub as a *Zippo*, because of how often the closed liquid oxygen system for the submerged running diesel caused fires. So, part of Chalk was glad the captain had marooned him and his team in the middle of the Atlantic. Drowning was better than burning to death. In the end, Chalk had been able to negotiate a decent rubber boat as part of the exit strategy. Captain Karkov originally proposed to get rid of Chalk and his team without ceremony through the torpedo tubes, but Karkov had a reputation as a black market transporter to uphold. That had earned Chalk better treatment, especially after he pointed out that disembarking the hard way meant that most of his strapping corn-fed boys would have gotten stuck in transit through the twenty-one inch diameter tubes. As Karkov saw it, the hastily inflated RHIB, and an intercept bearing to the slow-moving boat just over the horizon represented the height of generosity. There was no question of refunding a single dollar of monies Chalk had prepaid for the ride.

Chalk told the operator manning the smoky Whirlwind outboard, "Better pour on the coal. We've got one shot to meet that boat, or we'll be out of fuel and adrift."

"You had to shoot Karkov's son."

The smartass helmsman was coming close to enjoying the same fate, but Chalk thought this fellow was fattest, and so was best held in reserve if they missed that boat, and snacks at sea came up short.

"The brat got into my files. He was going to blab to daddy about our mission," Chalk said.

"Wouldn't he have seen the asset during the exfil?" This helmsman was growing less appetizing and more expendable by the minute.

Chalk answered, "By then we could've taken the crew down easy-peasy. A submarine's a floating choke point. Anybody puts their head through a hatch, off it comes. Those Ruskies are all drunks. It would've worked."

His four other operators checked their weapons and peered ahead into the gloom. Chalk's temperament was failing. His personality was decompensating at a furious rate since he had stopped taking his antipsychotic meds a year ago. Getting shot in the head on a previous gig, even the glancing blow he had suffered, which sent shards of bony shrapnel into his brain to inoperable depths, only made things worse. His quack of a surgeon told Chalk it was a miracle he was alive at all. Chalk, on the other hand, believed it was his personal manifest destiny to survive.

The helmsman was nattering again. "Albatrosses are unlucky." He nodded at the great bird ghosting in and out of view in the claggy moonlight around their boat.

"We'll see who's lucky tonight," Chalk snarled.

He drew his Mossberg tactical shotgun from the waterproof duffle, racked it, and fired once. The left wing of the albatross spun loose and fluttered down behind a wave, while the body and other wing splashed closer and sank.

CHAPTER 20

"YEP, THAT'S CHALK," Ellis said as the surveillance screen in the wheelhouse went dark. "Mean as a snake."

Mr. Gannet, despite the available UAV replacements, seemed put out at the treatment of his pretty drone.

Chalk was an old acquaintance of Blackshaw and Ellis. On behalf of a corrupt United States senator, he had attacked Smith Island to recover property stolen by Blackshaw's father. In the process, Chalk abducted LuAnna to gain leverage over Blackshaw's fierce defense of Smith Island. Chalk treated LuAnna with horrendous brutality resulting in miscarriage of her first pregnancy. The Smith Islanders had united to drive Chalk back into the Chesapeake, but at a grievous cost in blood. Months later, the psychotic operator had reappeared at the center of a savage human trafficking scheme, and once again, Blackshaw and Ellis had put up strong but costly resistance and prevailed, certain in the knowledge Chalk was dead at last. It was now clear such was not the case. *Bystander of Man*, and all souls aboard her were in danger. A devil was coming for them.

Ellis said. "Let's tool up. Mr. Auk is former HITRON."

Blackshaw was impressed. HITRON is the Coast Guard's Helicopter Interdiction Tactical Squadron, essentially a team that could put a sniper in the air aboard a Dauphin chopper to stop a gofast surface vessel from bringing illicit cargo to American shores. The shooter and pilot worked as one. After warning shots, the sniper could destroy the target boat's engine, or suppress personnel from a moving helicopter despite turbulence aloft and waves below. Since the firing geometry of these interdictions changed by the millisecond, Blackshaw knew Mr. Auk had to be a sniper phenom.

"'*Force from Above*,'" said Blackshaw, repeating the HITRON motto.

Mr. Auk looked abashed. "But Mr. Blackshaw is DEVGRU."

"Was." Blackshaw was telling a truth as much as he was putting distance between himself and the service. He wanted no discredit cast over his comrades because of what he had become since getting out of the Navy.

"Indeed," said Mr. Auk. "'*The Only Easy Day Was Yesterday*.' I'd be much obliged for a chance to see your work."

Ellis studied his friend for any hesitation, any sign that Blackshaw still scrupled against violence as a civilian; perhaps a second chance to take down his nemesis would win the day. There was a pause, but it was brief.

Blackshaw said, "If I recall the gun locker, you don't have a Barrett."

"The Robar is what I trained with. It's good enough for me," said Mr. Auk.

"And by trained," said Ellis, "he means he trained every gunnery sergeant who now oversees the HITRON's Naval Aerial Gunner certification program."

"You're a granddaddy," said Blackshaw to this legendary soldier. "Robar it is. Ellis, if I could take a spot up on your radio mast?"

"Mi barco es su barco, brother."

CHAPTER 21

"WE HAVE TO be close," Chalk shouted. Man, this was damn big water.

There was an earsplitting clang in the old motor as several pieces of the Whirlwind's cover spun off. The engine coughed, belched even more smoke, then stalled. The two-stroke din gave way to the hiss and roar of great growlers rolling and breaking all around them.

"What the—" Chalk was rendered speechless at the sight of the large caliber bullet hole in the engine cover. He felt sure he'd been in this situation before. He scoured his damaged mind to remember the details. All he could recall was a corrosive sensation of dread seeping through his nerves. Now it was back, and it came with a chilling full-body sweat. Panic almost overtook his natural state of fury.

Then his team began to die.

CHAPTER 22

LUANNA HATED DOING this. It felt like an awful abrogation of the separate spheres, the individual lives that she and Blackshaw had taken care to preserve despite being lifelong best friends, crazy-in-love for years, and married. She reached deep into her bottom bureau drawer, and opened the false back panel. She removed the encrypted satellite phone she had asked Ellis to get for her months before, just in case. She paused, filled with the trepidations of second thoughts, and went ahead and dialed.

After a few rings, Michael Craig answered the phone.

LuAnna said, "Do you know who this is?"

"Your Royal Highness, after tapping your fiancé's phone and email for three months, and determining what a total unfaithful jerk he is, I seriously doubt more surveillance is going to change the result. Unless you've broken it off, and would like me to look into someone new?"

"Not quite, Mike. Wow, I didn't think you handled crap like that."

"I'd handle railroad cars full of crap like that for the millions I earn doing it. You would, too."

"We're not the same."

"So you're blowing up my phone to give me judgy career advice."

"Of course not. My opinion isn't advice."

"Is the big guy okay?"

LuAnna wondered how to answer that. "Define *okay*. He is who he is. He is how he is."

"Good talk. Give him my best—"

"Hold it. I need your help."

"Imagine." Craig was not making this easy. It's a wonder Blackshaw was friends at all with such a prickly guy. "You going to fill me in?"

"You can recover key stroke histories on computers, right?"

"You could have a hundred mile airgap on a forty-year-old Trash-80, and I could do that. Unless it's your guy's computer. Then no. No way. Not happening. Understand?"

"Pretty much lost me after *You*. But I take it that you can do what I'm talking about, and no, the big guy doesn't own a computer." LuAnna thought that next to Michael Craig, porcupines were snuggly. "I'm talking about a laptop belonging to a certain Feeb. It's on an encrypted network, of course, but that's not a problem for a man of your talents."

"Is this about Travis?"

"A-firm."

"Does the big guy know you're doing this?"

"I was sitting right there the last time he called you."

"Answer the question. Does. Ben. Know."

"Nay-firm on that."

"Then no. I've poked around, and by all the signs, this thing is too hot. Way too big. I'm getting older. I don't like drama as much anymore."

"I can pay."

"Not enough."

LuAnna paused for effect. "You're pissing me off Mike."

"Get in line."

"Mike, listen to me. Does your wife know what a total hound you were before you met her?"

It was Michael Craig's turn to pause, but it sounded like he was having trouble talking, or breathing, or swallowing—maybe all three. Then he said. "Everybody has a past. Nicole understands that."

"I'm sure she does, in a nice general way. I'm talking gory details, like what the big guy's told me about you. Like, *The Donkey of Kirkuk*."

"Hearsay. Inadmissible."

"*The Flaming Rash of Tal Afar*?"

"That was poison oak from when I was on leave."

"*The Veiled Ladies of Panjab*."

"There was only one woman."

"Because the other two were dudes. Put Nicole on, Mike."

"I can't believe he named this—this crap." Craig was crumbling.

"Right? They're like punch-lines around our place, except you're the one who's going to get punched. Or shanked. Or de-peckerated in your sleep."

"Okay. Give me a name."

"Pershing Lowry."

"Executive Assistant Director for Counter—"

"Yes. Him. I need his history so I can get his password, and hack his files. Everything he's got on Travis's death."

"And you're going to do this from your phone? They'll be on your doorstep in under thirty minutes." Craig pressed his point. "Lady prison's not so nice. Is that where you want to have your baby?"

LuAnna hadn't thought things through that far.

Craig said, "I'll do it. I'll get the files. They'll never trace me. But you have to keep quiet about the other things. Swear."

"*The Cameltoe of Kabul.*"

LuAnna heard Craig cussing as he hung up on her.

CHAPTER 23

MR. GANNET TOSSED the blood-sprayed prisoner down on the afterdeck of *Bystander of Man*. From his AA-12 automatic combat shotgun, Mr. Auk banged a twenty-round drum of high explosive shells into the inflated sponsons of the RHIB. As the fat air tubes burst and collapsed, Ellis shoved the RHIB away from his yacht with the boathook. The sea turned and took the sinking boat with its complement of corpses. Each of Chalk's operators had been killed by a single .50 caliber bullet through the head, courtesy of Blackshaw. Two big waves, and the raft of carnage was gone—into the night—into the deep—and on to oblivion.

Blackshaw climbed down from the radio mast with the heavy Robar RC-50 slung over his shoulder and made his way aft.

"What the fuck you Commie assholes!" blustered Chalk, his face riven with the gory blowback from his dead comrades. "I'm an American cit—"

A kick from Ellis's boot prevented Chalk from finishing his Pledge of Allegiance.

Mr. Auk swapped his shotgun's empty drum for a fresh one, and said, "That was as pretty a piece of shooting as ever I've seen, Mr. Blackshaw."

Chalk froze on all fours. Then he looked up, his nose flattened, teeth broken, eyes ablaze. "Blackshaw! You're dead!"

"Happy to disappoint."

Chalk reared and lunged at Blackshaw, fingers hooked into claws. Mr. Gannet set his boot down hard between Chalk's shoulder blades, flattening him to the deck. For good measure, he brought his other boot down on Chalk's right hand; finger bones popped as they broke.

"Temper, laddybuck," suggested Mr. Gannet.

Chalk rolled onto his back clutching his bad hand in the good one. He was laughing. Blood frothed at the corners of his mouth. "Haakon squealed. You've been tracking me since Fort Clonque!"

Blackshaw told Ellis, "Reckon you over-kicked him. The boy's babbling."

"I don't give a shit!" howled Chalk. He rapped his knuckles against his head. "Titanium, thanks to you."

Ellis was tempted to interrogate Chalk, but thought better of it. Tipping Chalk to any line of inquiry might provide this vermin more intel than it earned, so he said, "Nice night for a boat ride."

"You'll never get it!" Chalk shouted. "They won't let you. And in three days, it's done. Until then, they'll throw everything at you. You're dead where you stand."

Blackshaw took a stab. "Travis Cynter doesn't think so."

"That SEAL belongs at SeaWorld. He's the last, and he'll never stop what's happening. You're all flaming idiots if you think you can. There's no time."

"Who wants to stop it?" Ellis ventured. It was hard to hold up his end of a chat with a lunatic, but it was fascinating.

"Okay. Sure. Okay. You want to cash in!" Chalk stood. His captors stepped back, but stayed ready to take him to the deck again. "I'll help you. You punk-ass shitbirds can't handle something this big by yourselves."

Blackshaw said, "Appreciate the offer, but I reckon we're doing a damn sight better than you."

"Not by half, boyo," said Chalk, spitting a tooth out on the deck. "You'll see soon enough."

Chalk took a fast step back, turned, and leapt for the rail. From its mount on the taffrail he bundled a horseshoe life-ring into his arms as he tumbled into the sea and disappeared.

Surprise prevented anyone from speaking for a moment. Mr. Auk stepped to the fantail with his AA-12 raised. He had his own views of the Man Overboard protocol.

Ellis said, "Hold on. The sharks'll get him."

"You got something against sharks," said Blackshaw.

After Mr. Gannet had sluiced Chalk's blood off the fantail, the crew gathered in the wheelhouse. Mr. Curlew, who had remained at the helm and missed most of the proceedings, was as disturbed by Chalk's arrival as he was astonished by his disappearance.

And Mr. Curlew had a report of his own. "Dawn in an hour. And we should raise Bermuda by then, too."

CHAPTER 24

LUANNA STEPPED OUT of the L.F. Wade International Airport into the sultry Bermuda afternoon and beelined for the waiting line of blue and blaze-green taxis.

Her driver, one Isabella Outerbridge, started the meter and asked, "Where're you going today Misses?"

"There's a jewelry store in Hamilton," said LuAnna, and she gave the name.

"Starting right in with the shopping then. Respect."

Sizing up her customer, Outerbridge maintained a pleasant patter about the sights along the way. LuAnna allowed herself to play tourist for the ride, tuning in for interesting facts, drifting off in thought at times to consider her next steps. The roads were narrow, often cut deep through the bedrock of rolling hills. Buildings or lush green tropical growth came right to the shoulders. She thought she would never get used to the sight of traffic hurtling at her on the right, especially entering a traffic circle clockwise, which made LuAnna catch her breath. She could walk Smith Island risking little more than an encounter with a nearsighted elder at the wheel of a golf cart. In Bermuda, the cars, trucks, and plentiful scooters seemed to weave in among each other as if by some grand design, but to LuAnna it tested her faith.

Roads on Smith Island, she mused, were more like paved pathways, and afterthoughts. The first folks to come to an island, and many who stayed, got around by boats. Then there are those who came to stay, who have little commerce with the waters around them. They are the road build-ers. LuAnna felt they would always be slaves to a landbound life—if you could call it a life—the importers, exporters, the fisherfolk and watermen, and yes even the pirates, they were truly free.

LuAnna wasn't sure what she was going to do. This was police work, and there were standard ways to approach this situation but, somehow, protocols seemed a poor fit here. Cynter's death hit her nearly as hard as it had struck Blackshaw. And it was clear the FBI was fragmented in their approach and struggling to make headway in the case, or there would have been no heavy-handed government visit to Smith Island. She had the name of a store. She had the name of a woman. At worst, she would enjoy a day in a foreign territory. At best, she might actually help Blackshaw find some peace. That thought made her chuckle, which made Outerbridge check her in the rear view mirror.

When Blackshaw deployed, peace was a relative thing, a question of the degree of uproar, the extent of the damage to property, and the number of bodies before all was said and done. She loved her man. He was reliable in his surgical applications of mayhem. With Blackshaw engaged on the mission, the mystery of Cynter's death would be investigated and solved. And Cynter would be avenged. Of this, LuAnna was also certain.

LuAnna glanced out the window, and a particular storefront caught her eye. On impulse she said, "Pull over here, please. In there."

Outerbridge seemed at peace with having her Hamilton fare cut short in St. George. "Starting your visit with a tattoo. Respect."

CHAPTER 25

CHALK AWOKE LYING face-down in the sand. Pink sand. His left arm was still crooked hard in a cramped angle through the horseshoe life ring, and the pain in his face and broken fingers throbbed without mercy. He read the name on the life ring. *Bystander of Man.* He would see about that.

A rooster strutted past Chalk's sand-caked face. At the same moment a ferocious odor penetrated his nostrils, he felt a tug on the cuff of his pants leg. With all his might, angled his head to see. He was greeted by the sight of a black tail flicking back and forth above a crap-smeared anus and a swollen, hairy, pendulous scrotum swaying too close to his nose. In his addled state, Chalk believed this was either Hell, or a flashback to his days at parochial school. He blinked, trying to clear the sand from his eyes. A goat, with its freaky pupils, stared at him from beneath dainty eye lashes; the fetid beast was trying to eat his khakis. Chalk struck out at the animal with his foot, expending his last ounce of strength. His vision went gray, then dark.

Chalk was mired in his recurring nightmare in which Ben Blackshaw thwarted his every effort to move, to climb, to succeed, to kill and win. Chalk counted a roomful of phantasmal cash with Blackshaw's face replacing that of dead presidents on every last bill. In a gallery filled with masterpieces Chalk yearned to steal, every painted face, and every signature, was that of Ben Blackshaw. In an unearthly harem, all the women were LuAnna Blackshaw clutching knives held out toward his vitals and privates.

With no idea how much time had passed, Chalk woke again to find that the goat had moved on to better pastures. He got to his knees. The world spun around him. He tottered, but remained conscious. He stood. Exposed to wind and wave, and dehydrated for untold hours though he had inhaled and choked, swallowed and vomited vast volumes of salt water all the while, at least he was on dry land. But where?

Blackshaw was a curse. A deadly gadfly who could never be shooed away. A rage welled up in Chalk's chest. The anger stiffened his spine. If Blackshaw were anywhere within a thousand miles, it meant the stakes of the mission were astronomical, and so Chalk had to be on the right track. Blackshaw stood between him and the blighted, spider-infested emotion that passed for happiness in Chalk's heart. He would finish this detail. Then he would finish Blackshaw and everything the Smith Islander held dear.

He took a few trial steps. It would be slow going; his feet barely budged, encased as they seemed to be in slabs of pig iron. The soft, loose sand above the waterline reared to Sisyphean heights like Sahara Desert dunes.

At last, Chalk was off the beach. He picked his way through a wall of lush plants and trees that all tugged at the salt-crusted remains of his clothes. The footing was firmer here than on the beach, and there was the welcome relief of shade, but the groundcover snared his ankles like heavy shackles.

After this death march of no more than a hundred yards, Chalk arrived at the shoulder of a road. It was the intersection of two roads, really, with traffic metered this way and that by a stop light. He stood back in the vegetation leaning against a palm tree, and from there he caught his breath, and assessed his position. A blue and blaze-green taxi pulled up to the light, its aftermarket brakes squeaking. And there, in the back seat of this cab in the middle of nowhere sat LuAnna Blackshaw. It was impossible. It must be fate, a chance at glorious vengeance. Bested by fatigue, Chalk surrendered consciousness and slid down the tree trunk to the ground.

CHAPTER 26

BLACKSHAW SUCKED AIR through the rebreather rig from Ellis's well-stocked shipboard cabinet of amazing toys. Mr. Curlew re-checked the settings for the gasses, and the secure placement of the CO_2 scrubbers that would allow the former SEAL to swim underwater toward the Bermudian shore without leaving a trail of bubbles on the surface.

Ellis tapped Mr. Curlew on the shoulder. "Give us a minute?"

Mr. Curlew aye-ayed, wished Blackshaw good luck, and left the small compartment deep in the bilges of *Bystander of Man*.

Ellis said, "Stamped passport?"

Blackshaw tapped a pocket containing a waterproof bag. "It looks perfect."

"Mr. Gannet's an artist. What can I say?"

"You think Chalk was coming here?"

After a moment's consideration, while he made a few yanks on Blackshaw's straps, Ellis said, "You mentioned Cynter, and Chalk didn't seem at all surprised. He's always got a money angle."

"True, but his money angles aren't little tiny, non-descript jobs. He's usually hooked in at pretty high levels."

"Exactly like those Feebs," Ellis said. "They don't nose around for penny-ante stuff. I'm worried you shouldn't go alone."

"Oh this is just recon. Take a look around and come on back."

Ellis Hogan and Blackshaw both knew this was a lie.

Ellis handed Blackshaw a dark waterproof bag. All the air had been squeezed out of it before it was sealed so it wouldn't throw his buoyancy off by expanding and contracting as he changed depth. The outline of the pistol inside was easy to see.

Blackshaw hefted the pouch and said, "Not my Bersa .380."

"Sig Sauer P226, 9mm, but I swapped in the chrome-phosphate-lined barrel. Reduced corrosion in the salt air. Single action. Reduced profile for fast—"

"Does it go bang?"

"All the live-long day, Ben. I hope you don't need it, but if you do, don't be shy."

"Any ideas yet, about that Haakon, or Fort Clonque that Chalk was rattling on about?"

Ellis assessed Blackshaw's gear while his friend stowed the weapon. "Not yet. We're still checking."

Under the rebreather straps and his buoyancy compensator, Blackshaw was wearing a RailRiders VersaTac shirt, and the mid-weight pants from the same line. A pair of light nylon boots was lashed to his weight belt. In those clothes, within minutes of swimming ashore on Bermuda, he would be as dry as any tourist out for a morning stroll.

Ellis opened the big hatch in the compartment sole. In the blue circle below sloshed the Atlantic Ocean. "We could still put you ashore by boat."

Blackshaw took in the compartment. "As far as I'm concerned, you have."

"We'll be standing by the satellite phone for your exfil. Do you have anything close to a plan you'd like to share? Anything we could help with?"

"I'd like to think so. If LuAnna calls, tell her I'll be back home in a day or two."

Ellis said, "Lying to her is bad business."

"You'll say the right thing. You sometimes do, anyway."

Blackshaw spat in his mask and fitted it over his face. With the mouthpiece clamped securely in his teeth, he leaned forward from the edge of the hatch, and dropped into the water.

CHAPTER 27

CHALK WOKE TO find himself under a clean white sheet. Had he died? Was he a ghost, or a corpse? It was another nightmare. As consciousness seeped back, he realized he lay beneath a high ceiling on a cot. The room was cool, and walled with big stone blocks painted an eye-searing shade of white. Through a door he saw and heard Black women and their children serving food at a long table. The aromas made him gag. The holy cross mounted on the wall told him this was some kind of church, or shelter. Maynard Pilchard Chalk was a goddamn foundling?

He peeked under the sheet. Even through the crushing pain in his head and aching jaw where his teeth had been kicked free, he saw he was clean, but naked. His crushed fingers still throbbed, but now they were splinted and bandaged. He sat up, and his bare feet recoiled from the cold floor. The nudity issue would need to be resolved. For the moment, he wrapped himself in the sheet and stood, looking for all the world like a Roman senator filled with important things to say. The women who noticed him through the doorway fell silent. Children saw the direction of their mothers' gaze, and they gawked, too.

"What the fuck are you looking at!" Chalk said. Or thought he said. His voice was a harsh rasp, and his parched tongue stuck to his remaining teeth.

A very sturdy woman appeared at Chalk's side and took him gently by the elbow. "You need to rest, friend. What's your name?"

"My name is Legion, you harpy! Where the hell are my clothes!" Chalk wrenched his elbow free, teetered, and caught himself by grabbing at the wall. His sheet fell free. The children howled with delight. Their mothers glanced away, unimpressed.

"There's a doctor coming to see to you," said the woman, draping Chalk in the sheet. He palmed the cell phone he had plucked from her pocket.

Chalk clutched at the pain in his head. He rapped his knuckles on the titanium plate, but got no relief. "Get away from me!"

A second woman with short gray hair brought Chalk a pair of pants, a shirt, and a pair of sandals. Nothing was new, but the items were all clean. Chalk staggered into her, mumbled a kind of apology, sat on the bed, and stashed her wallet beneath the mattress.

A third woman, tiny, thin, placed a steaming plate of rice on the table by the bed, along with a cup of water and a spoon. The rice was dotted with small pieces of meat. Chalk hoped it was the goat from his welcoming committee earlier in the day. He thrived on conflict, on rancorous opposition. He was Chalk. He met his own needs, amply, ably. Where was the fear these women should be showing him as an unkillable operator? These gestures of charity were a confusing humiliation.

The three women headed for the door. As the first woman drew the door closed, Chalk croaked, "Where am I?"

The second woman who had brought the clothing whispered, "Shipwreck—"

The third woman said, "Mad—"

The first woman answered, "Bermuda. You dress and eat, maybe rest some more, and let's see what the doctor says about you. You're not going anywhere today."

Chalk waited to hear the lock on the door click, entrapping him. The sound never came. Incredulous, Chalk dropped the sheet, shuffled to the door. No, not locked. He peeked out. Everyone was eating. There was laughter. There were smiles. The children seemed to have manners, or a healthy fear of their mothers' reach. Chalk closed the door against the din.

He sat on the bed and ate. He took small bites at first. The meat was seasoned. It was delicious. His appetite recovered, and he ate faster, worried there wouldn't be enough. With every grain of rice and every bit of meat devoured, Chalk eased into the clothes. The fit was good, if not perfect. At least he wasn't naked anymore.

His strength returning, and with it his native fury, Chalk considered his situation. He had to escape from here to finish this operation. There was a kitchen. There would be knives.

CHAPTER 28

THE PATIENT SURFACED from a twilight saw-tooth range of mountains as sharp and tall as anything on Mars. Yet the dream of those crags faded and left him with the ache of a man watching his home disappear as he departs over the horizon. The high windows in the room were dark.

Another medical technician, a man older than the one before, was moving through the ritual checks and replenishments of his intravenous fluids. The foot wound was rebandaged. His undressed head wound was inspected. The enfeebled Patient tried to resist, but the technician didn't even notice. The Patient felt more like a meal being prepared than anything sentient, living, or otherwise human.

At some point in this routine, the Patient became aware of another person in the room. With an effort, he turned to get a better look at the newcomer, who wore a suit and tie, and acknowledged his presence as only as an infidel would.

"Hi asshole. I've been waiting. We're going to have to dial back on your poppy juice. You look way too cozy."

The medical technician swabbed out the Patient's mouth with the little sponge on the stick, and dropped it into a red plastic bag marked *Incinerator*. His captors were either conscientious, or managing all traces of his DNA.

The newcomer spoke again. "I'm Screed. I know who you are so don't bother talking. I know your English is okay, but you don't like to speak it very often. It's all in your file. So just listen. We'll be moving you again in a few days. Get this. Some touchy-feely dipshit suggested we send you an Imam with a rug and a Quran so you could get your prayer on, but you're an animal, and I said no. We're going to keep a pulse in your body, but your brain and whatever's left of your soul is your fucking problem. I was thinking we lace your sedative with some high octane LSD, and then send in a dog or two to keep you company. Big dogs. Mean ones. I thought that would get your attention."

Screed stood, and dusted off his hands as if he'd finished a job involving dirt.

"I'm going now. I have to find some hungry, horny dogs for you. I'm thinking we need to flip you over once in a while to avoid bedsores. I'd let my K-9 unit toss your salad, except I don't let them eat filth."

The Patient marshaled his strength and whispered, "Kill—"

Screed laughed. "You going to kill me? Those days are over. Or you mean I should kill you. Trust, asshole." Screed drew a pistol, cocked it, and pressed the barrel to the Patient's temple. The metal was warm from Screed's armpit holster. Screed's breath was hot on the Patient's face. "If the order comes down, I'll do it myself."

PART II
SIOBHAN-CHICA-WOW-WOW

CHAPTER 29

THE TATTOO PARLOR was a bust. Almost. LuAnna had folded a print-out of photograph 102-L from Cynter's autopsy so that only the faint *Siobhan* outline was in view. She didn't want to be arrested for flogging porn. She thought it odd that the pretty young woman wielding the needle gun had no ink in sight on her, nor any piercings, nor loopy expanders in her earlobes.

LuAnna said, "I was wondering if you recognize this work."

The woman, who said her name was Critter, glanced at the photograph. "Not sure. It looks like *au-and-sausau* work. You from the Department of Health?"

"What's *au-and*—whatever you said?"

"Traditional Pacific Islander tools. Not machines." Critter pointed to her inking gun. "*Au-and-sausau* is tapping a serrated bone comb with the ink on it with a stick. Old School. Not legal now. Too hard to keep the tools clean. It's a two-person job, which cuts into profits. A *tufuga ta tatau* master does the work. A *solo*, probably an apprentice, wipes up ink and blood during the session. Hurts like hell."

"This guy's as tough as they come," said LuAnna.

"Come on," said Critter. "Show me."

"Whatever do you mean?"

"The rest of the photograph. Show me."

"Just between us girls," said LuAnna, unfolding the picture.

At first, Critter smiled in appreciation of Travis Cynter's equipment. Then she went pale, almost covered her hand with her mouth.

LuAnna said, "It's something. Critter, are you all right?"

"Bastard."

"You know him?"

Critter said, "Not personally. My girlfriend had a fling with him. See the freckles and moles like a little face? That, and the—" Critter held her palms apart to indicate a prodigious size, "—that's what she said. Has to be him. He dumped her."

"Who is she?"

"Did he dump you, too?" Critter asked. "Why don't you have a normal picture of him?"

LuAnna's mind raced to come up with any explanation besides the truth.

Critter studied the photo again. "He's dead, isn't he."

LuAnna nodded.

"Mindy won't be too upset about that," Critter said. "Are you absolutely sure you're not from the Department of Health, or the police?"

LuAnna said, "I promise you I'm not."

Critter decided. "Okay. Mindy's a *solo* for a *tufuga* in Hamilton. I wasn't supposed to say. She loves the old ways. Except when your ex comes in to get a tattoo of a new girl's name. What an asshole. Is she in trouble? You don't think—"

"No," said LuAnna. "But we're trying to figure out what happened to this man. Can you tell me where to find Mindy?"

Critter jotted down an address, and asked, "When are you due?"

"A few weeks yet."

"Mindy says a woman getting a *malu* tattoo, from her knees up to her butt, hurts worse than having a baby."

LuAnna said, "Mindy's wrong. Losing a baby hurts worst of all."

CHAPTER 30

BONAMY SCREED SCOURED the dark web for any clue about his next steps. Staying worlds ahead of his superiors, anticipating their next moves before they had even conceived them had made his rise faster than most. But his current fish was huge. A whale. And he needed extra-long distance foresight to stay on top of a situation that seemed static for now, but could get kinetic any second.

His predecessor at Langley, Maynard Chalk, had constructed Black Widow, a search engine that could move, spiderlike, throughout the known web and infiltrate any site no matter how heavily it was firewalled or encrypted. Screed's problem was finding Black Widow.

Chalk's old shell company, Right Way Moving & Storage, had a public, sham website. That's where Screed focused to find the way into Black Widow, but after weeks of probing it, digging into its code line by line, he hadn't cracked it. Chalk had been as cagey as he was insane. On the Packing & Crating page of Right Way's site, there were several tabs for disposable materials. Screed rolled his curser over the Bubble Wrap tab, and at the bottom of that page he saw a small fill-in field appear. He hadn't noticed it the hundred other times he'd explored Chalk's final digital footprint.

Screed had Chalk's full dossier next to him, and he began hand-cranking anything conceivable as a password to open Black Widow. The question for Screed was, how nuts had Chalk been when he had created the password? If he had done it before the most recent downward spiral over the last year that had led to his death, would it be something banal or plain stupid, like a birthday, or a childhood pet's name? What if Chalk had changed the password after shattering through his personal looking glass in a later fit of paranoia? Maybe the password was changed automatically from a list, or according to a pattern, like a Fibonacci sequence. Screed knew it could be anything. And how many chances would Screed get to try before the site locked him out? Even bank websites and Smartphones had a lock-out feature after too many incorrect attempts. What the hell was Chalk's *Rosebud?*

Screed started typing. His first try, he entered *password* in case Chalk was less a mad genius defending Black Widow, and more sophomoric. His failure was greeted by the sound of flatulence from his computer. *Classy, Chalk. Classy.* At least no attempt counter appeared. Maybe Chalk hadn't built one in, knowing that in his lunacy, remembering his password might take a few tries. Screed forgot his passwords now and then, and he wasn't barking mad. This was going to take time. Time Screed didn't have. But if he got lucky, he'd reward himself by visiting the Patient again. That was always fun.

CHAPTER 31

THE WATER CLEARED and clouded as sea life bloomed into view and faded. In Blackshaw's mind there was no doubt that the Caribbean offered far better visibility to a diver than the Chesapeake on its best day. He swam on, often checking his wrist compass and folding what he saw there in with his understanding of how currents and tides would affect his line toward Bermuda.

Ellis had ordered *Bystander of Man* to a dead stop three miles off shore. Moments after Blackshaw dropped out of the bottom of her hull and swam clear, the twin screws had started turning again. Blackshaw had watched her rudder swing to port, and the yacht turned north toward open water.

He glanced below from time to time, watching for the first signs of the bottom rising as he made his way toward shore. He kicked his long Cressi fins gently, and with no landmarks, he was barely aware of his progress.

Then he heard the engine. He couldn't identify its make or model even remotely, which surprised him, but it was a single diesel motor, and big. He scanned the surface, confident he was deep enough to avoid being struck as the approaching boat passed him overhead. With the sound growing, he wondered why he still couldn't see it up there.

On one of his scans, the vessel finally caught his attention as a darker shape in the distant gray. It grew, and Blackshaw had trouble trusting his eyes. It was a submarine. As it drew closer, Blackshaw saw the rust, barnacles, algae, and tendrils of sea grass undulating behind its conning tower. This vessel was like none he had seen before. It seemed incredible to him that this sub was the source of the combustion engine noise. A submerged boat usually moved with quieter electric or nuclear power. Somehow a diesel engine was rumbling away inside that thing, but it was at least fifty feet deep. There was no snorkel device trailing up to the surface through which to draw air down to the engine. Even so, a stream of bubbles rose up behind it.

Blackshaw watched the sub's bearing, which he guessed would take it past him sixty feet away. He judged it was under two hundred feet long, quite small by modern military standards. And it was a naval vessel, or had been. The port bow was grooved with two closed torpedo tubes. Blackshaw assumed there were two more on the starboard side. As the sub's course reached its closest point to him, he thought he saw a red Russian star underneath the algae coating on the tower.

Blackshaw watched the sub's screws whirl out of sight into a wall of gray and blue. A slight pressure wave washed over him, and soon, even the sound of that strange engine receded. He was baffled. He took a bearing off his compass, checked the time for a gauge on the tidal movement, and continued swimming.

Blackshaw knew it didn't take long for any ocean-going ship to look like hell without regular, energetic maintenance, especially below the waterline. Even in the gentler brackish waters of the Chesapeake, he had *Miss Dotsy* up on the hard for bottom paint every year. He'd even considered a boatlift to slow the algae growth and keep her smooth and quick, but he'd never hear the end of it from his neighbors; it was too fancy a contraption for Smith Island. Salt, flora, and fauna were a destructive trio, but with this sub, the factor of time also played a role in her looks. She was quite old. Something in Blackshaw's study of the Soviet-era navy was tugging at the edges of his memory.

He drifted into a meditative state listening to the way the whisper of air through his rebreather kept a kind of rhythm with the slow undulations of his fins. *Rebreather.* The word kept playing in his mind. Blackshaw kept swimming.

CHAPTER 32

LUANNA TAXIED TO the Hamilton street corner nearest the address Critter had given her in hopes of chatting with Mindy, Travis Cynter's ex. The tattoo shop was closed. That seemed strange to LuAnna. It was late afternoon. Sure, they likely did most of their business in the evening after Happy Hour, but a sign posted on the door said the joint should've been open already.

She walked around the block until she arrived at the entrance to an alley. Halfway down the narrow passage, she found the back door of the tattoo shop. She knocked. No one answered. She was going to try the door, but noticed blood on the wall. A hand print oriented as if it were made by the left hand of someone on the way out. The thumb of the handprint was pointed inward toward the door.

LuAnna's heart sped up. She backed away from the door, and glanced down the alley in both directions. She saw no one. Just as important, she saw no surveillance cameras recording her presence, and no nosey eyewitnesses peering down at her from the apartment windows looming overhead on both sides. No surprise, the door was unlocked. LuAnna went in.

The lights were off. She found herself in a back hallway that led to the shop's front studio area where light from outside poured in through a big picture window. Nothing like getting tipsy, glancing through the glass, and seeing a tattoo in progress to whet a body's thirst for ink. LuAnna never made it to the main studio area.

The door to a supply closet stood ajar. LuAnna pushed it open, but it stopped halfway. Something blocked it. She reached in and flipped on the light.

They were lying face down; their hands and ankles were bound. The first was an older man with a wispy gray beard. The doorstop was a nice looking woman, perhaps in her thirties. Her sleeveless shirt revealed a shoulder tattoo that read *Mindy*. They had been tortured. Torn out fingernails were strewn about the floor like bloody beetles. Their throats had been slashed deep, almost to the spine, by someone strong, crazy, or both. The blood had pooled, but there were spatters, likely feathered arterial spray beyond the edges of the larger puddles. A shitty way to die.

LuAnna nearly jumped out of her skin when someone yanked hard on the shop's front door. Some customer, maybe with an appointment, maybe a walk-in. She used her shirttail to wipe her fingerprints from the light switch as she turned it off, got into the alley as calmly as possible, and ambled away into the afternoon.

CHAPTER 33

THE CORALS WERE beautiful. Some fanned, and others were head-shaped. Blackshaw imagined he saw the coral bust of a beautiful Spanish woman with a filigreed mantilla in her anemone hair. Trigger fish and clownfish brought other splashes and dashes of color to the blues and grays of the water.

Blackshaw knew he was reaching the cruise ship jetty; soda cans and other tourist ejecta littered the bottom. There were no ocean liners in port at the moment. He reached the breakwater, turned right, and swam to its end. There, he did a hairpin left turn around to calmer waters between the jetty and shore. Ten minutes gentle swimming later, Blackshaw reached the netting. On the other side lay a watergate into the grounds of the old Royal Naval Dockyard.

Blackshaw removed his rebreather, but kept breathing through it. He changed his fins for the boots he'd brought along. When all his gear was bungeed fast to a sturdy coral, he shut the rebreather down, and pushed for the surface floats of the net, exhaling as he rose. Without pausing, he rolled over the top of the net, grabbing a breath of air as he went. It was early, but there was still a risk someone might have seen him. He jackknifed down again, and swam toward the watergate. Now, he was not alone.

Two gray shapes rushed at Blackshaw, twisted around him; one of them thumped him in a playful way in his chest. They were dolphins, from the attraction housed in the old stone buildings of the dockyard. A third dolphin joined the underwater inquiry. Blackshaw pressed on toward the watergate. He felt like a man coming home after a long absence to three big Chesapeake Bay Retriever pups desperate to greet and to play.

Inside the watergate, Blackshaw surfaced. The dolphins arched and puffed next to him, popping up to eye him above the water. He swam on to one of the meshed-off inner pools in which several other dolphins glided. Blackshaw climbed out onto a walkway, stood, and sorted his clothes as water drained around his boots. The warmth of the morning began to dry his VersaTac shirt and pants. Now he needed to wait until someone from the dolphin attraction came to open up for the day and disarm the door alarms.

CHAPTER 34

HOURS LATER, SCREED was still trying passwords to break into Chalk's Black Widow. He was reaching the end of the Chalk dossier, from which he had hoped to find some clue to his predecessor's inner workings. The Patient in the other room was the lynchpin for an American coup d'etat, but how to exploit him to best effect, that roadmap lay locked inside this digital safe. No one disputed Chalk had been insane, yet few could argue against his blue sky brilliance.

Screed typed *Lily*, the first name of a dead senator with whom Chalk had once worked, and got the same flatulent fanfare he'd heard after every attempt so far. He typed *Morgan*, to the same rude noise. He turned the computer's volume down. Why hadn't he thought to do that before? Screed was furious with himself.

He hurled the Chalk file in a fit of petulance. Midflight across the room, it opened, and documents fluttered down like dirty snow. Screed leaned back in the chair.

On a whim, he sat up again, and typed *F-A-R-T*. On the screen, the Right Way Moving & Storage page disappeared, and was replaced by a spider web graphic with a black widow in its center spinning a struggling insect into a sticky fajita of death. Chalk had created an audio password reminder for himself. Screed stood and whooped in conquest. One of Screed's men put his head in at the door, and retreated upon being shown the muzzle of a gun.

Screed began his study of Black Widow. The dossier littering the floor was nothing more than a redacted fortune cookie compared to the machinations now unfolding before Screed's eyes. He was desperate to continue reading, nearly helpless to pull away, but there was some housekeeping to do. He had to know more about how Black Widow worked.

Screed opened the log-in history, and could not stop staring. Someone had been using Black Widow not three hours ago. He scrolled to the last memo added during the session. It was a record of an infiltration to an FBI database. Screed's heart raced, then hammered. The target file was an autopsy report on the operator Screed had killed just a few days before. And there was another surprise. The most recent initials in the Black Widow infiltration log were the same as all the ones before. MPC. Maynard Pilchard Chalk was still alive. Screed called for high level surveillance on all Chalk's former associates, and all of the old Right Way Moving & Storage lines of communication. Chalk had been a god in black-ops circles. Today, he was a loose end.

CHAPTER 35

LUANNA HAD CHECKED into a hotel in Hamilton, and kept a very low profile. She watched the news, and on the late edition, word of the brutal double murder was rocking the airwaves. There was no word of any suspect, nor of any witness being sought for questioning, pregnant or otherwise. Good. Police were not aware of LuAnna's intrusion onto the crime scene. If they were, they weren't saying.

The next morning, she had breakfast in her room, and read the on-line edition of the *Royal Gazette* with the television on in the background. Stephanie DeSilva's coverage of the investigation did not seem to be moving forward, though the inquiry was still in its early stages.

LuAnna wondered how the one woman she wanted to speak with had come to such a grim end just hours ago, possibly even within minutes before finding her. Someone was working out ahead of LuAnna, fitting the pieces together, and erasing leads. The FBI file on Travis Cynter's death could be one source. A person who knew Cynter with a buck-naked intimacy could be another catalyst. LuAnna was in a race against a keen energetic mind, but one hell bent on covering tracks and creating new false trails.

She pulled Cynter's cuff-link from her pocket. Reasonably certain the cops weren't looking for her, she needed to take the next step. She showered, dressed, and went down to the lobby. Though the jewelry store wasn't far, her feet felt tired and swollen. She treated herself, and found a taxi in front of her hotel.

The Alexandra Mosher boutique was a study in functional beauty. Both a workspace and a showroom, to LuAnna it felt open and inviting with bright clean lines. It was a far cry from the gory tattoo parlor. This place was for well-heeled clients.

There was a lovely blonde woman with a golden tan seated behind a corner counter. Tools of her jewelry making profession lay scattered on the table between magnifying glasses fixed on small stands for close-up work. She looked up and smiled when LuAnna approached.

"May I help you?" The woman stood graciously without giving the least impression that LuAnna was interrupting her work.

"I hope so." LuAnna had the cuff-link ready in hand. "Could you tell me about this piece? I found it, and it seems such a precious thing. Are you the designer?"

"And chief cook and bottle washer. Alexandra," she said, extending her hand. "You recognized my work?"

"No, but with the pink sand inlay, and it being so pretty, it didn't take me long to Google you right up."

"Where did you find it?" Mosher's eyes gleamed. She enjoyed a mystery.

"On a beach," said LuAnna. "You've got a teensy-weensy serial number on it, I see. Do you know who bought this? I'd like to return it."

A cloud crossed Mosher's face. "Yes, we do have a record. It lends a bespoke feel to the pieces."

"Sure! Reckon it bespokes the heck out of them morning, noon, and night. So, between us girls, who bought it? I bet they're hoping to wear the pair this Friday night. Won't they be happy to get it back!"

Mosher examined the cuff-link, then did a look-up on her computer.

"This is awkward. We keep our client list confidential," Mosher said. "If you were here when she bought it, of course, what could I say, but—"

LuAnna smiled. "We have to keep it bespokish. I understand completely. A lady doesn't want her name bandied about even in the most polite circles." LuAnna took a risk. "Here. You take it." She laid the cuff-link on the counter and smiled. "I know you'll see it finds its way home."

CHAPTER 36

BLACKSHAW WOKE TO a nudge from a trim young woman in a sleek black one-piece bathing suit sporting the logo of the dolphin attraction. He was seated against a wall with his head on his arm-wrapped knees. The woman had a bucket of small fish in her hand.

"They need more time on the fire for my liking," he said, standing up. By now his clothing was completely dry.

"How'd you get in here?"

"A little too much party last night. Must've gotten lost in the dark." Blackshaw looked genuinely panicked when he said, "*Liberty of the Seas*. I'm sure late getting back aboard. That's the way out, right?" He backed for the door.

The young woman said, "The *Liberty* left yesterday!"

"Oh my *blessing*!" squawked Blackshaw, and he ran out through the gift shop, and disappeared into the growing crowd of tourists on the street.

CHAPTER 37

LUANNA LEFT THE Alexandra Mosher boutique and sought the restroom of a café across the street. Pregnancy was playing hell with her bladder. She emerged and took a seat at a small table where she could watch the boutique's entrance. She nursed an ammonia coke with small infrequent sips, as much because she was not sure of its effect on her burgeoning baby as to prevent having to pee again. She didn't know how long this stakeout would take, and she didn't want to leave the store unmonitored for even a second. It might all be moot. The person who bought that cufflink could be anywhere in the world right now.

She hadn't called Blackshaw. He had not reached out to her, either. She enjoyed a little solo time, but wondered if she should've filled him in on what she'd learned from her visit to Molly Wilde's place.

After a half-hour second guessing herself, LuAnna felt vindicated when her hunch was proved right. A chic woman in her late thirties or early forties rounded the corner near the boutique and went inside. Her red hair was neatly snatched into tortoiseshell barrettes. Red's sunglasses glinted with a high-end logo on the temple bars. Her white dress fit her curvy figure with tasteful lines that betokened a couture designer. Her purse and her open shoes were also elegant without screaming for attention. Red had money, but beyond letting the world know this in the most subtle ways, she had nothing further to prove. Her hurried gait said she had something important on her mind.

LuAnna left money on the café table and took a spot on the sidewalk near the store. She felt like an actress waiting for the cue to stroll into her scene. Red was twenty minutes in the boutique before she emerged in some kind of daze, but without a shopping bag. As LuAnna approached Red, she noticed she was dabbing at her eyes and nose with a tissue.

The women passed on the sidewalk. LuAnna turned and said, "Siobhan? Travis said you were gorgeous, but wowzy!"

CHAPTER 38

CHALK SPENT THE last of his stolen money on a taxi to the Great Head Battery, even though he was waiting for a plane. He had slept rough overnight in a hedge, and woke early covered in insect bites, his fractured fingers and other hurts pulsing with pain. To kill time until the early flight arrived, he strolled the hilly winding paths of the old fortification, stepping off as if to examine some artifact or gun emplacement whenever a tourist or fitness nut bounded into view. At the expected hour, Chalk made his way back to the enormous nine-inch coastal guns, sat down, and contemplated the sea like a peaceful man without a care.

So, Cynter had been on Bermuda. That tattoo chippy had divulged that much. Apparently, he'd been there for several weeks, looking for something, for an asset, on behalf of the U.S. Government.

Chalk grew wistful. He'd been a good government bag man. He was a kingmaker back when he worked with Senator Lily Morgan. The money, the operations, he'd been the absolute mogul of Morgan's proxy wars. Of course she'd been crazy as a shit-house rat, but he'd always been able to work with it, exploit the chaos, and cash in on it. It made him feel alive. Then she got greedy and turned her back on him. She froze him out of her harebrained agenda when the Blackshaws took him down and revealed the terrible truth, that Chalk had feet of clay. When she became the Secretary of Homeland Security and still didn't pay him his due, he came around to collect. She got her two bullets down in that inferno at Dove Point, and then Chalk gave her creepy kinked-out husband two bullets more.

Chalk had to climb out of this slump. Revenge was delish', but half a year on from capping Lily Morgan, Chalk was sitting on a Godforsaken rock in the Atlantic in somebody's borrowed clothes. How low he had fallen! He had to admit, interviewing that girl and her geezer tattoo guy, and cutting their throats, had been a bright spot in an otherwise unhappy stretch.

"Mr. Chalk."

Chalk roused himself out of his funk, and got up to face his new companion. "Who the hell are you?"

There before Chalk stood a tall woman, beautiful, head completely shaved with a proud set to her back and her chin. She gripped the handle of a roller suitcase, but she carried its full weight in one hand without using the wheels.

Her smile was broad. "Call me Blessing."

"Maybe you should tell me who the hell you are," said Chalk. "I've never seen you before. If I had, I'd remember."

"I worked at the Denver office of Right Way."

"The farm team. Good to have somebody from the old crew on deck. What'd you do back in Denver?

"Oh, some filing. Some typing," said Blessing with modest confidence. "Worked some tasty psy-ops voodoo on that chucklehead who shot up the mall."

Chalk brightened. "And got the senator? That was you? We made a fortune. The Libs screamed their horseshit about sensible gun control and any shop-owner with AR-15s on the shelves sold out ten times over before that one died down. I figured Right Way made a million bucks for every corpse that day. Strong work, Blessing."

"Good times," she said with a nod.

"Gimme," said Chalk, holding out his hand for the case.

Blessing said, "Perhaps we should go somewhere less public."

"Okay. I need a hotel, some grub, and a shower."

"Fair enough. I have a rental in the lot over there." Blessing turned, and carried the case toward the road.

Chalk padded along beside her long stride as best he could in his ill-fitting shoes. "Blessing. You're as good as your name."

CHAPTER 39

BLACKSHAW DIALED HIS micro sat-phone. It was smaller than the usual sat-brick because its battery had been taken down to the barest functional minimums to make the unit compact. The shrinkage had come at a price. Without a recharge or swap-out, this battery pack provided less than fifteen minutes of talk time. So be it. Blackshaw had worked hard to get himself into position on Bermuda, but he still needed his, or rather LuAnna's hunch verified.

Somewhere in a White Mountain cave, Michael Craig picked up the line. "Rocco's Pizza."

"Large double-cheese, onions, sausage for delivery," said Blackshaw.

"You're outside our driver's range. We could do carry-out, no problem. I'm glad you called."

"I don't think you ever said that before. Got anything cooking on what we talked about?"

Craig said, "You're the ones with a bun in the oven. It's good you and LuAnna are taking some time away together."

"We're not. What are you talking about? I meant Travis. What'd you learn?"

An older couple strolled past Blackshaw and eyed his shady bench in Hamilton's Victoria Park. Blackshaw stood, and walked further down the path followed by a polite *thank you* from the gentleman as the couple took over the bench.

"I got some data on Travis yesterday. But today, everything about him prior to his death is gone. They've burnt up Travis's digital trail. Poof! It'd take an army to do this kind of job. The message is, he didn't exist before. He doesn't exist now. So watch your step. You know he was still DEVGRU."

Blackshaw stopped walking. "Sure. He told me he was Team 5. Group 1."

"When he got dead," said Craig. "Before that, he was Task Force Blue. Team 6, from 2010 through 2012."

"And there's nothing left on the web about him."

"He's been scrubbed off the planet. Of course, my gear clones everything I look at including yesterday's data dredge. And there're some hard-copy records here and there that anybody could get to, but a digital wipe like this, that's the way to blank out quick inquiries. It means something's happening on an accelerated timetable. Whoever's doing this doesn't care what somebody's more time-consuming legwork would eventually turn up. Light-speed fingertip data is their big worry. So I've been looking elsewhere."

"At things other than Cynter's record," Blackshaw said.

"Exactly. You're not going to dig this. There was this gig back in '08. I designed a search bot for JSOC."

"Do I want to hear this, Mike?" Blackshaw glanced around for eavesdroppers, found none, and felt foolish as though he were making a bad job of a kindergarten pantomime.

"Probably not. While the op was running, I refined the bot's search criteria, but I was still mining big data from all over the world. I had to hijack half the Company's processing power of their entire network."

"I'm sure they loved that."

"They begged me to. It was really their gig. They had a target. They couldn't find it. They came to me through JSOC."

Why didn't Craig sound proud? Why did he sound anxious?

"That's a high value target," Blackshaw said. "Did they tell you what it was?"

"No. They just kept feeding me search criteria. Item after item, with a prioritization of each one, you know, which item to filter for first, second, three hundredth, it was nuts. Always changing. And sometimes they'd have me clean house, and start over, and build a completely new model."

"So what's the issue? You said this was in '08. That's a while ago. I mean, what happened back then that's so hurry-up today that they'd squeegee Travis like that?"

Craig was so nervous it made him talk in circles. "I said they *commissioned* the bot in 2008. I ran it for three years, sometimes updating it thirty, forty times a day with new inputs from the spooks and culling obsolete criteria. Then in 2011, the bot pinged once, and they pulled its plug. They cancelled the entire program."

"Didn't they pay you?"

"You paid me, my taxable citizen buddy, but yes, I got all of what I was due."

"Mike, the battery on this phone's right puny. What's the problem?"

"I didn't turn the bot off," said Craig. "I just forgot. I run ten, twenty ops at a time. I was so glad to not have to update this one. And right after the gig was shut down, Nicole and I bailed on a trip to Rio, like that day, to celebrate, and I never thought of the technical side of it again. I left it running with the same criteria it was searching for when the Company killed it."

"You're a dirty bird, Mike."

"It was an accident. But it's been going this whole time. Well, a week back, it pinged again. It shouldn't have done that. The mission was over. I didn't know what the hell it was, it's been so long."

"What was the criteria?"

"One thing woke up the whole search. It refocused the bot's other criteria until it pinged."

"Okay Mike. What was it?"

"Disposable medical supplies for a renal patient. For dialysis. Blood group AB negative, as it happens. In Bermuda. I backtracked. Before it pinged in Bermuda, it un-pinged in the UK."

Blackshaw grew impatient. "Okay, that's a rare blood-type. What's an un-ping?"

"It's when the bot detects that the full set of criteria has gone dark all at once, like a digital black hole."

"So maybe the guy just died," said Blackshaw. "That was the un-ping."

"Not likely," said Craig. "It happened just before the ping in Bermuda, where the criteria all went hot again. From the un-ping to the ping, maybe seven hours. How long is a flight from Heathrow to Bermuda?"

Blackshaw asked, "And this is what got your bot to ping again?"

"There were other criteria, a whole constellation, but that's what started up the algorithm that was supposed to be shut down and obsolete as of 2011."

Things Michael Craig had said began falling into place in Blackshaw's mind. He asked, "So when in 2011 are we talking about? When did the Company pull the plug on your op?"

"I rechecked to make sure. It was early May. Thanks, Honey."

"What?"

Through mouthful of food, Craig said, "Nicole brought me a sandwich."

"Tell her *hey* from me," said Blackshaw.

"So how's LuAnna doing? Where is she? Have you talked to her?"

"You never ask about her, Mike. Why are you asking about her? You nev—Mike?"

The line was dead. Blackshaw checked the battery meter on the phone. It still had a few minutes left but he could hardly trust it. Like an aircraft fuel gauge, the meter was only mil-spec'd to be accurate when power was completely drained.

Blackshaw ambled out of the park deep in thought. Travis Cynter was DEVGRU at a critical time during the war in Afghanistan. He had survived, and moved on to other gigs. But at some point he had stumbled on something he shouldn't have, something about the operation that Michael Craig had been running for JSOC and the Company until 2011. May of 2011.

Blackshaw felt like he was kicking pebbles and not seeing the whole mountain. He wandered Hamilton like this for nearly an hour. Then he rounded a corner and could have sworn he saw his wife, who was back in Maryland attending her baby shower.

CHAPTER 40

PERSHING LOWRY TAPPED on Molly Wilde's door in her Calvert office. He obeyed her command to come in. She brightened upon seeing him.

"This is a treat," she said. "Wait. Am I in trouble?"

"Of course not. But we should talk about our intruder." Lowry closed the door and sat in the knock-off Eames lounger that Molly had picked up for quick siestas at work.

"What're you thinking?" she asked.

"We should recruit her. Sign her up."

"Seriously?" Wilde said. "I'm barely good with looping either Blackshaw in on this weird back-channel basis."

"I should have made it clearer that I was kidding," said Lowry. "What's your assessment of this—case, for want of a better word."

"A dead SEAL on a small tidal island, cause of death possibly British sniper bullet. Two-tap coup de gras from a 9mm with no rifling match in the system. And a lady in Cynter's life named Siobhan who's important enough to get her name tattooed where she can read it if he was naked. Said tattoo—unfinished. Oh, and somebody shot a stallion on Assateague Island around the same time of Cynter's death."

"That's fresh," said Lowry. "Is it related? Recover a bullet?"

"No bullet. Wounds indicate a large caliber. Probably fragmented. I do have an agent with a metal detector working the scene, so that might turn something up. It's worth noting the pony died from a head shot."

Lowry took this in. "Any sign of Ben Blackshaw?"

"No. Not yet," said Wilde. "We've got Smith Island surveilled, but between private boats, ferries, and a quick hop to Tangier Island where there's an airstrip, I'd say the cordon is more like a sieve."

"It's possible LuAnna Blackshaw has been of service again, not by anything she said. More from what she's done. I find it helps to read around her."

"Okay, what's she done?" asked Wilde.

Lowry produced two plane tickets from his inside jacket pocket. "Yesterday, she flew to Bermuda."

CHAPTER 41

BLESSING WAITED IN the hotel lobby. She had given Chalk her keycard, and he was upstairs taking that much needed shower. He would dress out of the suitcase she had brought for him, his Get Out Of Dodge, or GOOD bag he kept ready. Then they would eat. Blessing punched up a number on her conventional cellular phone.

Bonamy Screed answered. "Do you have him?"

"Yes. He's cleaning up," said Blessing. "He was so glad to see me it was touching. Are you sure it's the same Maynard Chalk?"

"I'm guessing your cover is solid," said Screed.

"As the Bank of England. A little mayhem goes a long way as a calling card with that one. I didn't tell him about the rest of the team."

"Good. Have you confirmed why he's there?"

Blessing thought for a moment. "He's trying to pick up the scent. He wants the asset for his very own. It might interest you; two tattoo artists are dead here. Murder. Talk of the town."

"The ones who knew Cynter?"

"Can't say for sure. They were bound, and their throats were slashed."

"That's Chalk. Christ, what a sloppy embarrassment. Sounds like he's scrubbing the backtrail as he investigates so no one can follow. Keep an eye on him," said Screed.

"Of course. I'll pick his brain meantime."

Screed said, "Please. We absolutely need to know how close he is, and who he's told. He's got access to the FBI file on the dead SEAL. The question is, can he make anything of it?"

Blessing saw Chalk emerge from the hotel elevator looking clean, pressed, shaved, and refreshed though still a bit knocked around. She told Screed, "I'll get what I can. Here he is. Right on time for his last meal."

She closed the phone and produced a beautiful, warm smile as Chalk approached.

CHAPTER 42

LUANNA AND SIOBHAN took a table at the same café across from the Mosher boutique. The server gave no indication she'd ever seen LuAnna before, let alone less than ten minutes ago. LuAnna thought that one was worth her weight in gold.

"You knew my name how?" Siobhan dabbed at her nose with a fresh tissue.

"Purely by accident. Alexandra checked the serial number on the cufflink first thing. She didn't mean it, but I couldn't help but see the screen when she looked up the owner."

"Buyer. I gave them as a gift less than a week ago. If Travis lost one, why did you bring it back here?" In her confusion, Siobhan wasn't processing well, and the inevitable lay far outside her ken.

LuAnna guessed that a shock, while unpleasant, might shake loose things that Siobhan might usually be too poised and discrete to reveal. "Hon, I've got some crap news. Travis is dead."

Siobhan did not wail. She just dialed up her work with the tissue, dabbing a little sign of the cross between her two eyes and her nose over and over again. "Oh my God. What happened?"

"He was shot. We don't know why, or who did it. He couldn't say."

"You're friends? Or were? Oh my God."

LuAnna sized Siobhan up before answering. "He and my husband served together. They were pretty tight. When the docs said they couldn't operate because the bullet was too close to his heart, or his aorta was coming apart or something, he just talked and talked about you to the last. We were lucky we got to say good-bye. I'm so sorry you didn't. Were you together long?"

Siobhan said, "No. A few weeks. A month. He was so good to me. My husband died four years ago and Travis was the first—you understand. The pickings on an island, even a nice place like Bermuda, they're a bit slim.

"Unless you get lucky," said LuAnna.

"Exactly. And I did. All the men in my circle were my husband's friends, some of them married. When Travis showed up, he was strong. Handsome. And he liked me. He was magic in bed."

LuAnna understood. She'd seen the wand.

"Live by the sword—" said Siobhan.

"Oh my blessing, was he trouble?"

"He was a soldier. He was in Bermuda doing something hush-hush. And he had a cruel streak."

"Travis? Really?"

"At first, it was romantic, his wanting my name on his body forever. He liked the old way of getting a tattoo. All that tapping and whacking and blood. He said it was traditional to have loved ones present when they got them because the process is a physical ordeal. I was flattered. Suddenly I was a loved-one again. Come to find the helper of the man doing the tattoo was his ex! I was mortified."

"Do you think she killed him?" LuAnna was struggling to play so dumb.

"Perhaps. Do you know that same woman was murdered just yesterday? It's all been a quite a shock."

"Seriously?"

"A stabbing. That Mindy woman, and the fellow doing the tattoo. Throats cut. You clearly don't watch the news."

"But you didn't think she killed him."

Siobhan said, "How could I know, really? You never said where Travis died."

"Back in the States. So who do you think would shoot him?"

"I think it had to do with his work. He was looking for something. He said it was a matter of honor, like his fellow soldiers had lost a Roman eagle, or standard or something. It was a bloody big deal, but he never said exactly what."

"Did he ever mention a name?" said LuAnna.

"No. We were so new, it was like the rest of the world didn't exist. Except once, now that I think about it. The only name he ever mentioned was Haakon. He said it on a phone call. Next day, he was gone."

"Haakon. Any idea who that is?"

Siobhan sat up straight with a realization. "I can do you one better. Travis was using my phone at the time. The call number is still in the log."

CHAPTER 43

THE PATIENT HAD to be dreaming. The medical technician, a blonde woman with lovely blue eyes was replacing expended IV bags with fresh ones, checking the lines, the rates of flow. All this was nothing new in his twilight existence.

But this technician was talking to him. They never did that. Not in months. And she was speaking Arabic. That touched him like music; her words were the most beautiful lyrics.

"My Prince. Can you hear me?" The woman checked the dressing on the foot wound that had reopened.

The Patient nodded once, afraid to believe his ears.

The technician said, "You are not alone. You have friends close by." She stopped speaking until the man in the bed nodded again. Then she went on. "Your captors have been keeping you heavily sedated. I am replacing the sedative with the exact same type bag, same labels, but it is filled with saline. Do you understand?"

Another nod.

"You should feel yourself wake up, my Prince, but when others are with you, you must remain as quiet as possible."

The Patient tried to speak, but his voice rasped, "Who are you?"

"That's not important, my Prince. Do you understand? You must appear to be sedated when others are with you."

The Patient said, "I understand."

"Within two days," said the woman, "we will free you. Three days after that, inshallah, you will be home where you will be welcomed. You will fight again."

The woman finished her tasks, gathered up the trash, and left the room.

The Patient felt a glimmer of hope for the first time in years. Then he wondered about the woman's words. Where was his home now?

CHAPTER 44

BLACKSHAW'S WIFE FASCINATED him. Here she was in Bermuda plain as day. And she was talking with a nice-enough looking woman like they were old friends. The woman was weeping off and on during the chat. But LuAnna didn't know anyone here, or so Blackshaw believed. LuAnna's companion showed her something on her cell phone, then rose and left.

Blackshaw was on the verge of heading down the sidewalk and sitting across from his wife in the chair just vacated. LuAnna left some money on the table, got up, and began walking away. Blackshaw's surprise at the table was spoiled, but he could still catch up with her. Then he saw Chalk.

The bastard had jumped into the sea and lived to tell about it. That vermin should have drowned. Yet he was walking down this sidewalk with a remarkable woman with a shaved head. He had already whistled up his support.

Blackshaw watched as LuAnna walked straight past Chalk. She wasn't looking for him. Clearly, she still thought he was dead. Chalk must have thought the same of her. It was obvious he didn't recognize his former hostage.

Then Blackshaw noticed three men following Chalk by about thirty feet. Operators, or agents. They were tailing him, stopping whenever he stopped, and looking everywhere but at the gorgeous woman at Chalk's side. At first Blackshaw thought the operators were there with Chalk on overwatch. From previous experience, Blackshaw knew Chalk liked his posse much closer, where they could stop bullets meant for him. Once, Chalk's statuesque companion glanced over her shoulder, checking on the tail. Then she side-eyed Chalk confirming he hadn't noticed. It was an amateurish move, but it told Blackshaw that Chalk had no idea the three operators were there. They weren't his men. They were hers.

Blackshaw jogged back through to the other side of the Par-La-Ville Park to find LuAnna.

CHAPTER 45

LUANNA WAS SHAKEN, and wondered if she could trust what she'd seen. She closed the door to her hotel room, double-bolted it, jammed the desk chair's back under the doorknob, and drew her folding knife. She backed away from the door, then checked the bathroom, including behind the shower curtain. She threw the sliding closet doors open, then swished the window drapes aside. She tried to slow her breathing. Her search complete, she knew that physically she was alone in the room. In the shadowy oubliette of her mind, Maynard Chalk was leering down at her from the trap door in the ceiling. She shuddered at the thought of him, at the beatings she'd suffered from his men a year ago. Her hip burned where they had cut her. LuAnna's soul cried out for the unborn baby that Chalk's torment had made her miscarry. Thank God he hadn't noticed her, hadn't somehow heard her heart hammering as she recognized him on the sidewalk.

Chalk was back, and LuAnna was carrying another child. She worked on her breathing again. The riptide of cortisol and adrenalin rushing though her bloodstream had to be terrible for this innocent baby, this God-sent wonder that was blooming inside her when she had lost all hope of motherhood. This time, she would do better. This time she would protect her child and win.

Someone pounded on the door. She held the knife at arm's length. "Who is it!"

"It's me, Hon," said Blackshaw his voice muffled by the door.

LuAnna caught her breath. "Ben! Oh God, Ben, are you alone?"

"Reckon so."

LuAnna dashed the chair away from the knob, unbolted the door and was in Blackshaw's arms in a second. She dragged him into the room.

"He's alive. He's here!" she said as she secured the door again. "Did anyone follow you?"

"No," said Blackshaw. "I watched the lobby, then the hallway. Hon, you're giving me a ten. We need a five."

LuAnna slapped Blackshaw hard, and slammed him against the wall. "Don't tell me what to do! Chalk's here!"

"I'm sorry. Lu' please, I'm here. We need to take it down a notch. Can we talk?"

LuAnna backed off of Blackshaw. He moved his head and neck with care. No damage from LuAnna's onslaught.

She went to the window and peered out. "I thought you shot him back at Dove Point. I thought of all the uncertain things in the world, the two facts I could trust were that you love me, and that animal was dead."

"When he showed up on the boat—"

LuAnna was on Blackshaw again. She had the front of his shirt twisted into two knots at his throat. "What—?" She tried to say more, but choked on the words.

Blackshaw talked as he gently unclamped her fingers. "We couldn't believe it. He was on a RHIB in the middle of the ocean with a tactical team. Like the Atlantic coughed him up. I put his team down, and then he was right there on the deck, howling and spitting like a mad dog."

LuAnna's voice was ice. "You were going to tell me you saw him—when?"

"I thought you were safe on Smith Island!" Blackshaw's indignation was almost all defense. Almost. "You didn't say you were coming here. You knew I was. You could've called. Ellis's boat has more radios than an aircraft carrier."

LuAnna backed off. She was honest, and knew she had her part in this confusion. She took a slow, deep breath. "You let him leave that boat alive?"

"No. He jumped off. Swagger die, he snatched a life-ring and back-flipped over the side. Anybody'd think he was crazy to hear him, and he was doing the decent thing killing himself, and good riddance."

"How did he survive?" LuAnna was quieter. "How does he live through terrible things while good folks we love get dead?"

"You didn't go to that baby shower."

"Oh hell no. I did drop in on that Molly Wilde and got a peek at her file on Travis."

Blackshaw raised an eyebrow—utter shock for him. "You two getting along?"

Mentioning her coup seemed to remind LuAnna of her own savvy strength, and this calmed her. As she had when she was an officer in the Natural Resources Police, she took refuge in an orderly reporting of the details. "Reckon not so much. There was a tattoo on Travis. Woman's name. Siobhan."

"Was that who you were sitting with at the café?"

"As a matter of fact." LuAnna was rallying. She pecked Blackshaw on the lips. "So you were watching over me. She and Travis were an item, but not for long. He was here recovering something. She said it was like a lost Roman Eagle, or something with that kind of honor attached to it. Any ideas?"

Blackshaw said, "SEALs are proud, but finishing the mission, and leaving nobody behind, that's pretty much what we do."

"Does that include losing an asset?" LuAnna said.

"An asset could be anything from a thumb drive to an agent on the ground in-country," said Blackshaw. "Take Chalk. He was raving. Talked about a fort. With more time, we could have developed Chalk as an asset.

"You mean torture him."

"That only works in the best of marriages. Who the hell is Haakon? Chalk said 'Haakon squealed.'"

LuAnna pulled out her phone. "I don't know who he is, Ben. But I got his number."

CHAPTER 46

THE PATIENT WOKE. For a moment he thought he had dreamed that the medical technician had spoken to him in his native tongue, making wondrous promises of freedom and assurances of fighting wars to come. Then he remembered something she had said, and it proved to be true. His thoughts were clear. A fog that had shrouded his mind and vitiated his will had lifted.

Screed barreled into the room carrying a large stained paper bag, and found the Patient dozing. "They say hearing is the last to go when someone dies. Who stuck around long enough to report that before crapping out, I have no idea. I'm assuming you're in there. I'm assuming you can hear me."

The Patient gave no indication Screed was right.

Screed said, "It makes me sick, how you're going to help real patriots out with some old fashioned regime change here at home. Probably makes you happy. The fulfilment of every screwed up dream you ever had, right?"

The Patient's mind raced. He was to help Screed replace a sitting president? It struck him he had no idea who was in the Oval Office today.

"To be clear," Screed said, "once you've played your part, you're done. Or maybe not. Which is worse? We kill you. Or we park you in Gitmo for the rest of your life. Mull that over."

The Patient wondered if taking down an American president would feel the same if he did it as a pawn, instead of as a warlord.

"Or maybe we keep you alive, and declare open season on your twenty-three children. And their children. And your wives. Put big irresistible rewards on all their heads. And every once in a while, we pay you a visit in whatever shit-hole we stashed you, and bring along a head for you to inspect. How about we do that until your whole line is wiped from the face of the earth."

The Patient stirred in spite of himself.

"That gotcha, you bastard."

Screed reached into the stained paper bag and with a flourish extracted a woman's severed head, holding it up by the hair. He said, "Let's start with her."

It was the medical technician who had spoken to him in his native tongue. Her blue eyes were open.

CHAPTER 47

BLACKSHAW'S SHOWER WAS hot and soapy. It was an unex-
pected luxury on this operation. LuAnna was checking the television for
news in the bedroom.

Toweling off in front of the mirror, noting all his scars, Blackshaw
said, "I'm getting old."

LuAnna said, "No, you're getting better at not dying."

Blackshaw said no more on the subject. "I saw an old Russian sub on
my infil."

LuAnna said, "Oh quit trying to justify all the gear and the swim and
all your hugger-mugger skulking. It didn't accomplish a thing."

"Swagger die, hon. And it wasn't sunk on the bottom. Sailed right on
by in front of me about fifty feet down."

LuAnna was quiet.

"And coming in like I did wasn't for nothing. I'm here, but officially,
I'm not here. You can't say the same."

LuAnna didn't answer.

"You know I'm right," said Blackshaw.

LuAnna was subdued when she said, "Lordy go to fire."

Blackshaw put his head into the room. LuAnna was transfixed by the
television. On the screen, a woman dressed like a waitress was speaking to a
reporter. The screen split, and half was taken up by a police artist's sketch
of LuAnna.

The crawl at the bottom of the screen read, "SIOBHAN GRIMES—LATEST STABBING VICTIM."

The waitress on the TV said, "Mrs. Grimes and the pregnant woman, they were both sitting right here not an hour ago. When I saw it on the telly, I couldn't believe it. It's horrible."

LuAnna said, "Shit. And I tipped that gal plenty, too."

CHAPTER 48

BERMUDA'S POLICE COMMISSIONER, Aldon Pressert, welcomed the two FBI agents into his office in the municipal building on the corner of Court and Victoria. Pressert wondered straight away if there might be a photo-op, particularly with the Executive Assistant Director for Counter Terrorism and Counterintelligence, Pershing Lowry, who was African American. Community policing was Pressert's legacy from the former Commissioner. Some positive press might help ease interracial tensions that hadn't really relaxed since '77, and the hanging of two Black men from the Black Beret Cadre, after their conviction for five murders, including Governor Sharples, and then-Commissioner Ducket. Not for the first time Pressert wondered why the last executions in the entire British Empire had to take place here on his patch. Senior Resident Agent Molly Wilde was a lovely thing in her own right, to be sure, and would be quite decorative in any picture published in the *Royal Gazette*.

Pressert kept his office temperature on the cool side so hot tea would always be welcomed no matter the season. His assistant served it—two lumps for the commissioner, and plain, neither sugar nor milk for the Americans—and retired closing the door on the way out.

Lowry said, "It's good of you to see us personally on such short notice."

"Bermuda is lovely this time of year," said Wilde.

"You could say that on any day from January to December, Agent Wilde, barring the odd hurricane. But you didn't come so far to discuss the weather."

"We're investigating a very sensitive murder case," Lowry said. "We think a person of interest in a murder—an American—might have come here to make contact with a Bermudian."

Pressert asked, "May I ask who is the victim?"

"A U.S. Navy SEAL by the name of Travis Cynter," said Lowry.

Pressert studied Lowry and Wilde for a moment. "But you're not Military Police of any sort."

"That's the sensitive aspect. We're not certain it was a strictly military operation on which he died. Not in the usual sense."

"Oh dear. Central Intelligence? NSA?" asked Pressert.

"When we have more information, we'll certainly be able to share more," said Wilde.

Pressert smiled. "I believe that's the nicest *Need-to-Know* I've ever heard."

"That wasn't my intent," said Wilde. "At this point, the motive for killing Cynter is exactly what we'd like to take up with our person of interest, to see if she can shed any more light. We can give you the number of the flight she arrived on yesterday."

"We know your Customs port of entry records are sensitive," said Lowry.

"As are your airport surveillance video feeds," said Wilde.

"It depends, of course," said Pressert, "on which feeds and records. On the airside, it's all privatized and handled by Airport Security Police. On the landside, it's handled by us at the BPS."

Wilde said, "A feed of the taxi stand would help us most for now, to see if we can get a line on her cab, and from there at least see where she went from the airport. Her name is LuAnna Blackshaw."

"And who do you believe Blackshaw wishes to contact?"

Lowry said, "We don't have a last name, but we believe the first name is Siobhan."

Pressert felt the blood drain from his face while his heart sped up, old sensations from his days as an inspector when a case was breaking. "Most interesting," was all he said. He brought up the 24/7 Bernews.com crime page on his computer.

"Are we boring you, Commissioner Pressert?" said Wilde.

"On the contrary," said Pressert, "not even my dear wife proved so fascinating as the two of you have done on such short acquaintance."

He turned the screen toward Lowry and Wilde. They saw the sketch of LuAnna, and the headline about the murder of socialite Siobhan Grimes pictured in better times in an evening gown at a charity event.

"I'd call this a development," said Wilde.

Pressert asked, "The sketch?"

Lowry said, "Commissioner Pressert, I think we share a person of interest. Meet LuAnna Blackshaw."

CHAPTER 49

CHALK BLUSTERED AT Blessing. "I told you, I never forget a face. Not for long anyway."

They had returned to Blessing's room so Chalk could scour the gore off his hands and swap fresh clothes from his GOOD bag for the bloody ones. A knife soaked in crimson water turning ruddy in the bathroom sink.

"But the woman you killed—", began Blessing.

"Linkage. She was connected to this whole mess. To Cynter anyway. The only Siobhan on this whole rock that'd make a SEAL's pecker stand at attention. Even her DMV picture gave me a DHO."

"A DHO?" Blessing knew she'd regret asking, and she was right.

"A Demi-Hard-On. She confirmed Cynter was here looking for the asset, didn't she?"

"She might have told you more if you hadn't practically lopped her head off."

"For God's sake," said Chalk, "I thought you had some grit. We'd clearly crossed that line between things she knew, and shit she was making up to stay alive. She'd say the sky was purple if she thought it'd make me happy."

"It might be above my pay grade, but do you know what the asset is?"

"It's huge. It's epic. Put it this way, I've held nuclear weapons in my hands, and hundreds of millions, even billions of dollars, but this asset is more valuable than all of it. It's a call to arms for every red-blooded jihadi on the planet. It's the start of the war to end all wars, because there's no one left to fight. And you're damn right it's above your penny-ante GS-2 pay grade. I'll tell you more when I need you to know more, but I don't think you're going to live that long."

"Always happy to serve, of course." Blessing was scanning the Bernews.com crime page where the Siobhan Grimes case was the biggest thing on the blotter after the double tattoo murders. "You've caused a stir, it seems."

Chalk dried the knife and pointed it at the computer screen. "Maybe so, but they're looking for her, not me."

"And she's the LuAnna person you thought was dead," said Blessing.

"Shut the hell up. If you'd seen the lighthouse—this is going back a year—blown completely to shit. No way she could've survived. But it's her all right. She's knocked up, which is double the fun. Plus, I ran into her husband on the water. Did you ever feel like your fate was inextricably bound up with another person?"

"Yes," Blessing said.

"Well that's total bullshit." Chalk swept the knife through the air as he ranted. "Sometimes people just get in your way over and over again until you cut off their fucking heads, drop them down a manhole, and burn their hearts to ashes with a flamethrower. That's why I'm seeing to things personally, and that bitch LuAnna Blackshaw is next."

CHAPTER 50

BLACKSHAW LED LUANNA down the hotel's emergency stairs. She had been careful to leave the room littered with brochures, her bag, and toiletries, as if she'd stepped out for a moment and hadn't scrambled to pack and disappear. The ruse could buy some time.

At the bottom of the stairway, Blackshaw disabled the alarm connected to the emergency door's crash bar; he went out first. A cook in an apron was enjoying a smoke in the alley behind the hotel. LuAnna was already in the alley when Blackshaw realized there was no door to the kitchen there. The waterman held still as the cook pressed a pistol to his head.

"We should talk," said the cook, who sounded Russian, not British.

LuAnna's knife was out, and jammed against the seat of the cook's pants hard enough to let him know just how sharp it was. "You'll be talking out your ass if you don't lower the gun."

The cook laughed, and took LuAnna's suggestion. She stripped the pistol out of his hand.

Blackshaw took the gun, glanced at it. "Tokarev. Old. Reliable. You looking to turn in my wife for a reward?"

"A fee. Only if you agree, of course," said the Russian. "But not to turn in. You need to leave Bermuda. I'm leaving Bermuda. You maybe want to hitch a ride. One million dollars."

Blackshaw said, "I'd need to make a call."

"Each," said the cook. "One million dollars each. Baby's no charge."

LuAnna said, "How do you know we're leaving?"

The cook said, "It's my job to know. And I watch TV. Two cab drivers came to me first about you. In twenty minutes, they'll be talking to the police—very good citizens. I have a Jeep."

Blackshaw said, "But you really drive a Quebec Class sub."

"Hah! My fame precedes me. Captain Rady Karkov, of the *Nabokov 672* at your service. Also ship's cook."

CHAPTER 51

CHIEF INSPECTOR HORACE Finton of the Bermuda Police Service accompanied Wilde, Lowry and the hotel manager down a quiet hall to the room.

Wilde said, "Your lead came from the staff here?"

Finton shot the manager a side-eyed look. "No. Hotels are notoriously uncooperative. Seems that guests craving privacy can offer better tips to the staff for being discreet than we pay in rewards. It was a cab driver. And not the one who picked Mrs. Blackshaw up at the airport. It was the one who dropped her in the vicinity of the tattoo shop where the double murder took place."

"LuAnna's batting a thousand," said Wilde.

The manager opened the door to the room and stood aside.

Lowry led the way, and said, "She didn't check out."

"As I said." The manager was watching their every move, still protective of his absent guest despite this clear betrayal of trust.

Wilde emerged from the bathroom. "All her stuff's here, too. But no passport."

Finton said, "No surprise. Visitors tend to keep passports on their persons as identification, especially if they have banking to attend to."

"Not that there's anything wrong with banking offshore," said Lowry.

"We enjoy complete financial transparency with the United States," said Finton.

"And there's this," said Wilde, holding up a short, straight, black hair. "In the tub drain. Not LuAnna's."

"Blackshaw keeps it high and tight," said Lowry. He turned to the hotel manager, "The tubs are scrubbed out between guests?"

The manager did not dignify Lowry's question with a reply.

"Make that *two* persons of interest," Wilde said. "LuAnna has to know she's being sought for questioning. So, what're they doing right now?"

"Trying to leave Bermuda," said Lowry.

"A pregnant woman and a former SEAL shouldn't be hard to spot," said Finton. "We have the airport, harbors, and marinas under surveillance."

"Oh good," said Wilde. "Then everything's going to be just fine."

The phone on the nightstand rang.

CHAPTER 52

BLESSING WANTED TO check in with Screed, but Chalk was now full-kinetic to end LuAnna Blackshaw. Unfinished business, he called it. A waste of time, Blessing would have said, except that if this woman had an interest in the asset, she too would need to be scrubbed. Blessing was uncomfortable finding herself in agreement with Chalk.

Chalk had used some kind of proprietary computer program to locate LuAnna Blackshaw's hotel. She had used her own name to check in. That was a surprise to Chalk, who expected more spycraft from his prey. Chalk grabbed a house phone in the lobby, and the hotel operator rang LuAnna's room. Blessing leaned in to listen. A woman answered.

Chalk said, "I want you to stay put right there. You and I need to have a talk."

"Okay," said the woman. "Anything in particular on your mind?"

To Blessing, this woman did not sound as upset as she should receiving a threatening call from a stranger like this.

Chalk said, "Do you know who this is?"

"Do tell," the woman said.

Blessing sensed something was wrong. "Hang up."

"We met before," Chalk went on. "Last year. We hung out—you, me, a few of my boys."

"Listen Sugar, I have an appointment for a massage, so if you're not going to tell me your name—"

"Hang up. Now!" said Blessing.

"It's Chalk! That's right. It's me. Big as life!"

A few guests glanced at Chalk and Blessing. Chalk turned toward the window facing the street.

The woman in LuAnna Blackshaw's room said, "I'm in 314. Maybe the massage can wait."

That's when Chalk gawked through the window at an elderly Jeep stuck in traffic in front of the hotel. He slammed the house phone down. "Damn!"

Blessing noticed the Jeep, the scruffy driver wearing an apron, the pregnant woman in the front seat, and the scarred god of a man sitting in back. The traffic light changed and the Jeep pulled away in a cloud of exhaust.

"Maynard?"

"It's them," spat Chalk. "We need your car. Now!"

"Who were you talking to?" Blessing started for the valet parking kiosk outside.

"Not the housekeeper. American," said Chalk. "She played it cool. I think she's Johnny Law."

Blessing hoped her three-man team had one guy in their car with the motor running. She had no way to tell them who to follow without tipping their presence to Chalk. At least they'd fall in behind her rental once the valet brought it around. What was taking so long!

CHAPTER 53

WILDE BLEW OUT of the elevator going a hundred miles an hour. Lowry was close behind, followed by Chief Inspector Finton and the hotel manager. While the elevator descended, Wilde had prepped the manager: find out which house phone had been used to call the Blackshaw room, and locate anyone who might have noticed who made the call.

The manager disappeared into an office behind the reception desk, and emerged moments later pointing to a bank of house phones across the lobby. He stopped and asked the clerk what she'd seen.

Wilde button-holed the concierge, one Abel Willingham, a tough nut with the crossed gold keys, or Les Clefs d'Or, of his international guild in his lapels.

Willingham said, "May I help you?"

"Did you see a man use one of those phones a moment ago?" Wilde said.

Willingham's face shut like a bank vault. "It's been a busy morning."

Finton vectored in on the conversation, "The fellow on that phone a few minutes ago is a person of interest. A man. Around—"

"Sixty years old," said Lowry. "Fit, excitable."

Wilde said, "He's wanted in connection with terrorist activity in the United States. Agent Lowry and I are with the FBI."

Though a terrorist would be bad for his hotel's reputation, it was clear that the concierge was not impressed by any credentials except those of Chief Inspector Finton. Willingham addressed only him, ignoring the Feds. "There was a fellow who announced himself in his conversation as Choke, or Chalk."

"Yes!" said Wilde. "That's him! Where'd he go?"

Willingham said to Finton, "He was with a rather striking woman, tall, her head completely shaved bald."

Finton said, "If the next thing out of your mouth isn't the direction taken by this Chalk and his bald companion—"

"Try Valet Parking."

"They'll have the make, model, and number plate recorded," Finton said. "We can get a description out."

Lowry asked, "Can somebody canvas the airport rental desks? We might get a better picture of all the players."

CHAPTER 54

BLESSING WAS AMAZED, watching Chalk work his Black Widow wonder engine on the small tablet from Chalk's case. She dreamed of inheriting this tool once Chalk was neutralized. With the tablet she could become Black Widow incarnate. At the moment, Chalk was looking at multiple camera views from Bermuda traffic intersections to the east of Hamilton, the last direction they saw the Jeep take. In fact, Chalk had cranked in a profile recognition protocol for mid-1990s model Jeep CJs. Black Widow was doing all the work.

"Eyes on the road, sister," said Chalk.

"Stay on Front Street?"

"For now."

Blessing said, "They might be making a run for the airport."

"Pretty sure their driver has other ideas. Karkov, that traitorous shit-bird, he's a water baby. Soon all the roads funnel into North Shore or Harrington Sound, but there're plenty of places to put in a boat."

"There's The Causeway, too," Blessing said. "Straight across Castle Harbour to the west end of the airport. Just saying."

"Crap." Chalk rapped the tablet screen. "Come on!"

Blessing asked, "Is the software or an app on the tablet, or do you just log in from anywhere?"

"There's no app for Black Widow, for Christ's sake! And why the hell do you care!"

A buzz erupted from the tablet. One of the small camera views expanded full-screen, showing a Jeep with three occupants pushing through the roundabout where Highland Road and Blue Hole Hill met.

"That's them!" barked Chalk, and he gave Blessing turn-by-turn directions from Black Widow, including a detour for construction.

CHAPTER 55

BLACKSHAW WAS ABOUT to ask Rady Karkov to pull off the road to check their backtrail when the Russian turned so hard he put the old Jeep up two wheels and plunged straight for a solid stone wall draped in vines. Blackshaw braced for the crash.

There was a loud rush and rasp of leaves as the Jeep tore into the vines. Karkov stood on the brakes and the wheels locked up and dug into the high grass in this concealed clearing. Karkov was out of the Jeep in seconds, and strode back to the clearing's hidden entrance.

Blackshaw asked LuAnna, "You okay?"

"Of course! Thank God this old crate still has its seatbelts."

Blackshaw followed Karkov toward the road. "There's a guy on the island we need to watch out for. Name of Chalk."

Karkov turned on Blackshaw, eyes ablaze with rage. "He's here! Maynard Chalk is here! How could he—give me back my gun. Please give it to me!"

LuAnna did as asked.

"Figured you knew him," said Blackshaw. "He showed up in the middle of the ocean—"

"I put him out in a boat. That cock-shit-bastard shot my son," said Karkov.

LuAnna said, "Oh my blessing! Will he be all right?"

"Yes, but not for some while. I should have killed Chalk when I had the chance."

"It's what most folks say of him." said Blackshaw. "The woman he's with, she's got a team backing her. I don't think Chalk knows. Three men."

Karkov said, "Five men went in the boat with him."

"Reckon those ones are dead, Rady. I can tell you that. But the other three—"

"If you don't know for sure, I'll assume they're on his side. So stupid that I must finish what the entire Atlantic Ocean failed to do."

Cars rolled past them on the road, but traffic was light.

LuAnna said, "Can we please keep the whole *getting away* thing in mind?"

Karkov said, "Of course, but we have to know the whole score, like you say."

After several minutes of random traffic whizzing by, Blessing's rental approached, Chalk in the passenger seat.

"That's him," said Blackshaw. "Knew he'd get on us."

Karkov drew his pistol, but Blackshaw stayed his hand. "I still need Chalk's answers on the death of a friend."

As they passed, neither Chalk nor Blessing noticed the three watchers peering from the roadside vines.

More cars went by, then Blackshaw spotted a yellow rental sedan with the three men he'd seen trailing Chalk and the woman. The open sunroof shed enough light on them to rule out any doubts. "That's the B-Team."

"Are you sure?" asked Karkov.

Blackshaw stepped onto the shoulder of the road, his Sig Sauer drawn. With a two-hand grip, he was calm and deliberate when he opened fire. Spiderwebbed cracks burst in the windshield. The car swerved and plunged into a ditch thirty yards past Blackshaw's firing position. Blackshaw jogged toward the steaming wreck.

Karkov caught up, grabbed Blackshaw's arm and held tight. "Your charming bride is right. There's no time. Not if I'm going to earn my fee. Let's go."

Moments later, Karkov drove LuAnna and Blackshaw fast past the wreck. Blackshaw glimpsed movement in the crumpled sedan's back seat, drew again, and put two more bullets into the car.

Rady Karkov laughed hard. "Persistent!"

LuAnna said, "Ben, stop that! Swagger die I'll take that gun away from you!"

CHAPTER 56

CHIEF INSPECTOR FINTON took a call over his bluetooth while he drove the unmarked sedan. Lowry and Wilde watched his face darkening with every second.

Finton ended the call and said, "St. David's Road. We've got a wrecked car and three dead."

Lowry said, "With all due respect, that sounds important, but don't you have a police constable who could catch that one for you?"

Finton said, "The Officer In Charge on the scene identified the car as one of two rented upon arrival at the airport yesterday by one Blessing Klyman who fits the description of the woman with the shaved head. Two of four designated drivers listed on the rental agreements are dead at the scene."

Wilde said, "This Blessing person is dead."

"No," said Finton. "None of the deceased is Klyman. She might be using the other rental with that Chalk fellow. We're trying to piece it together. Apparently, shots were fired."

Nine minutes later, police constables waved Finton's car through a cordon to the crash site.

The wrecked car had two men in the front seats who had just been pronounced dead by an EMT. A third person, a young Black woman, lay dead on her back at the shoulder of the road. Wilde bent low to examine her remains first.

Lowry studied the wrecked car. "Both struck in the head, both also struck in the chest."

"That's some fancy shooting," said Wilde. "The girl's GSWs are right side, head, neck, shoulder. Overkill. Sloppy. Wallet's still in her purse."

Finton said, "This car crashed when the driver was shot. The front passenger was also killed then?"

"So says the windshield," said Lowry. "Four shots through the front."

"Blessing Klyman arrives with three men," said Wilde. "She takes a car, meets with Chalk. The three others have a separate car."

"An auxiliary team of some sort," Finton said. "Back-up."

"I like that," said Wilde. "Look here. There are two shots through the left rear side window. And some spatter back there, too."

Lowry said, "That could be spatter from the front seat victims blown into the back."

"True," said Wilde bending over the car. "But a quick look here, and I see one hole in the lower back seat cushion. And a low, close-up arterial horsetail. Two bullets through the side window, one hole low in the cushion."

Lowry said, "Two shooters?"

"Or one shooter," said Wilde, "and two different firing positions in sequence.

Finton said, "Shall we say someone, perhaps the final listed driver, was in the back seat, and was struck by a round."

"Maybe he was hit twice, and one was a through-and-through," said Lowry.

"I see. Quite possibly, yes," Finton said. "We'll have to recover the bullets, compare them, to determine how many weapons were in use."

Wilde said, "And he's the one who gets out of the back of this wreck, flags down that girl, carjacks her, shooting her three times."

Finton said, "We'll find out what she was driving from her ID, and put a BOLO in place."

Wilde spoke softly to Lowry. "Any thoughts on who can stop a moving car like this, and hit everyone in it?"

"Where there's a Mrs. Blackshaw—" said Lowry.

"A Mr. Blackshaw might not be far behind," said Wilde. "The folks in this car are linked through Blessing Klyman to that freak, Chalk. Even if he hadn't said his name on the house phone, I'd never forget his voice from that double kidnapping scene this spring."

"Spooky, talking with you from a boat offshore in the fog," said Lowry. "Tossing that fishing lure your way."

"Even without the damn fog and that lure, I wouldn't forget his voice. Not in this lifetime," said Wilde, pulling her blazer closed against a chill only she could feel.

CHAPTER 57

BLACKSHAW NOTICED KARKOV was taking the corners more slowly, but didn't complain. Because they had pulled the Jeep into the concealed clearing, now Chalk's car was somewhere ahead. A police response to Blackshaw's take-down of the B-Team's car was forming behind them. A BPS car, with lights and sirens flashing and bleating, rounded a corner rushing toward them, and passed en route to the crash.

"Captain Karkov, sir, where the hell are we going?" Only Blackshaw would've known from her voice that LuAnna was still nervous.

"You know the old American Navy Air Station," said Karkov.

"I got all the brochures, but it's the airport now, isn't it?" LuAnna said. "We just drove past it."

"We're going near there," said Karkov, as he slowed to take another turn. "You know the tourist caves?"

LuAnna said, "Read about them too, but we haven't been."

"You must! Very pretty. We're not going there either," Karkov said, helpfully explaining nothing.

Four minutes later, Karkov pulled over on the shoulder. A stout, dark-skinned older woman emerged from a lane, waved, and smiled. "Hey Captain," she said.

"Mrs. Cox!" said Karkov as he got down from the Jeep with the engine still running. "You're more beautiful every time I see you!"

Mrs. Cox beamed, "Be quiet you flatterer!"

Karkov kissed the woman's cheek, and goosed her bottom, making her yelp. "Is everything aboard?" he asked.

"My grandson got a pig this morning. So big! I hope your men left something for you. Who are these then?"

"Friends of mine," Karkov said.

Without asking, Mrs. Cox placed the palms of her hands gently on LuAnna's belly, and closed her eyes. LuAnna held still, clearly not wanting to be rude, but not loving this attention either.

Mrs. Cox said, "Strong boy. Big man some day. Quiet. Unpopular with men of bad character."

"Thank you?" said LuAnna.

Mrs. Cox removed her hands. "But you missed breakfast and lunch, dear. Make sure the captain feeds you up proper."

The strange woman climbed behind the wheel of the Jeep, blew Karkov a kiss, and drove away.

Karkov laughed. "You got the Pequot Sonogram!"

"Pequot," said Blackshaw. "As in—"

"Yes! The Indians!" said Karkov. "Pequot, Wampanoag, Arawak, all sent to Bermuda as slaves by the British almost four hundred years ago from your New England. Isolated for centuries here on St. David's Island. Mixed and married some, yes, but they still remember who they are."

"Sounds familiar. Is Mrs. Cox ever right?" LuAnna asked.

"Is she ever right?" said Karkov. "She's never, ever wrong! You're baby's going to take after his parents. Big pains in the ass! Come this way."

Karkov walked behind an overhang of lush vines to rival any tropical jungle—and disappeared.

"Captain?" said Blackshaw.

Karkov's distant voice echoed, "Come! Much to do!"

Blackshaw led LuAnna around the green wall and came close to pitching headlong into a grave-shaped hole in the ground. Catching himself, he saw steps cut into the rock down the side of the opening.

LuAnna said, "You're sure there's no bounty on us."

"Reckon it wouldn't come close to his transport fee."

LuAnna didn't seem so certain. "Okay. Best get on with it, loverman."

Blackshaw drew his Sig and stepped down into the earth. He had to duck his head down as the carved stairway turned to the left. Then a string of feeble bare lightbulbs traced the wall down a further twenty feet. LuAnna's footing was sure as she followed.

In addition to the carved steps, the passage had been enlarged enough from a natural fissure in the rocky substrate to allow Blackshaw and LuAnna to walk almost upright. The passage turned a sharp right, and they emerged in a large cavern to a surprising sight. Except for a ledge about ten feet wide, the enormous space had no floor. It was all water, still as a mirror. And in the water lay a submarine made fast to iron rings secured in the rock walls. Crewmen carried stores up a narrow gangway from the ledge to the deck, where more men lowered them through a hatch. Two men were failing to persuade a very large, stubborn pig to cross the gangway.

Karkov had just made the ledge. He turned and called, "Welcome to my port away from home!"

"Jules Verne!" Blackshaw yelled. "*The Mysterious Island!*"

"A favorite of mine, to be sure, but no," said Karkov. "This was an American sub base until the subs got too big and fat to fit inside. Very secret. The sea entrance lies far below low tide! And when the American Navy left, then great things, wonderful things like this place were soon forgotten by everybody, except Mrs. Cox! One day, I pick up her son far out at sea. His fishing boat—swamped. She repays me with a memory of this place, and now the *Nabokov* and I come and go as I please—okay mostly at night."

Karkov was vexed by the men shoving the squealing pig toward the gangway. He drew his pistol and shot the animal three times. "*Chashushuli* for dinner tonight!"

CHAPTER 58

BYSTANDER OF MAN was equipped with a state-of-the-art communications array. Knocker Ellis Hogan kept his boat loitering beyond the horizon to the north of Bermuda where the sensitive antennae could still snag the island's digital news feeds. Mr. Curlew, Mr. Gannet, and Mr. Auk, peered at the monitor with their captain.

"And he hasn't called once," Mr. Auk said.

Ellis said, "Last I saw or heard of him was right before he went down through the hell hole into the water. He swims like a fish. He should be all right."

"I only met her the once, of course," said Mr. Curlew, "But isn't that a sketch of Mrs. Blackshaw, and her wanted for questioning in three murders?"

Mr. Auk said, "That's no kind of baby shower I've ever heard of."

"I'm thinking that one didn't even go to a baby shower," said Mr. Gannet.

"She fibbed to us!" said Mr. Curlew.

Ellis could not suppress his laughter. His crew was reminding him of the Smith Island Council of Elders, a wily pack of rogues given to bloody-minded sarcasm.

"It does seem she's been busy, and not exactly off the radar," said Ellis.

Mr. Gannet suggested, "We go in, Captain Hogan? We clear them off?"

"No sir. We sit tight. We sit tight until we hear something."

CHAPTER 59

CHALK BARKED AT Blessing, "Slow down!"

He was staring once again at the tablet, but at a different screen from the traffic intersection surveillance cameras. This was a map of Bermuda, zoomed in to an area of coverage extending laterally a thousand yards in all directions. Chalk shrunk the tablet screen's field of view, and now there was a red dot pulsing off to the right just two hundred feet away.

"Hot damn!" Chalk was elated. "I can't believe it! The tracker I slapped on Karkov's scum-bucket when he tossed me in the soup, it's still pinging away. Thought for sure it'd fall off."

"And Black Widow picked it up." said Blessing.

"It's faint as hell, but—shit! Stop! Do a one-eighty and go back nice and slow. Must've passed it."

At Chalk's order, Blessing pulled off the road onto a lay-by and shut the car down. Chalk got out, and like a teenage boy exchanging his first texts with a girl far out of his league, he strolled into traffic staring at the tablet. Cars braked, skidded, and honked, and when Chalk gained the opposite shoulder, the vexed drivers moved on their way with obscene epithets and gestures. Blessing, on the other hand, caught up with Chalk at a trot when it was safe.

Chalk rounded a mass of ground shrubs and stopped short. Blessing bumped into him, she was following so close.

"It's a hole," Chalk said. He tossed the tablet aside, and drew a pistol. "Got a funny feeling about this."

"Let's get on with it," said Blessing, pulling a gun of her own.

"Yeah. If it's Blackshaw or the Devil himself down there, I'm going to fuck his shit up."

CHAPTER 60

CHIEF INSPECTOR FINTON pulled over when he saw the second car described in Blessing Klyman's rental agreement in the roadside lay-by. Wilde and Lowry climbed out of the car when he did. During a lull in the traffic, they all heard the gunfire. They followed the sound across the road, and into the vegetation. More gunshots echoed out of an open maw in the earth.

"We should call for back-up," Finton said.

"Even with a hundred officers, only one could fit down there at a time single file," Lowry said.

"Single file it is," Wilde said. She drew a gun and a small pocket flashlight, then took her first step down the carved stairs.

"See here!" Finton blustered with a head full of chivalric thoughts swirling around Wilde's gender and pregnancy.

Her eyes blazed at Finton with pent-up anger, but she didn't stop descending.

"Chief Inspector, with all due respect, it's no use," said Lowry. "We both know it's your patch, but she knows the players."

Finton relented. From the set of Wilde's shoulders, it looked dangerous for him to do otherwise. He followed her down the stairway. Lowry brought up the rear, glancing over his shoulder every few seconds to check for other operators who might be following them in.

Finton could barely see around Wilde in the narrow rock defile. He saw her tuck her torch away as she assessed the string of lightbulbs. Two more gunshots rang out from below.

CHAPTER 61

WILDE WAS GLAD Finton checked himself at Lowry's well-timed suggestion. She didn't need a second battle front opening up just when her concentration on this descent had to be at its sharpest. Two shots rang from farther below, but she kept moving in a slow steady step-by-step advance down toward a fight she could not see.

She came to a corner where the lighting brightened, and a change in the acoustics suggested a very large chamber close by. She bent and peered around the corner.

Chalk and a woman who could only be Blessing Klyman were crouched on a ledge behind crates, their pistols drawn. Chalk was changing his gun's magazine. The rest of the space was like a small underground harbor, with a museum piece submarine rusting at its moorings. On the aft deck, two of the sub's crew lay bleeding. One was trying to crawl forward to the conning tower. The other lay still.

At the top of the conning tower, a man in an apron was shouting in Russian, perhaps to rally his crew, perhaps to curse Chalk and his companion. Taking cover in a hatch in the foredeck, Wilde recognized Ben Blackshaw. He squeezed off two shots at Chalk's position. If Wilde opened fire, Chalk would be pinched between her team, and Blackshaw and the sub crew.

Wilde said, "Chief Inspector, is this where you say something legal?"

Finton shouted, "Lay down your weapons! You're under arrest, charged with disturbing the peace, discharge of unlicensed weapons, attempted murder—"

All eyes turned to the high opening in the chamber wall where Wilde, Finton, and Lowry crouched.

"Oh hell," said Finton.

Chalk, Klyman, and all the Russians opened fire at the law officers. Bullets splintered the rock walls. As Wilde staggered back into Finton, she saw Blackshaw burst from the forward hatch and leap from the sub toward cover on the ledge. Then Lowry hauled Wilde and Finton deeper into the tunnel; they tumbled on top of him.

From behind the embattled trio farther up in the tunnel toward the surface, a shot boomed like a cannon in the passage; a lightbulb overhead shattered from splintered rock.

"Damnit," said Finton. "And that would be our carjacker, Klyman's registered driver number four."

Lowry turned to face the way they'd come, crouched, and waited. He heard steps recede. The last carjacker had turned and fled.

CHAPTER 62

BLACKSHAW PRAYED LUANNA was below decks and out of harm's way; Chalk and his operator were laying down a hellish barrage of gunfire. Most of Karkov's crew had assumed the submarine cavern was safe from this kind of attack, and had been loading stores aboard without benefit of side arms. Two crewmen were dead or dying, and now there was law enforcement hollering from the entrance, and no other way out.

When Chalk, the operator with him, and Karkov's men all rounded on the cops and started shooting up at them, Blackshaw thought he recognized two of the interlopers—those Feds, Wilde and Lowry. They must have ridden into Bermuda on LuAnna's trail. The allegiances were shifting as fast as the bullets were flying. Blackshaw drew the line at shooting at Lowry and Wilde, but the distraction the Feds provided gave him a moment to close on Chalk.

Blackshaw launched from the sub's forward hatch, got as much speed as he could on the algae-slimed deck, and jumped toward the ledge. He made it to the edge, but his feet whipped out from under him in a slick of that pig's blood. He bounced off a stack of crates and caromed into a pile of large bags of flour. Rising to his knees, he fired a snapshot at Chalk, but missed. Karkov had a height advantage up there in the conning tower above the ledge, but he was potting his suppressing fire at the mouth of the passage to the surface. Somehow, the law scared Karkov worse than Chalk.

With Karkov keeping the Feds checked at the top of the stairs, Chalk took advantage of the Russian's distraction and fired up at the conning tower. Karkov fell back, and Blackshaw worried for his ride. A moment later, Karkov stood again, blood from a bullet's grazing at his shoulder. Gone was his Tokarev pistol. Instead, he gripped an AK-47 set to full auto, the big banana magazine emptying at Chalk's position. The din in the cavern was ear-shattering. The reek of propellant hung acrid in the air.

Chalk hunkered low, but exposed his head between two boxes. Blackshaw fired, and the shot went home. Chalk's head snapped to one side. To Blackshaw's amazement, Chalk reached a hand to his torn scalp, and laughed at the bloody fingers he pulled away. The titanium plate in his skull had saved him.

Chalk yelled, "Nice try, Ben! Why are we fighting like this? You should hop on over here, and leave that weird Chesapeake hillbilly life in the dust. It'll kill you if I don't."

Blackshaw fired again, but missed.

Chalk shouted, "You people, your stick figure family on the back of your minivan—it's nothing but a catalog for serial killers! Come on! You love the adrenaline! I can dish it up by the gallon, my man!"

Brave crewmen bolted out of the forward and aft deck hatches, sprinted for the mooring lines and freed them. Bad timing. Karkov was swapping magazines in his AK, and failed to cover their dash with suppressing fire. The crewman on the stern had leaped over two fallen comrades to get to his mooring line, but after three shots from Chalk on the return sprint, he fell next to them and slid into the water.

Chalk yelled, "Dammit, Ben! You want Cynter's killer. I want the asset. We need to make common cause here. We're on the same side!"

Blackshaw fired at Chalk again. The bullet caught him in the notch at the base of his throat. Chalk pawed at his new stoma, coughed blood from his neck and mouth, and fell to his side, his eyes fixed on nothing in particular.

Karkov was in a panic. Blackshaw had no idea what the captain screamed in Russian down the conning tower hatch until the water around the submarine frothed with air rushing out of the ballast tanks displaced by water rushing in. Karkov had ordered "Dive!" though Blackshaw was still on the ledge.

Compressed air hissed into a single diesel engine to turn it over; the motor rumbled when it caught. The sub began to sink. The decks were awash when the gangway floated off. Blackshaw was still pinned down on the ledge by the Feds shooting from the access tunnel. Soon, only the top of conning tower remained above the surface.

Now at eye level, Karkov shrugged and shouted, "Sorry, Ben! Can't wait for you! Keep in touch! Your wife will be fine! Oh and no refunds— you have million-dollar transport credit with me. Redeem anytime! Except now, of course!" With a final burst of machinegun fire at the entrance to the surface passage, Karkov dropped into the conning tower hatch.

In a false lull of gunfire, Blackshaw ran hard at the conning tower—it was narrow, and was much farther from the ledge than the foredeck had been when he leapt ashore. His blood-slicked boots slipped again, and his jump fell short. He grabbed the conning tower coaming by his fingertips.

"Blackshaw! Freeze!"

He glanced over his shoulder; Wilde was halfway down the steel stair from the surface tunnel's opening into the cavern, looking at him over her gunbarrel. Her pistol banged three times, striking the tower; rust and bullet fragments stung him in a thousand places. He hauled himself over the coaming into the tower, and grabbed at the hatch as a crewman was closing it. He wasn't fast enough. The hatch clanged shut. Water poured over the top of the tower. In fifteen seconds, he'd be swimming. In sixty seconds, he'd be shot dead, drowned, or in handcuffs.

With the water lapping at the hatch, it opened again. Blackshaw peered down through the water cascading in. Karkov was sheepishly gesturing for Blackshaw to come below.

LuAnna had a pistol jammed hard into the captain's neck. She yelled, "Ahoy, Honeyboy! Best get yourself down here quick—it's a long half-swim to hell!"

Blackshaw scrambled down through the hatch and pulled it shut behind him, spinning the operator wheel to dog it tight.

CHAPTER 63

WILDE LOOSED MORE shots at the sinking conning tower. She was on the verge of lowering her gun when Blessing broke from cover on the ledge, ran three steps, and dived into the water.

"Dammit!" Wilde fired blind at the water where Blessing disappeared. "Anybody got her?"

"Molly!" shouted Lowry. "Stand down!"

She stopped pulling the trigger only when the magazine was empty, the pistol's slide stayed open, and her brass rolled smoky circles on the ledge below.

Finton said, "She'll not get very far."

"Persh, I was protecting Blackshaw's cover."

Lowry said, "Please don't say that. Chief Inspector Finton, Blackshaw isn't an official confidential informant of the FBI. We needed to interview him with LuAnna."

Wilde said, "I didn't see her. Did you?"

Wilde descended to the ledge, kicked Chalk's gun away, and nudged his body with the toe of her shoe. "Christ. The paperwork. I need some fresh air."

CHAPTER 64

BLACKSHAW SHOVED KARKOV against the wall of the conning tower, hands at his throat. "We had a deal!"

A sailor in the cramped space pressed a gun to Blackshaw's head. LuAnna jammed her pistol in the sailor's ear.

Karkov put his hands up in surrender and choked out, "Everybody! Everybody calm down! There's no deal if I am dead, or you are dead, if anybody's dead! And for this moment, I must be in the control room, to guide *Nabokov* to sea. Special knowledge of twisty tunnel. So no killings! Please, everybody lower guns. Please!"

LuAnna and the sailor slowly pulled their guns away. Blackshaw released Karkov's neck. Karkov rubbed his throat, and then shimmied down the ladder into the control room. Blackshaw followed, taking in the stifling odors of unwashed men, diesel fuel, and onions. The sailor graciously gestured that LuAnna could go next. She made an ungainly descent into the compartment below, with its snarl of pipes, gauges, valves, and other controls lining the bulkheads and overheads.

Karkov navigated the sub, ahead slow, through the vast gallery. He said, "We go into tunnel three minutes. All stop. We come up in a large chamber. Very dark. No electricity for light. No stairs to surface. Nice and cozy-cozy. We wait."

"Wait for what?" said Blackshaw. "We need to go!"

"Night!" Karkov said. "The water is so clear. The tunnel mouth is deep, but not so deep. *Nabokov* might be seen from the air. We come out later in darkness, dive for deeper water, cone of confusion grows—*Nabokov* disappears."

Blackshaw was in no position to argue.

Karkov asked, "You don't ask how long we can stay down. How long battery lasts for electric motor."

Blackshaw said, "That's a diesel running. Zippo Class subs run on a closed liquid oxygen system. Like a big rebreather unit, but for an engine, instead of a man."

"You're right! Very good!" Karkov seemed happy to have his ship so well understood.

Blackshaw went on, "It's the only time the Russians were flat-out ahead of U.S. sub technology, and they mothballed them all by the 1970s."

For a moment, Karkov was sobered by Blackshaw's assessment. "True. A shame. Still, *Nabokov* is still running beautifully today!"

The concerned looks of the crew might have been founded on the loss of comrades in the firefight, or maybe they did not share Karkov's confidence in the old boat.

The captain navigated the sub through a short series of timed runs and turns, then ordered Stop Engine. "Now we surface."

Compressed air was valved into the ballast tanks. Neutral buoyancy changed to positive. The depth on the gauge that everyone was watching crept up, then held steady.

Karkov smiled. "We are here."

An unholy banging on the hull rang in their ears. Three bangs, then silent. Then four more blows.

Blackshaw could tell no one had a clue what it was. "Who ordered pizza?"

CHAPTER 65

SCREED AIMED THE video camera at the Patient. He had used the bed's controls to raise the groggy man into a higher sitting position. Judging by the image in the monitor, a bedside spot for the tripod would offer a closer, more intimate shot of the subject. He repositioned the camera.

"I know you can hear me," said Screed. "Play possum all you like. You don't have to say anything right now. This is just for B-roll."

Screed rubbed his knuckles back-and-forth hard against the Patient's sternum, evoking a tired, miserable groan.

Screed brightened, and said, "There you are. Thing is, over the last couple days, I've lightened up on your sedatives. But we've been giving you some new stuff. Around the clubhouse, we call it Squealer. A hundred times better than *burundanga* at messing with your free will, and it doesn't zonk you out like Scopolamine, which'd just as likely kill you before it got you talking."

Screed saw the Patient's eyes twitch behind their lids as if he were in REM sleep. They even opened for an instant, then closed.

Screed said, "I thought so. Now, I want you to imagine all the things I'm going to have you say when the time comes. I want you to picture in your mind the faces of all your faithful when they hear the most outrageous, deep, dark secrets pour out of your hairy face."

The Patient stirred, tried to raise his hands, but couldn't. Leather cuffs at his wrists and ankles, and a strap each across his chest, hips, and knees held him still.

"Sorry buddy," Screed said. "Going easy on the sedation means you get real restraints. Your new nurse will help if you start feeling the itchies from the morphine. He'll be only too glad to help. I will say he's got seriously big fingers."

The Patient stirred again, and grunted.

"I know just the thing," Screed mused. "I know exactly the first thing I'm going to make you say. I going to start that camera—maybe today, maybe tomorrow—and I'm going to make you say—your name."

The Patient thrashed against his restraints for a few seconds, then went limp.

A burly medical technician lumbered into the room.

"Oh he's okay," said Screed to the tech. Then he turned to the Patient. "Hey, your new nurse is here. You know, the guy with fingers like mutant kielbasas? Yes, sir. I think it's time for your sponge bath."

CHAPTER 66

CAPTAIN KARKOV SCALED back up the ladder into the conning tower, with a crewman from the dive plane station close on his heels with a flashlight. Blackshaw and LuAnna heard the hatch in the compartment above open to a larger echoing space outside, followed by sounds that would translate into consternation in any language.

Karkov's voice came down from above. "Blackshaw! Aft deck hatch! You and two men!"

Blackshaw let two *Nabokov* men lead the way aft to an escape trunk. They opened the lower hatch, climbed into the tight space, and opened the outside hatch. One of the crew passed Blackshaw a flashlight. He put his head out of the hatch, and saw Captain Karkov at the top of the conning tower shining his light down onto a mound of something on the deck. The crewman with Karkov was climbing down a set of rungs welded to the outer skin of the conning tower. Blackshaw trained his light there as well.

A tall woman lay on the deck next to the body of one of the crew Chalk had shot. The corpse's foot was wedged tight in a ballast tank vent, and had been trailing the sub like a macabre balloon behind a child. The woman had control of the man's gun, but she wasn't aiming it. In a half-drowned stupor, she raised the pistol and struck the hull with the gun's butt.

Blackshaw sprinted to her side before she became more alert. He wrenched the gun from her grasp. The crewman from the conning tower dealt her a solid kick in the ribs. She had used his dead comrade's body to cling to the sub. He clearly thought his friend deserved better than serving as his killer's belay.

Blackshaw looked up at Captain Karkov. "It's your boat. Does she stay or go?"

"Can she pay, do you think?"

Blackshaw said, "I don't see a wallet, but who carries cash these days. If she was with Chalk, she's connected."

Karkov decided fast. "Okay. We have some time here before it's dark enough to run for the open ocean. Bring her below."

CHAPTER 67

AGENT PERSHING LOWRY sat in the leafy shade at the mouth of the cavern's stone staircase with Agent Molly Wilde, their feet dangling over the edge of the entrance.

"That was a submarine. An actual submarine. I don't have an early case of baby brain, do I?" Wilde said.

Chief Inspector Finton returned from the road. "They're on their way. All my local units are still at the carjacking."

Lowry leaned over the edge of the crevasse and glanced down at the blood of the injured carjacker who had fled after firing one shot. "That last one's still at large."

Finton said, "I've reported him as well. If he's lucky, the police will get to him first."

"But the sub," said Lowry, "I've never seen anything like it. Chief Inspector?"

"As a constable, I heard the odd rumors from fishermen. Thought they were holdovers from the days of the Naval bases. Yours and ours. Never took them seriously."

"I can't sit like this," said Wilde standing up. "My ankles'll swell like grapefruits."

A stout woman with dark skin came into the clearing bearing a tray with a pitcher of lemonade and glasses filled with ice. She said, "I'm Mrs. Cox, and you poor things look so thirsty."

She placed the tray on a rock with a level top, filled the glasses and handed them to the officers. "I heard noises. Shots. Is everyone all right?"

There were thanks and yums all around for the lemonade, but it fell to Finton to answer Mrs. Cox's question with one of his own. "Have you ever seen strangers here before? Recently?"

"Aside from you? No offense mister constable sir, but St. David's and the BPS don't always mix so well or so fine. And now you're here. I heard about the car crash, about the dead. And now I'm worried. I heard the guns. Please. My grandson's not at home." Tears welled in Mrs. Cox's eyes as the sound of ambulance sirens swelled in the distance. "Is my family all right? Are my people okay?"

Chief Inspector Finton couldn't point to police crime scene tape and shoo Mrs. Cox away, especially when he was holding a glass of her lemonade, which was delicious. He recognized this woman as a pillar of this community. He risked all. He told the truth. "The shots you likely heard, Mrs. Cox, many of them were ours. We engaged with hostile, armed, foreign elements. They were wanted for questioning in the recent murders in Hamilton, the two at the tattoo shop, and Mrs. Grimes. Some of them escaped. The rest are deceased."

Lowry and Wilde were mesmerized by Finton's storytelling. Finton had done this kind of Public Information Officer work before, and he was good at it. He was deliberate, but instilled confidence that all information would be conveyed in its proper place, in the right order, at the proper time, and even the most difficult questions would be answered.

Mrs. Cox listened with patience. She sensed hard news coming.

Finton went on. "What I am about to say might be more difficult to hear than the gunfire. There was a car stolen on the road several miles from here. The driver, a St. David's resident, was shot. I regret to say she did not survive her injuries. She was pronounced at the scene."

Mrs. Cox hung on every one of Finton's words. "What is her name?"

"Ruth Minor."

Mrs. Cox sat heavily on the stone, knocking the tray and its pitcher of lemonade to the ground. "The one who escaped, he's in this Ruth Minor's car?"

Finton asked, "Quite likely injured, armed, and dangerous, very likely in this area. I'm terribly sorry. You knew the victim? Does she have family here? Could you help us inform her next of kin?"

Mrs. Cox stood. There was a quaver in her voice as she looked down on the wrecked tray of refreshments. "What a mess I've made. No, sir. I don't know Ruth Minor."

When Mrs. Cox caught sight of Molly Wilde's rounding pregnancy, her face regained some of its life. She gently placed the palms of her hands on Molly's belly, and said, "Oh my dear, she will be a wonder. She will be strong. She will fight, and make you so proud of the battles she will join and win."

Mrs. Cox took withdrew her hands with a sad smile, bent to pick up the pitcher and tray, turned, and walked out of the clearing without another word.

Deep in Molly Wilde's soul, she wondered if Mrs. Cox had heralded a girl who would soon come into the world, or if she had eulogized one who'd just departed it.

CHAPTER 68

LUANNA STRUCK THE woman's face once to rouse her from the torpor of the nearly drowned. The sound of the impact had a confined feel there in the officers' bunk room of the *Nabokov*.

The woman's eyes opened, "Slap me again, it's the last thing you do."

"Reckon I like your spirit. But that wasn't a slap." LuAnna chuckled to herself. "Lordy no, I was just waking you up. What's your name, Hon?"

"Blessing."

"Pretty name, Blessing. I'm—

"LuAnna Blackshaw," said Blessing. Dazed as she was, she seemed smug, too.

"Wow, that was some stunt! How'd you come to catch hold of that dead fellow on deck?"

"I swam into the tunnel as far as I could," said Blessing. "Found an air pocket. Treaded water. The sub came along. I hitched a ride to where you found me. I thought I was dead."

Blackshaw stepped and stooped through the bulkhead, and sat on the opposite bunk. "You're not dead, if you can come up with a million dollars American."

"Don't be ridiculous," the woman spat out.

"Her name's Blessing."

"That's a fair bit of freight to load on a person," Blackshaw said. "Especially if you're keeping company with Maynard Chalk."

Blessing's laugh was grim. "I was sent to kill him."

"That so? Then you're welcome. Not for nothing, at least two of your three-man team are dead," said Blackshaw. "And if that third fellow's not dead, he's surely not feeling too spry."

Blessing's eyes betrayed surprised.

LuAnna said, "I think a more interesting question than your bank or lack of it, is who ordered you to kill Chalk?"

CHAPTER 69

MRS. COX'S GRANDSON had finally come home. He and several friends had located the vehicle belonging to the carjacking victim, Ruth Minor. They had found the injured carjacker himself lying close by in a hedge, a gunshot wound to his leg, and a bullet dent in the trauma plate of his ballistic vest. He had taken a wrong turn deep into the heart of a St. David's neighborhood, gotten lost, gotten out of the car, and collapsed. He would live to regret it, but not for very long.

Now, this last man of Blessing's B-Team was trussed in a sturdy straight-backed chair with ropes that cut off the circulation in his arms. His hands were swollen and purple from the wires twisted around his wrists. A crude dressing had been applied to the leg wound to forestall his untimely death. The dressing, the ropes, these were all he wore now. His clothing had been cut away. More things that he valued would soon follow.

Mrs. Cox came into the room dressed in mourning black. She took a seat opposite her captive. She studied the man in the chair, the man whose want of a car had brought him to cross paths with the young woman, Ruth Minor, and murder her in cold blood. The man looked back at Mrs. Cox through swollen eyes. In taking him, Mrs. Cox's grandson and his friends had been rough.

Ruth had been a good girl, strong and beautiful. She had studied hard. Her grades were as good as they could be for a girl who also worked cleaning hotel rooms before she finally graduated with her GCSE. She had wanted to go to college; perhaps earn a degree, or a certification in the hospitality industry, which would have suited her warm and caring ways. Relatives in New England, distant Wampanoag Indian relatives, had already promised Mrs. Cox they would take in her lovely granddaughter, Ruth Minor, if she wanted to study in the States. That girl was on the right path. Until she was stopped dead by the man who was now roped into the chair.

Mrs. Cox had a knife. She had spent the last hour honing it. Many years ago, the blade had been broad and heavy. After hundreds of thousands of turns across the sharpening wheel, it was now so thin, it was the merest idea of a blade; it was a wisp of steel wraithing out of a sturdy wood handle.

Mrs. Cox had nothing to say to this destroyer. Nothing to ask. No plaintive *how could you*, or *how dare you*, or *why*. He could offer no answer that would bring her granddaughter back. If Ruth Minor had died quickly, Mrs. Cox would take great care to make sure this man would still be alive in several days. By the end of several days, he would beg for death if he had a tongue, if he still had lips. But by the end of several days, his death would still be one week away. Mrs. Cox was skilled and practiced. Mrs. Cox was patient. Mrs. Cox was in a rage.

CHAPTER 70

BLESSING WAS SITTING up, sipping. Captain Karkov, his shoulder wound bandaged, had given her a cup of warm onion broth. Warm, not boiling. Though Blessing might not have realized it, there was nothing left within ten feet of her bunk that could be used as a weapon. The reek of onions in the small compartment was potent.

Blackshaw asked her, "Who wants Chalk dead?"

LuAnna added, "Some of us thought he already was."

"At Dove Point," said Blessing. "The fire there. And yet he survived. We were surprised, too."

"How did a fellow all tarnished like him still have a job?" LuAnna asked. "He still had funding?"

"From some elements overseas," Blessing explained. "Enemies of State. Chalk had become more troublesome than when he worked for Lily Morgan back when she was a senator. Killing him was overdue housekeeping."

"Whose house, Blessing?" LuAnna was charming, but persistent.

"Who's Haakon?" Blackshaw asked.

Again, Blessing seemed surprised. She covered by taking a sip of onion broth.

Captain Karkov put his head through the hatch. "Dark. We're going through the rest of the tunnel to the ocean. Oh, please ignore scraping sounds of the hull on the tunnel wall. I sometimes don't get the turns timed right. Is she staying aboard, or swimming?"

Blessing hastened to say, "Chalk was working for fringe factions."

Blackshaw appreciated Blessing's willingness to talk. He said to Karkov, "She stays aboard for now."

Karkov disappeared aft to the control room.

Blessing said, "There's a group that wants to embarrass the current administration and start a war."

"Congress? Nothing new about that." Blackshaw said.

"No. This group has an asset that could make it happen. If Americans don't scream for war first, radical Islamist factions will likely rise up—"

"Like Isis?" LuAnna asked.

"Bigger," said Blessing. "A coalition of Isis, Al Qaeda, Al Qaeda in the Arabian Peninsula, Al Shabaab, Boko Haram. A larger, concerted war effort on their part would mean business for the military-industrial complex. My people want the massive orders like the good old days. The small, fractured fronts against low-tech terrorists are great for small arms, transport, body armor—squad level ordnance and matériel—but it's not great for big ticket items. Hard to justify buying an aircraft carrier to throw at nineteen Saudis with civilian pilot licenses, right?"

LuAnna asked, "What kind of asset could stir up a holocaust like you're talking about?"

"It's not a what. It's a who," Blessing said.

"It's this Haakon," said Blackshaw. "Chalk mentioned him."

"No," said Blessing. "Haakon's a nobody."

"Look, honeygirl, we're trying to find out who killed Travis Cynter," said LuAnna. "Is the name familiar?"

Blessing sat up straight, and swung her feet off the bunk to the deck. She asked, "What about Cynter? Who's he?"

"He was a SEAL. Got tagged on an off-the-books style mission on Dog & Bitch Island, near Ocean City in Maryland," said Blackshaw.

Blessing shook her head. "I mean, who is he to you?"

"He was an old friend."

Blessing said, "Okay. In that case, I saw your friend die."

"Help me understand what you're saying," said Blackshaw, mastering his temper. "You saw him dead. Or, you watched him die after he was shot? You witnessed his getting shot? Paint us a picture."

"I was standing next to the man who pulled the trigger. Cynter wanted to take control of the asset from my boss." Blessing drained the cup of onion broth. "Your friend was operating forward, solo, on U.S. soil; he wanted the asset, and let's say my boss didn't care for it. But it wasn't personal."

"Who is your boss?" Blackshaw asked.

"Screed. Bonamy Screed," said Blessing.

"Hey Captain Karkov!" Blackshaw shouted.

After a moment, the Russian put his head back into the compartment where the chat was taking place. "What? This is not a good time, Ben Blackshaw. I have an eight degree left turn combined with a one degree down-bubble coming up in—" Karkov checked his stopwatch. "—in forty-two seconds."

Blackshaw drew his pistol. "Blessing here, she's tapped out. No bus fare. So she's swimming after all. Thought you'd like to know."

Blessing lunged at LuAnna, head-locking her. She stood and backed away with LuAnna wrestled in front as a shield, eyes wide with fear.

"What the hell!" LuAnna shouted. "Shoot her!"

Blackshaw fired, catching Blessing in an exposed knee. Blessing screamed, and LuAnna twisted away. Blackshaw pulled the trigger twice more, and Blessing dropped. The haze and smell of propellant mixed with the reek of onion soup as her last meal flowed out with her blood on the deck.

Captain Karkov appraised Blessing's corpse. "Your lucky day, Ben Blackshaw!"

"How you reckon?"

Karkov grinned with pride. "Number three torpedo tube still works, and it's empty, empty, empty! I think she'll fit okay."

The captain retreated to the control room again to see about the complicated upcoming turn.

"Ben," said LuAnna, when they were alone with the corpse, "Blessing didn't tell you who the asset is."

"She didn't have to. I already know. But she's an accessory to Travis's death."

Blessing's left arm moved on the deck as she groaned. Blackshaw shot her in the head.

He said, "It's sinking in, that Chalk's dead. I think a part of me might miss him."

LuAnna side-eyed her man. "Remember when I told you to share more of yourself with me?"

Blackshaw nodded.

"I need you to shut up for five minutes on Chalk. Maybe a couple weeks. Far as I'm concerned, it's high time Chalk was dead. It needed doing. I'm glad you're the one did it. But please, you can shut the actual hell up about missing him."

CHAPTER 71

RESIDENT AGENT WILDE took the call from Chief Inspector Finton. When it was over, she said to Lowry, "They found the woman's car."

She and Lowry were seated in a small bistro in Hamilton, taking a break after a marathon session of filing reports for Finton and the Bermuda Police Service on their activities so far. Wilde had thought the FBI bureaucracy was ponderous. Now she believed it was kindergarten-simple compared to the administrative requirements of a constitutional monarchy.

Lowry looked up from the coffee that had just been served. "Where?"

"It was abandoned on a sandy stretch between the end of Ariel Road and Cox Bay."

"Is that on St. David's Island?" Lowry added another cube of sugar to his coffee.

"From what I gather, it isn't."

"What about the carjacker?"

Wilde said, "They haven't caught him."

"How far can he have gotten? It's an island," Lowry said. "Any word on Blessing, and her men?"

Wilde frowned at Lowry. "My office practically set up a task force on that bunch. Shots fired overseas, Chalk and two other Americans dead. That's the headline, whatever criminal activity they were up to. Dead Americans. You realize that."

"Not to mention the tattoo shop victims, and Siobhan Grimes."

Wilde said, "I couldn't tell from Finton if he still wants the Blackshaws extradited for questioning if they turn up back in the States, or if he's ready to hang it all on Chalk."

"He's doing what he can toward that, testing Chalk's Laguiole pocket knife for the Bermudian victims' DNA."

"Do we have to fly back tonight, Persh?"

"And miss being called on the carpet for this mess tomorrow? By dammit, I better not see Ben Blackshaw again anytime soon."

Wilde was surprised. Lowry never swore. Now she realized he wasn't good at it.

He went on, "You said it. Three Bermudians with their throats cut. A former aide to an assassinated Secretary of Homeland Security likewise killed in a firefight—"

"That was line of duty. Self-defense—"

"And two American operators shot dead in a car, likely by Ben Blackshaw himself—"

"He does have the chops for it," Wilde mused.

Lowry would not be interrupted. "—a third operator missing, and wanted for questioning, and none of this conveniently taking place on U.S. soil, except for the murder of one Travis Cynter, a highly decorated Navy SEAL who died for all we know on an unsanctioned mission very much on U.S. soil, and no real idea why! Damn!"

"What's really bothering you, Persh?" Wilde felt his frustration, and was trying to lighten the moment. She didn't expect a serious answer.

"Molly, I wanted to bring you here for our honeymoon. To Bermuda. The pink beaches. The beautiful weather. Now, after all this blood and stupidity, I just can't. It's utterly impossible. I might not even have a job after tomorrow."

In the rush of romance, her pregnancy, new job titles, moving in together, and this case, Wilde had nearly forgotten they weren't already married. Her heart swelled with love for this man.

CHAPTER 72

BLACKSHAW HELPED KARKOV and two crewmen lug Blessing's remains forward to the *Nabokov's* torpedo room. A fifth man followed behind with a mop and bucket, swabbing where the body bled on the deck.

Since the Quebec Class carried no spare torpedoes, it had a maximum of only four shots on a patrol before needing resupply. Blackshaw didn't ask why torpedo tube three was empty, or if the others were loaded. They were in a rush. The captain had only three minutes on this course before the final turn in the tunnel to open ocean. The Russian must have had implicit faith in his second in command to run this section of the rocky gauntlet without a collision.

Karkov himself made sure that the number three tube was sealed on the outboard end and pumped dry before opening it. As the tube hatch swung open, some water drained into the compartment. The outboard seal was leaking.

"On a count of three?" Blackshaw said.

Karkov said, "A moment. I find head-first works best."

It was awkward, turning the body end-for-end in the small space, but they managed it, and packed the dead operator into the tube. Blackshaw picked up Blessing's fallen left sandal, and tossed it in after her.

Karkov closed the inboard hatch, flooded the tube, and said, "Would you like to say a few words, Mr. Blackshaw?"

"I'd say burial at sea is too good for her as it is. Let's not make a bad joke of it."

"I agree with you totally and completely," said Karkov as he threw the firing lever. Air hissed into the torpedo tube to eject the body. "Shall we say, two hundred thousand added to our fee for disposal of inconvenient remains?"

CHAPTER 73

THE BRIDGE OF *Bystander of Man* was abuzz. Mr. Curlew had laid in a course for the unremarkable rendezvous fix in the open ocean where Blackshaw had directed them via satellite phone five hours before.

Ellis was engrossed on a secure computer tablet typing encrypted instructions that Blackshaw had provided for the transfer of two point two million dollars to a bank account in Kowloon. It was a large sum for most. For Ellis, the task was a bigger annoyance than the figure. He loathed filling out forms of any kind.

Mr. Gannet was observing a monitor showing an image of the empty sea where Blackshaw and LuAnna were supposed to meet them. His new surveillance albatross drone was loitering at the designated position now two miles away and beaming images back to the yacht.

Mr. Gannet said, "Nothing. There's nothing out there for miles. Are you sure you got the latitude and longitude correct, Captain Hogan?"

Ellis said, "Reasonably sure, Mr. Gannet. Is your bird at the right spot?"

"I used the same numbers you did, sir. The very same."

"So we hold our course for there," said Ellis.

Mr. Auk entered the bridge from the boat deck. "The cutter's ready to lower whenever you say, sir."

"Not yet awhile, Mr. Auk. Don't want it over the side if we have to change plans on the fly."

"Understood, sir," said Mr. Auk, who poured himself a mug of coffee from the urn that was always full or brewing.

"Captain Hogan." It was Mr. Gannet, sounding amazed as he stared at the drone's surveillance screen . "I believe—"

"You believe what, Mr. Gannet?"

"I believe that's a—periscope."

CHAPTER 74

SCREED WAS WORRIED. He unloaded, and reloaded the magazine of his pistols, first his Glock 17, then his compact Glock 26 Gen 3; he did this the way others doodled on notepads, or squeezed stress balls.

Blessing had been radio-silent for twelve hours. At first, even in close contact with Maynard Chalk, she had found ways to send up a signal of some kind, a text, a coded or encrypted phone call. Of course, since she was operating under cover posing as Chalk's ally, Screed couldn't keep her on a tight leash. She had to maintain the appearance of serving only Chalk.

Even so, it was entirely possible her cover had been blown. Chalk, psychotic in the best of times, also had a brilliant mind, and a lucky streak a mile wide. Granted, his erratic behavior recently was outstripping anything his psychotropic meds could subdue, if he were even taking them (Screed had it on good authority that Chalk was completely non-compliant with his all prescriptions, except his damn cholesterol pills.) Certainly, Chalk's luck had cooled from his glory days. That said, to insure Chalk would not meddle with Screed's operation any more than he had, Blessing's killing hand was necessary. So, where the hell was she?

In his office a few doors down from where the Patient lay, Screed sent Blessing's phone a discreet signal alerting her of the need for a check-in. If he didn't hear back from her in a few hours, he would be forced to assume the worst: Blessing was compromised. Chalk had interrogated her, and terminated her. Further, it had to be assumed Chalk knew about the location of the Patient; that would require repositioning everyone until it was time to pull the trigger on the public side of the op, the side that really mattered. Screed almost chuckled at the notion of actually needing the services of Chalk's old cover company, Right Way Moving & Storage. But that was only if Blessing didn't respond.

Screed reloaded the Glock 17, and tucked it in the holster under his arm. He checked his watch. Only a minute had passed since he sent the signal. He dialed a satellite phone number for the chase boat he had sent to exfiltrate Blessing once her sanction against Chalk was complete. The C-Team aboard the boat would have to stand by in case Blessing surfaced needing help.

CHAPTER 75

MR. CURLEW'S VOICE was calm. "I have a surface radar contact coming in at high speed from the south. It's bearing is toward us, not toward that periscope."

Ellis studied the radar. "No, there's no return on the sub yet. Ahead full please, Mr. Curlew. Mr. Auk, I'll need the RHIB over the side, and you in it. Get to the rendezvous point. When you have the Blackshaws, put them aboard here at the aft passerelle, and show them directly to the helideck."

"Blackshaws to the pad, aye Captain." Soon after Mr. Auk was on deck, the davit winches could be heard lowering the high speed RHIB into the ocean.

Mr. Gannet said, "If they've got sonar aboard the sub they'll hear fast-turning screws, from us and that boat. Do you want eyes-on, Captain Hogan?"

"Yes, please. But I have a feeling it's Bermuda Police investigating us. Likely some blowback from the Blackshaw family vacation making them get all edgy about unidentified vessels. This is getting somewhat—international."

Mr. Gannet adjusted the controls of his albatross, starting its high torque electric ducted fan for a quick climb higher above the waves for a better view across a longer distance.

After several tense minutes Mr. Curlew said, "New radar contact—airborne. From the north northwest. Oh my. Two hundred knots plus."

"Thank you. This is going to be close," said Ellis.

Mr. Curlew announced, "And now I've got a radar return from the surfaced sub, and Mr. Auk is right there."

Ellis left the bridge, and went forward on the yacht's Portuguese bridge with binoculars. "I've got them!" he shouted aft through the door. "The sub's barely hull-up, decks awash. The Blackshaws are on the foredeck." After a moment, "And now Mr. Auk has them aboard. Please close on Mr. Auk and the Blackshaws quick as you can."

"Aye, sir," said Mr. Curlew, refining his course and mashing the throttles forward.

Mr. Gannet said, "Here's that fast boat, sir."

As Ellis checked the monitor showing the albatross drone's-eye view. It was as he feared, a patrol boat. Ellis said, "It's not BPS. Can't see any markings. Hold it. Is she changing course? They were coming for us a minute ago."

"Must have seen the sub's radar return show up out of nowhere," said Mr. Curlew. "That should buy us some time. Not much, but some."

"Oh damn," said Ellis, still looking through the binoculars. "That patrol boat's going straight for the sub. The sub's crash diving. Still too slow. Jesus, the boat's going to ram the thing! What the hell!"

Ellis watched in horror as the patrol boat raced over the sea where the sub's conning tower had just disappeared below the surface. The boat's forward way checked suddenly and hard, and it was shunted to port as if it had struck a rock. A great rush of bubbles welled up and made the sea boil white.

"Mr. Curlew, how's that fast contact from the northwest looking?"

The helmsman answered, "Slowing, but still inbound. Two miles."

Ellis said, "That's my ride. Mr. Curlew, Mr. Gannet, this is where I'll leave you for now. As soon as the Blackshaws are on that pad, that helicopter you've been tracking will touch briefly, take the Blackshaws and me aboard, and boogie. Best you don't know where."

"Orders, Captain?" asked Mr. Gannet.

Ellis looked his crew. "Head north out of Bermuda's territorial waters as fast as *Bystander of Man* can go. That patrol boat might be messed up below the waterline from ramming the sub. You head straight back to port in

Ocean City. But if that boat turns out to be BPS, and gives chase and catches you, play dumb, and sit tight imagining your lavish Christmas bonuses from me. Let them impound this boat, no resistance. It's just a boat. Six angry international attorneys armed with lots of bluster and folding money will have you sprung in no time."

"And what if she's not Bermuda Police Service?" asked Mr. Curlew.

"I'll sort it out from aloft."

Ellis shook hands with Mr. Curlew and Mr. Gannet, and double-timed back to the small helideck. Blackshaw and LuAnna were just hitting the top of the passerelle with Mr. Auk, who'd tied up the RHIB below. From the northwest, a sleek Eurocopter EC155 with its four-bladed main rotor and shrouded tail rotor, wheeled in for a landing. The sole pilot sported a white beard, and on his sleeve, a yellow Norman shield with a black backslash and horse head silhouette; it was the insignia of the 1st Cavalry Division. He greased a touch down so gently, he could have caught a grape between the nose wheel and the deck and not squeezed out a drop of juice.

The rear cabin door slid open. Another wizened man with a 1st Cavalry insignia on his sleeve and an unlit, pencil-thin cheroot clamped in his teeth, stepped back to help LuAnna aboard. Blackshaw assisted from behind, earning a yelp and a slap from his bride. Last, Ellis saluted Mr. Auk in farewell, boarded and took a seat in the plush leather cabin.

The helicopter rose and turned in the air, but the cabin crewman left the big door open. He lowered a compact GE M134 electric six-barreled Gatling gun on its mount from its stowed position near the overhead.

"What's going on Ellis?" Blackshaw shouted over the aircraft noise.

"A patrol boat went for the sub," said Ellis.

"Karkov's sonar guy heard it. Shot at her?" LuAnna asked.

"Looked like a ramming," said Ellis, donning a set of headphones hardwired to the intercom. He handed a pair each to Blackshaw and LuAnna. Then he said to the pilot, "Mr. Harrier, fly us past that patrol boat, but give Mr. Merlin room to work his magic."

The helicopter swung low in a large circle around the patrol boat, which was itself carving a large curved wake as if its rudder were damaged and the helm was not answering properly.

Ellis said, "Mr. Merlin, I ask you. Does that look like a legit government patrol vessel to you?"

Ellis had no sooner asked this, than two crewmen emerged from the bridge of the patrol boat, and opened fire at the helicopter with machine guns. The bullets flew wide of the mark.

"That answer your question, sir?" said Mr. Merlin.

Ellis grinned. "Light those bastards up, if you would."

"Not if you'd care to do the honors, sir." said Mr. Merlin.

Ellis traded positions with Mr. Merlin, took aim with the minigun, and squeezed the trigger. The six barrels whirled into a blur to the accompanying buzz of a thousand mad hornets. A plume of smoke belched out and trailed aft from the muzzles while a cascade of brass cartridges fell away. A torrent of bullets ripped out of the sky.

Ellis had gauged the relative motion of the helicopter and the boat to perfection. First one, then the second shooter on the vessel below was sawn into pieces by the hail of bullets, sending blood and limbs into the scuppers to drain red down the white freeboard of the boat. Without halting the burst, Ellis walked the stream of bullets aft to the three big outboard motors, destroying them one by one, and starting a fire from ruptured fuel lines. That boat was dead in the water.

Mr. Merlin jabbed a finger at a hatch on the boat's bow. "There's another one coming up forward! And he's got a SAW!"

"Now you see him—" Ellis was grinning now.

He lifted his finger from the minigun's trigger and took a split second to train its sights at the man struggling to hoist a Squad Automatic Weapon through the forward hatch. When he was sure of his aim, Ellis opened fire again. The operative's entire head and upper torso were pulped to stewed tomatoes and bone before he dropped back through the hatch and out of sight.

"—and now you don't."

Blackshaw said, "Might be a little late, but who were they?"

"Gravely mistaken about my patience," said Ellis. "Mr. Harrier, we'll secure for cruise, and head to shore."

The pilot acknowledged the order, gaining altitude and speed as he bore west toward the U.S. mainland. Mr. Merlin stowed the minigun up by the overhead, and slid the big cabin door closed.

Ellis took a hard look at Blackshaw for the first time since boarding, and said, "Your cheek. You're bleeding."

LuAnna produced a tissue from somewhere, licked it, and dabbed at Blackshaw's face. "It's not his blood," she said. "It never is."

CHAPTER 76

BLACKSHAW RECLINED IN the Gulfstream's spacious main cabin with Ellis. LuAnna was taking advantage of the shower and fresh change of clothes in the private aft cabin. Ellis had ordered Mr. Harrier to land the Eurocopter at Atlanta-Hartsfield Airport, where they immediately boarded Ellis's Gulfstream 650 which was waiting there, fueled, with the galley stocked.

"You sure you know who the pilot is?" Blackshaw asked his friend. He had every reason. There'd been one flight the year before when they found that a hostile operative had poisoned Ellis's actual pilot, commandeered the plane, and tried to murder Blackshaw, wounding Ellis in the process.

"It's our buddy Dale!" Ellis named the first officer whom they had forced at gunpoint to replace the captain who'd been killed.

"I thought Dale hated you," said Blackshaw.

"Seriously. With what I pay him? No, we're pals." Ellis leaned into the aisle and shouted forward, "Hey Dale, say hi to Ben!"

Blackshaw craned his neck around, and saw a raised middle finger from the cockpit's left seat.

"It's *you* he doesn't like," Ellis confided. "But you'll notice I took the cockpit door off just in case, so we can see who the hell's really driving."

"Belt-and-suspenders, Ellis. I respect that."

"Maynard Chalk is well and truly dead?"

"I clanked a round off a titanium plate in his noggin," Blackshaw said. "Then I shot him again, base of the neck."

"I bet he felt that," said Ellis.

"Reckon he did. Then he tipped over dead like he meant it."

Ellis stared at Blackshaw. "You don't think he's dead. You're superstitious. Ben, I never took you for the type to credit ghosts."

"Just because the circus left town doesn't mean they took all the monkeys," Blackshaw said.

"Still see things from time to time, do you?"

"People mostly, same as always. Ones I notched up in the service, and since. Like they're angry, and waiting for me on the other side. A while back, there were two bodies I never recovered from a place I had to hole up. I'd wake up in the middle of the night, and they'd be sitting there in my compartment, just playing cards and ignoring me. Then one of them looks at me. I know that bastard wants to deal me in."

"There's always an open seat at that game," Ellis said.

"Used to think I was the only one who saw—things. A week at the VA, and I knew I wasn't so special."

"The dead are never done with us," said Ellis.

"Reckon not 'til we've joined them." Blackshaw looked out the window at the ocean far below.

LuAnna emerged from the aft cabin toweling her hair dry. She paused at the moving map screen on the bulkhead. "Nova Scotia. En route to Paris."

"It's the great circle route from Atlanta, but we'll refile soon enough to land at Alderney," Blackshaw said. Seeing LuAnna's puzzled expression he went on, "Gurnsey. Channel Islands. Fort Clonque. Haakon. It's where that land line number you showed me is wired"

"I know where the heck we're going, Ben. I'm pregnant, not stupid. Just wondering if there's enough runway for this big bird on that little patch."

Ellis brightened. "There's three runways, LuAnna! I figure if we stick all of them end-to-end, we'll have plenty of room and to spare."

"You do know that's not how it works," LuAnna said.

"Of course, hon. I'm old, not senile."

LuAnna went to the galley refrigerator and grabbed a bottle of spring water. She said, "Swagger die, Ellis, that is the last beer you drink in front of me until this baby's born."

"Copy that," said Ellis before draining his glass with a friendly mix of pleasure and spite.

"About this Haakon fellow?" asked LuAnna. "Who is he when he's at home?"

"Okay, on Ellis's boat, when we took Chalk aboard from the life raft, he blamed somebody by that name for snitching on him. Then Chalk mentioned this fort in just about the same breath," said Blackshaw. "We've been working backwards from where Travis died."

"There's none too many Norwegian kings of that name," said LuAnna. "I was hoping we'd have a little something more than a Google search to point the way." LuAnna was quiet for a moment before she spoke again. "Ben, back on the *Nabokov*, you said you knew who the asset was that got Chalk all riled, and maybe got Travis killed. But you never said who."

Blackshaw said, "I could be wrong."

"You were sure enough to shoot Blessing more than once," observed LuAnna.

"She admitted she was an accessory to Travis's death, hon. She had to go."

Ellis said, "A year ago, you'd be all in my face about due process, Ben. You might be snuffing folks who could help you make a case against the one who killed Travis."

"Oops."

Ellis asked, "What about the name Blessing said before you—unblessed her?"

"Bonamy Screed," said LuAnna.

"Blessing said Screed leads whatever fringe group thinks they've got a personage who the radical troops on both sides can rise up and rally around, or rail against—"

"Like I said, it's your phantom asset," said LuAnna.

"Reckon if he doesn't get the big military orders rolling again, he's about as good as a ghost." Blackshaw mulled what he'd just said, and went on. "Screed must be a coalition builder, but he also manufactures opposition, too."

"A black-ops lobbyist working both ends," said LuAnna.

"A self-licking ice cream cone," said Ellis. "He runs an echo chamber."

"Sounds like Chalk's next of kin," Blackshaw said. He leaned back his chair, and closed his eyes.

LuAnna looked up from a web search on her phone and said, "If this one is the same Bonamy Screed, you boys are not going to believe how high this goes."

CHAPTER 77

SCREED WAS INCENSED. From a distress call, he learned his C-Team on the fast boat had been cut to shreds by a civilian helicopter with a black-ops sting. Two survivors had full thickness burns over 60 percent of their bodies. Their kidneys might hold out, or the guys might die in the next twelve hours. Either way they were useless, and the boat was disabled. There'd been a submarine. A sub! And Blessing was still not picking up.

Moving the Patient now would be a problem. Screed had instructed the beefy medical technician to increase the Squealer dosage, but there'd been a reaction. A side effect. The Patient had been weeping non-stop for nine hours. Screed had rolled video of this obscenity just in case he could spin it to advantage somehow in the future, but this maudlin appearance of repentance would not fly. Screed needed the Patient angry as instructed, and on message as scripted, in order to light off the global conflagration desired by his clients. This blubbering mess wouldn't foment any kind of notice in the news beyond a mildly compromising scandal. So everything was riding on this Patient's performance. Screed was beside himself with anger, but his fury meant nothing on the world stage.

The intravenous line pumping Squealer into the Patient's arm was removed and replaced by a flow of conventional sedatives. That was done two hours ago, but still the tears, the sobbing continued. Screed almost felt embarrassed for the Patient. The world's most colossal monster was now a pathetic geezer with all the fight of a corpse.

Screed put his head in the Patient's room. The medical technician shrugged at Screed, and blotted the Patient's mottled face with a tissue.

"Has he chilled out?" asked Screed.

"I thought he was slowing down for a few minutes. He was even snoring. But then the waterworks came back like Niagara Falls. We're going to need more Kleenex."

"Shit," said Screed. "I think we broke him."

CHAPTER 78

LOWRY AND WILDE had been invited to sit by the FBI's Director, Sid Hornsby. They found the chairs comfortable, despite the fact that the agents were perching only on the edges of the seats. Lowry sensed that if Wilde were not visibly pregnant, Hornsby would have been happy to leave them on their feet. Hornsby was not pleased. But he was otherwise alone. There was no one from Human Resources overseeing the conversation. This meeting was not a firing or a demotion. Not yet.

"Where are we?" said Hornsby. "Pershing? Might as well start with the butcher's bill." Hornsby had read all of Patrick O'Brian's Aubrey-Maturin seafaring novels, and some of the books' antiquated language had crept into his daily usage.

Lowry's mouth was dry. That was another sign of Hornsby's unhappiness. No offer of bottled water from the fridge by his desk. Lowry listed, "Travis Cynter. Maynard Chalk. Both dead. Blessing Klyman is missing."

"She was what, to whom exactly?"

Wilde offered, "We're not sure. She was an NSA operative under cover with Chalk's group a year ago. Then she drops off the map. She made contact with Chalk in Bermuda, but there's also evidence she was accompanied there by a three-man team, and we aren't sure if Chalk was aware of their presence before things went south. Also, there's no record of Chalk's entry into Bermuda through Customs."

Hornsby locked eyes with Wilde, but spoke to Lowry. "Is she cleared for all this?"

"Absolutely," Lowry replied.

Hornsby glanced at Wilde's belly as if it were an affront to his Calvinist Puritan work ethic, and said, "Where's that three-man team?"

"Two are dead, by whose hand we're not certain. The third one, who's likely wounded, armed, and dangerous, has so far escaped a tight Bermuda Police Service cordon following a fatal carjacking. Despite the manhunt, he remains at large."

"A manhunt on Bermuda. Jesus, they could knock that out before elevenses," said Hornsby. "Who do you think killed Blessing Klyman's two B-Team guys? Best guess."

Lowry took this one. "We had visual contact with a U.S. citizen, a former SEAL, name of Ben Blackshaw. His wife, LuAnna Blackshaw, was a person of interest wanted for questioning in several murder cases on Bermuda."

"Several! Meaning what? Two? Five? A baker's dozen?" Hornsby's unhappiness was boiling up into anger. "How'd they get involved?"

Wilde said, "Ben Blackshaw has served as an ad hoc Confidential Informant on Bureau matters in the past."

"Ad hoc. Explain."

"Meaning, when he feels like it," said Wilde. "It's not ideal, but his help has aided in closing some difficult cases."

"Do I want to know which cases, Molly?"

"Do you want deniability, sir?"

"Forget the Blackshaws," Hornsby said quickly. "Like as not they were just a couple in Bermuda on vacation, right? And those B-Team bozos who clearly aren't FBI—" Hornsby waited a moment to be sure no one was going to contradict him. "They had some kind of internal falling out, resulting in two deaths, and a guy missing, and a carjacking. Right?"

Wilde said, "The three men accompanying Blessing Klyman arrived through Bermuda Customs at the airport, as did Mrs. Blackshaw. But as in Maynard Chalk's case, there's no record of Ben Blackshaw arriving in Bermuda through Customs."

Hornsby could barely look at Wilde. "Jesus! If it crosses your mind to come out and ask somebody about deniability on a topic, which practically begs for a special prosecutor all by itself, you don't then go on and on about said topic to the point that I want to jab ice picks in my eardrums, so I actually have the deniability you seem to think I'd want. 'No Congressman Ass-Ream, I did not hear Senior Resident Agent Wilde discussing this international cluster, which by the way was not under the oversight of any FBI Foreign Liaison Office, as my eardrums were bleeding into my collar.' Next time, Molly just bring the ice picks! Now, who do you like for those several other murders you mentioned? The Bermudian civilian ones."

Wilde's eyebrows ticked up, and she glanced at Lowry for direction. His face was expressionless. She asked, "You want me to continue?"

Hornsby stood. "Since my triplet daughters are all entering Seven Sister schools in the same year, I guess I can't exactly quit, go home and put my feet up and still pay their tuition, so sure—hit me."

Wilde said, "There were hallmarks of psychotic and overwhelming brutality, with all three victim's throats not so much cut as hacked back to the vertebrae. Each victim was in some way connected with Travis Cynter. We think it was Chalk conducting an investigation his own way."

"Were Chalk and Cynter buddies?" Hornsby asked.

"Cynter was trying to gain control of an asset that Chalk himself wants. Wanted."

"God knows I hate to ask," said Hornsby, "but what is the asset?"

Lowry said, "Still not sure. I received an interagency request from a friend at the NSA. They needed human-derived intel to verify some disturbing chatter."

Hornsby asked, "Why you? Why us? Why not the CIA?"

"The request came from somebody in S32," said Lowry.

"Tailored Access Operations," said Hornsby. "That's computers. Overseas. Again, why us?"

"Because the trace on the chatter led from an ally, the UK, straight back to U.S. soil," said Wilde.

"So what!" Hornsby bellowed. "That's still NSA S35. Special Source Operations. That directorate's all domestic all the time!"

"And so, it wasn't for the CIA," Wilde explained.

Hornsby settled down. "So we've got a half dozen folks dead or missing, including a decorated SEAL, some Blackshaws, a Blessing, and that wingnut Chalk, and multiple national security agencies in a lather, with an international angle leading back here someplace, and an unknown asset whose purpose is—what?"

"Scandal at the highest levels of government," Lowry said.

"So—business as usual," Hornsby summed up.

Wilde didn't want to speak, but the report was still incomplete. She said, "There was a Russian submarine."

Hornsby's face went purple. "What the hell!"

Lowry said, "It was rather small, and quite old. Likely an old surplus buy, or perhaps stolen. It submerged and was lost through a large improved natural tunnel leading from a former hardened U.S. Naval sub base in Bermuda out to open sea. Blackshaw escaped in it."

Hornsby put his face in his hands. "Got a line on that sub? Or Blackshaw?"

"No, sir," said Wilde. "But a Gulfstream 650 belonging to a known associate of Blackshaw rendezvoused with this same associate's Eurocopter in Atlanta. The G650 is now airborne with a flight plan filed for Paris."

"Who has that kind of bank? You two do know you're suspended as hell, don't you?"

"It's not a great surprise," Lowry said.

"It's a Director's Suspension," Hornsby said. "It means it's effective immediately, but I don't have to get the paperwork in to HR for four days."

Lowry's expression told Wilde this kind of disciplinary action was new to him.

Hornsby went on, "Of course, during those four days, I have no idea what you two are up to, except you can't mope around your offices. Off limits. You might stay home. You might take a trip someplace. Drop out. Lay low while I assess this amazing crater you've dug for the bureau. Maybe overseas? Who knows. Up to you. Not my problem. In four days, we talk again. See where things stand."

"Yes, sir," were the only words Wilde could say.

Hornsby reached into the fridge by his desk and pulled out a two bottles of water. "Want a couple for the road?"

Outside Hornsby's office, Wilde cracked her water bottle open and took a long pull.

Lowry said, "Director's Suspension?"

"That's totally not a thing," Wilde confirmed. "We're damaged goods. If we can finish this in four days, maybe we keep our jobs. If we fail, the already damaged goods get shit-canned."

"So, if we were a bit rogue before—" mused Lowry to himself.

"—Now we're *officially* rogue," finished Wilde. "Which is also not a thing."

CHAPTER 79

LUANNA TOOK IN the scenery of Alderney as their taxi brought them into town from the airfield. She said, "This place is so old, and quiet, and beautiful. I hope to be like that someday."

Blackshaw said, "You've got beautiful nailed down already, but if you were quiet, I wouldn't know what to do."

LuAnna smiled and snuggled closer to Blackshaw in back.

"So sweet," said Ellis from the front seat. "And here I am without my insulin."

"You're not diabetic," said LuAnna.

"I might be if you two don't have a fight, or let me shank somebody evil, or let me have a beer sometime before that child is born."

The taxi passed through to the other side of town, and onto a windswept road. They drew closer to a large mansion surrounded by a great broad lawn that ended in rocky bluffs overlooking the English Channel.

LuAnna fixed her sights on the house. "Now that's a fort."

The driver, who until now had shirked all responsibilities as a tour guide, said, "That's a mansion, dearie."

He drove them past the attractive structure, and down a lane toward the sea. The causeway ahead was partially awash with foamy waves. Beyond it was a low and forbidding spit of rock topped with gun emplacements and barracks made of quarried stone. The driver piped up again. "Now that—that's Fort Clonque."

LuAnna turned to Blackshaw. "There's a pattern here. First, you invited me to hole up with you in a nasty abandoned New York basement."

"It was close to shopping," Blackshaw said.

"Big deal. We were sitting on millions of gold, but we were stone cashbroke. And next there was that date in a wrecked ship."

"Water views for days."

"And now, this old rock," said LuAnna. "You're batting a thousand, hon."

Blackshaw said, "And I'd feel just awful if you weren't a volunteer each and every time."

CHAPTER 80

SCREED WHISTLED UP a fresh team of operators to go forth, hunt down, and eliminate any and all pursuers. The trio that assembled before him in his office seemed tough, cool, and crazy enough for the job. Their resumes were perfect. Long military service terminated in Bad Conduct Discharges for excessive levels of violence well beyond stated rules of engagement in Iraq, Afghanistan, and Syria.

They had worked together since their BCDs on several wet black-ops both overseas and at home in the States. Spider was a fireplug of a woman, with blonde hair buzzed to nubs and a habit of gnashing her teeth on a toothpick. Roach was a tall red haired lout who cleaved to his Viking ancestral tradition of Berserker attacks. Bodies in the wake of his engagements had often required the sorting of parts and some reassembly before burial. Tick was smaller, Black, wiry, and completely mean. He tempered his caustic personality only to the point that his colleagues would not murder him in his sleep. Torture was part of his current modus operandi. Likely, torture had also been part of his childhood.

Tick asked, "So you're looking for us to LURP overseas to defend an asset you've got here."

A Long-Range Reconnaissance Patrol was old school lingo for going deep into the enemy's territory and ruining his day.

Spider looked at her two comrades before she said to Screed, "You must have serious intel on a specific target set."

"That, or they've got missiles targeted here," Roach said.

Screed didn't feel the need to discuss his hack of Chalk's Black Widow search engine with all its keys to sites throughout the dark web, nor to disclose his trap and trace on the complete mess in Bermuda. There were Blackshaws involved. That name was cropping up in more and more missions as Screed delved into Chalk's past. The FBI also seemed to be getting a look at Screed's operation, but he wasn't about to draw fire by waxing senior agents. At least not yet. The FBI was not nimble enough to datamine specifics, form a task force, and execute a sting before the Patient would be finally thrust onto the stage of worldwide media. As Screed studied his options, he needed to start the conventional world war his clients wanted, collect his pay, and quickly fade away.

Screed answered Spider, "Yes, I've got intel. I'm a hundred percent on it. It's good."

Spider's glance at Roach and Tick said nothing was a hundred percent certain, and Screed was a fool.

Roach asked, "Where're we talking about?"

"Channel Islands," said Screed. "Alderney. There's a fort."

"Made of blankets and cardboard boxes?" said Spider.

"I'm dead serious. It's a Victorian era fort. The Nazis had it for World War II. It's not exactly the Guns of Navarone. In fact, it's a bed-and-breakfast now. But there's a team zeroing in on my business here. That's their next stop."

"How many?" asked Roach.

"Three. Maybe more," said Screed.

"Righteous hard?" Tick asked.

"One's a former SEAL. Another is the SEAL's wife, who's former Natural Resources Police. She's bigtime pregnant."

"She's going to squirt us with breast milk!" Roach was beside himself laughing.

"You sure you need all of us for this?" Tick asked, chuckling.

"Last one's an older guy, former MACV-SOG." It sobered the trio when Screed told them that. They were from a younger generation of soldiers, but they'd heard the stories. Anyone who survived the Studies and Observations Group missions in Vietnam and lived to old age was tough, smart, and not to be taken lightly.

CHAPTER 81

BLACKSHAW LED THEIR way through Fort Clonque's gate as the taxi sputtered away. Puffs of sea foam floated across the open spaces, or swirled into larger wobbling drifts in the fortress's corner eddies where wind pushed in and spent itself against stone while looking for a way to move on.

An older woman with wisps of gray hair escaping her bun stepped out of a doorway with a housekeeping cart parked close by. She was just warm enough and showed just enough teeth in her smile not to be brusque when she said, "You'd be the Hogan group."

Ellis confirmed it.

"I'm Nora, and you can drop your things through that door to the dining room across the courtyard. No one else is staying tonight. Everyone from last night checked out. Your two rooms will be ready soon."

The small dining area was appointed with two long tables, with benches on both sides, like a summer camp or a soldiers' mess hall. There were pass-throughs in the thick wall to the kitchen where trays could be fetched and placed on the dining tables. A foody humidity hung in the air like a restaurant kitchen during off hours.

With the luggage deposited in the dining room, Blackshaw bellied up to a large coffee urn steaming in the dining room corner and drew a mugful. It was strong and hot. Ellis and LuAnna declined his offer to fill mugs for them.

LuAnna said, "I'm going to chat with Nora. People say the craziest crap to pregnant ladies."

When LuAnna had pulled the heavy door closed against the chilling sea breeze, Ellis asked, "What do you think?"

Blackshaw took a sip of coffee before he answered. "Nora seems to be a type. Do you think she's the full-timer here?"

"Good question. She might be retired MI6."

"You got the smart of that," Blackshaw said. "This nice quirky little tourist stop has *black site* written all over it."

"You going to tell me who you think the big asset is, Ben? Not like you to keep secrets." Ellis chuckled at a private joke.

Blackshaw seemed deflated as he considered Ellis's question. "I think you already know."

"Maybe I do," said Ellis. "Is that what's eating you? Go easy on yourself. It wasn't your mission."

"The guys who did go out, they believed they got the job done. They were proud of it. But they got conned. And now they're most all dead. Look at what Travis was willing to do to set things right."

Ellis changed his mind about the coffee and drew a mug of it from the urn. "You're going to find the asset and finish the mission."

"Of course. Wouldn't you?"

Ellis said, "That depends on who gave the order to take the mission sideways. Don't you wonder who had the power to operate forward like that, and change the outcome, in spite of a whole team of SEALs sitting right there?"

"The leader is likely to be the one who pulled it off," Blackshaw said.

"Oh, I agree. But Travis is the conundrum, even if he's not pulling the strings."

"How do you mean, Ellis? He was trying to make things right."

"Come on Ben. I know he was a good guy when you knew him. But ask yourself, how did he know he had to make things right?"

Blackshaw thought about that. Ellis drank his coffee and waited. Finally, Blackshaw said, "Travis knew about the problem with the mission because he *was* the problem with the mission. He took it in a different direction himself."

"Guilt can be a terrible thing. It can eat at you," Ellis said.

"So he had to make things right, or die trying," said Blackshaw. "But who was pulling the strings?"

"Who indeed, Ben. Who'd do such a thing? To figure out that, we need to know why."

CHAPTER 82

FBI DIRECTOR HORNSBY waved the Deputy Director into his office, and then to a chair. The man sat, looking tense, and waited. He knew enough not make small-talk with his boss, who disliked such drivel with the intensity of a pragmatist with a sliver of the Martinet stabbed into his soul.

Hornsby said, "I think we have a problem."

"When you say problem—"

"I mean a fucking mole. Somebody inside the bureau, or maybe at State, somebody who's running an op that should be a CIA thing, but it's happening on U.S. soil, so the bureau's on the hook."

Hornsby's subordinate sat up straighter at that, and said, "How can I help?"

"Lowry and Wilde are dealing with the murder of that dead SEAL. You heard about it?"

"Yes," said the underling. "Everybody heard about it. I didn't know we caught it. It's not a matter for military jurisdiction? They usually like to handle these things in-house."

Hornsby said, "The jurisdictional question alone is a Gordian knot in my rectum. Frankly, I think there's a former SEAL working the case, but not officially. There's some kind of asset in play, but we don't control it. Do you trust Lowry and Wilde?"

"I respect them. I feel better knowing for certain they're handling things. Let me know what I can do," Deputy Director Bonamy Screed replied to his boss.

PART III
THE PRINCE

CHAPTER 83

LUANNA PUSHED IN through the door into the small fortress mess hall flicking sea foam from her hair. Ellis spooned sugar into his coffee. Blackshaw was staring out a window. He turned to LuAnna.

LuAnna said, "All that pretty weather's going to shit the bed in a minute."

Blackshaw said, "You're like a Botticelli Venus rising up from the sea."

Ellis said, "All that's missing is the half-shell."

"Nora was none too chatty?" Blackshaw asked.

"It's what she didn't say. I helped her make up our bed," said LuAnna. "It's a nice room, a big bathroom right there."

"What didn't she say, Hon?"

LuAnna looked cross. "Do not rush me. Nora stepped out to the cart for the little soaps, but she didn't have any there either, so she took off across the courtyard to wherever you keep little soaps in an old fort. There's a door off our bedroom. Not a closet. Locked. But the door wasn't pushed all the way closed."

"Lu?" said Blackshaw, with suspicion in his tone.

"Or maybe I 'loided it open with a credit card. I don't recall exactly," LuAnna admitted. "The door being opened, I saw it had medical equipment in it. Used, but clean. Not all dusty. I didn't get too good a look. I closed the door before Nora came back in. That one's a piece of work, she is."

Ellis asked, "No idea on that medical stuff?"

"Oh, no idea at all. It was intravenous delivery type pumps, but bigger. Not just a hook for a bag, though there were a couple of those, too,"

LuAnna said. "It all looked like my Aunt Marcie's hospital room when her kidneys were crapping out on her."

LuAnna saw Ellis trade glances with Blackshaw. "Boys," she said, "I think it's high time you fill me in."

Blackshaw stalled, asking, "What about Nora was bothering you?"

"She's on the job."

"A cop?" asked Ellis.

"Or a spook," LuAnna confirmed. "She's asking all nice questions about us, and gabbing on about the fort's history. Then I asked her about Haakon."

"Tell me you didn't do that," said Blackshaw.

"He's why we're here, right? Well Nora, she went from Mary Poppins to Lady Macbeth in a split second. Thought she was going to catch like gas, but she reined it in, stuck a sweet-as-pie smile on the front of her head, and said she was going to see to a few things, then we should all head over to Room 3 and we'd have a chat."

"Why not here?" Ellis asked.

"What's in Room 3, and what's she doing right now, LuAnna?" Blackshaw asked. "Calling in the cavalry?"

LuAnna grinned. "She's looking in on Haakon. Making sure he's up for visitors. He keeps a little poultry farm on the main part of the island. Don't laugh, but he's the eggman around these parts."

"Goo goo g'joob," said Ellis.

CHAPTER 84

ELLIS RAPPED ON the heavy wooden door of Room 3. Nora opened up, and stepped back to let them file in.

This was a small chamber. In a worn wing chair sat a man in his seventies, with an enviable head of gray hair and piercing blue eyes. His neck was heavily bandaged. He had a blanket draped over his legs to ward off the chill.

"I'm Haakon," said the man in the comfortable chair. His voice had been deep at one time, but now he sounded as though he had laryngitis. It was so pronounced that Ellis had to work hard to suppress the urge to clear his throat. "Nora said you wanted to speak with me."

Nora drew a heavy looking Webley top-break revolver. "Let's take a moment to put down your weapons first."

Ellis said, "Ma'am, we're not here to cause trouble. And in the interests of time, it'd take us a good five minutes to offload all our cut-and-bang."

From beneath the covers, Haakon pulled out his own pistol, and suddenly Ellis was staring down the cavernous barrel of a Walther P99.

The old man rasped, "Time well spent, don't you think? Get on with it."

Under the watchful eyes of Nora and Haakon, Blackshaw and Ellis slowly drew two pistols apiece, as well as two knives.

LuAnna withdrew her main pistol, a SIG, from her waist holster, and two more backup guns including her little Jetfire, from a pair of ankle holsters. By way of explanation she muttered, "I'm fighting for two."

Nora said, "We've had some dodgy sorts visiting of late. And since nobody ever knows Haakon by name before they get here, I daresay you've already raised a few eyebrows from here to Vauxhall Cross."

LuAnna, recognizing the address, said, "You're MI6. And that room you were fixing up is bugged?"

Nora's expression said *what did you expect?*

"And this room too, I reckon." LuAnna glanced around for little microphones.

Ellis asked Haakon, "What happened to your neck?"

The older man hissed and rasped, "A fellow came looking for one of our former guests who'd already checked out. We had our orders. He, apparently, had his. He was about to get the upper hand when Nora barged in guns blazing. He escaped unharmed, I'm afraid. Wish I could say the same but I'll be up and about like new in no time."

"Not if you know what's good for you," said Nora with equal measures of menace and worry.

"Was it Maynard Chalk?" Blackshaw asked. "Nutty as a fruitcake, and likes the sound of his own voice?"

Haakon smiled. "Formally introduced himself, yes, and then said he was going to cut my throat if I didn't tell him where the asset went."

LuAnna said, "Guess you didn't—"

"Clearly not," said Haakon.

"—but you're going to tell us," LuAnna finished

Haakon looked at Nora, waiting for something. The old bedside phone double-buzzed. Nora answered it with just her name. She said, *yes ma'am* twice, and then cradled the receiver.

Nora said, "I'm authorized to tell you this: we were not made privy to the asset's identity while he was on site. He had his own team of minders, and the asset was kept in full quarantine. That said, you'll have our full cooperation, but we will all be completely disavowed from the top down, whatever happens next."

Ellis waited a moment, then spoke up. "The Prime Minister said something else."

Nora nodded. "She said, *good hunting*."

CHAPTER 85

TICK, ROACH, SPIDER and the pilot watched the Channel Islands creep toward them over the horizon. Screed's team had been airborne for the last ten hours, with only a single stop at Bournemouth to swap the plush Dassault Falcon in which they had crossed the Atlantic for the utilitarian CASA C-212 Aviocar cargo propjet.

Roach sat down again after looking forward out the windscreen. In the twilight, he had seen the monstrous towering cumulus cloud ahead with its anvil top drifting downwind. They had all seen the jagged lightning ripping up the air.

Roach bent his long frame around a computer tablet into which local weather, including winds at various flight levels, was being processed to calculate the right spot to initiate their HALO jump into Alderney. If they exited the CASA directly over Fort Clonque, powerful currents of air out of the west would require tracking their freefall hard into the wind, making the insertion, especially the short canopy ride, dicey and imprecise at best. Exiting the plane at high altitude, and opening extremely close to the earth reduced problematic drift; jumping well to the west of the target meant they could ride downwind during both freefall and the brief insertion phase under the chute.

The pilot, a contract hire from an overseas security firm, called to his passengers, "Blowing like hell up here. Your spot's going to be over the Atlantic."

Roach passed the tablet forward to the pilot, who reviewed the jump's plan view for the spot coordinates, and the jump profile for the altitude.

The pilot fed the coordinates into his flight management system and configured the plane for a climb. He said, "Hope you got your long johns on, you sorry bitches. You're getting out in the middle of that storm."

The deck angle tilted nose-up. Despite the growing turbulence, Spider and Tick checked each other's rigs, especially the pins from the ripcord that held the parachute containers closed. Once Tick cleared Spider's rig for the jump, Spider did the same gear check for Roach. Then they checked the readiness of their own weapons for the tenth time.

After a half hour's rough climbing in a wide circle, the pilot leveled off. He shouted, "We regroup at the airport in two hours. If you're not there by then, fuck the lot of you, and I'm gone. Three minutes to jump!"

Spider looked at Tick for a moment before she pulled off her nonrebreather mask, through which she'd been inhaling one hundred per-cent oxygen. She said, "I got a feeling about this one."

Tick pulled his mask aside, laughed and said, "Me, too. I feel like there's some killing to do, and some beer to drink."

"Absolutely," said Spider, not quite convinced. "That's the plan."

The rear deck door, like the clamshell loading ramp of the much larger C-130, began to open to the failing light like an enormous maw. The wider it got, the more the wind roared, and the deeper the gale's wet and chill blasted through the cargo bay.

The team stood and made one last gear check, and switched to breathing from their small oxygen bottles strapped to their gear. Then they crept aft toward the void, keeping their knees bent, and their grips tight on any handhold they could find as they went, because of the turbulence toss-ing the deck beneath them. After every flash of lightning, they were blind for a moment, with only the wind, the wet, and the dim red lights of the cargo bay to tell them how close they were to the edge of the ramp.

The three operators looked each other in the eye to make sure they were all heads-up and ready for what was about to happen. It was then that Spider surprised Tick. She dashed their oxygen masks aside and grabbed Tick by the neck with both hands and kissed him hard on the mouth, the tip of her tongue flicking deep around his molars. It was awkward with their helmets and goggles, but there was no mistaking her desperation and fervor. Roach's eyes went wide, but like Tick, he had no time to process what was happening.

A second later, the pilot turned the jump light to green, and the plane bounced through a violent pocket of windshear. The operators' usual orderly exit went to pieces. It was as if they were being shaken like soft gingerbread cookies out of a large tin into an open fire hydrant.

CHAPTER 86

HAAKON THE EGGMAN had questions. Nora had helped him to the dining hall across the courtyard, but not before the Americans had recovered and holstered their weapons with Nora's blessing. Haakon was now nursing a cup of tea. Blackshaw and Ellis stuck with coffee, while LuAnna sipped tap water that was delicious with minerals.

The older man growled, "So Chalk mentioned me by name."

"And the fort," said LuAnna.

Haakon went on, "And that's how you traced the asset here."

"Chalk must have figured out the asset was going Bermuda some-how," Ellis said.

"People like to chat over at the airport," said Nora. "If Chalk picked up the tail number of the asset's transport aircraft, finding out where it landed is the work of a minute or two on line."

"Chalk cut up rough in Bermuda, did he?" said Haakon, suspecting the answer.

"Three dead that we know of," said Blackshaw. "But he didn't survive."

"Then on a personal note, I thank you."

Nora said, "So Chalk never got his hooks into the asset."

"I don't know about you," said LuAnna, "but you keep calling the guy at the center of everything *the asset*. It's Bin Laden. Travis and the boys didn't kill him. They thought they got him, but they didn't. Somebody fooled them. And the only way Osama survived is if he was hit with some fancy rounds that put him down, but didn't kill him. And I'm sorry, but there's only one person who likely had ammo like that, likely made by DARPA, and it was probably Travis Cynter himself. So it's no wonder he felt so bad. No wonder he went rogue to set things right, knowing his team was all dead believing they'd done their duty. The only question is, who put Travis up to it, and where the hell is Bin Laden now?"

It was as if LuAnna had broken a spell with her truth.

Blackshaw would have had something to say, but from the courtyard, the crash of guest room doors being smashed open in quick succession distracted him.

CHAPTER 87

THE HALO JUMP was Tick's worst ever. After Spider's kiss on the aircraft's ramp, and the shit-show of an exit, he'd struggled as he fell through the storm to get his oxygen mask secured again. After a few breaths, his mind cleared and focused enough to realize his glowing wrist compass was whirling faster than his altimeter was unwinding. He was in a flat spin.

Tick fought down panic, gently arched belly-low, and twisted his body, angling arms and legs to bleed off most of the spin. He finished the correction with just his hands deflecting enough of the 125 mph terminal velocity air he was ripping through to roll him out on the right heading of 100 degrees. Spider and Roach were someplace to his left, heading at 90 degrees and 80 degrees by their compasses respectively to give them plenty of clearance from each other. There were to regroup once under their canopies.

With his legs extended, and his feet at shoulder width, Tick spread his arms straight out from his shoulders like a T; the iron cross position would slow his descent, while still allowing him to track horizontally across ground, or in his case at the moment, the English Channel. A compass was fine, but he needed a second to get oriented with the island. Through the rain, he saw the larger cluster of town lights ahead and to his left. An instant later, he located the remote lights of the fort. A quick altimeter check. Nineteen thousand feet. Time to get serious.

He rolled his shoulders forward, swept his arms back and up, bent a little at the waist, and pointed his toes. The wind tearing past him changed pitch as his flat track picked up speed. The rain beat harder at his goggles, then in a flash of lightning behind him, he blew out from under the precipitation into clear air with the fort below. He bent at the waist more, trimmed back his arms, cleaned up his legs to plunge into a hard delta; he covered less ground than in the flat track, but he was killing altitude like a meteor.

He eased out of the dive, slowed his free fall, and pulled the ripcord. He was swooping under the square parachute canopy for less than fifteen seconds before his toes touched the flagstones of the fort's inner courtyard. Six seconds after that, he was out of his rig, gun up, kicking doors and collapsing sectors inside the guest rooms with Roach. He didn't ask Roach where Spider was. If she wasn't there beside them, something had happened to her on the jump. Tons of suck for her. Tick was now on a mission with a two-man team. But where the hell were the targets?

CHAPTER 88

HAAKON TOLD NORA, "We should nip downstairs, don't you think?" Nora nodded and pulled open a low, narrow wooden door with iron fittings and a Gothic peak.

Their host held the door while Nora led off down a stone stair with a flashlight she snatched up from a nearby shelf. LuAnna followed her. Ellis and Blackshaw went next, with Haakon bringing up the rear after a moment's delay. They felt, as much as they smelled the reek of mold and damp trying to cling to their skin through the chilly air. The sound of another guestroom door shattering reached them as they descended.

Blackshaw whispered over his shoulder, "There isn't a submarine down here, is there?"

"No, why on earth—" said Haakon.

"Nevermind," the waterman said.

From the tunnel above, they all heard the courtyard door into the mess hall smashed to pieces.

Again, Blackshaw spoke to Haakon, "Sounds like you left that door open up there."

"Perhaps just a bit." The old eggman seemed coy.

They all continued down the curving stone stairs until Nora's flashlight illuminated jail cells with stout iron bars. The air was even colder here.

"Dead end?" asked Ellis.

Nora said, "Not at all. Those stairs from the mess down to these cells were for feeding prisoners. There's another stair into the courtyard, and one more down to the watergate, but that's almost always flooded these days even at low tide. Climate change."

LuAnna whispered, "You might want to keep it down, honeygirl. Don't want them to find us."

Haakon said, "On the contrary. We'd at least like them to follow us."

At first, Blackshaw suspected Haakon had betrayed them. He noticed the look on the old man's face seemed puckish.

"What did you do?" said Blackshaw.

Haakon replied, "I suggest everyone cover their ears and open their mouths. The concussion, you see—"

CHAPTER 89

ROACH SPOTTED IT. An arched doorway at the back of the fort's mess hall. It was ajar. Roach gestured toward it, and Tick nodded. Since the rest of the mess and the kitchen were clear, except for a three steaming mugs and a water glass, Tick figured that door was the only other way out.

Roach pushed the little door open. A fragmentation grenade that had been wedged at the top of the door dropped at their feet. The safety lever flipped up. Tick and Roach dived away from the powerful little bomb as men. They landed as bloody mist and lumpen chunks of meat and shattered bone.

CHAPTER 90

THE COURTYARD DOOR was well-oiled and opened quietly with an easy push from Blackshaw's hand. He left the doorway first. Ellis followed on Blackshaw's heels, turned, and cleared the parapet wall above and behind them. Haakon came after Ellis, with LuAnna trailing. Nora backed out of the door making sure no one was coming up the stairway behind them from the prison cells below.

Haakon said, "Nora, one for good measure, don't you think?"

Nora removed a fragmentation grenade from the pouch pocket of her long, thick sweater. She pulled its pin, and tossed it back through the door down to the dungeon. As the grenade clacked down the stairs, she slammed the door, shot the iron bolt, and said, "Frag out, my dears."

Everyone was already hustling away from the door just in case the ancient iron fittings and oak timbers shattered from the shock wave. The grenade exploded with a thump they could feel through their feet. Smoke pulsed up through two ventilation flues, and somewhere in the distance, a window shattered.

"Lovely thing about a good stone fortress," said Nora. "Grenades can't do a thing to the décor."

The five spread out across the courtyard, carefully approached the mess, and entered. LuAnna was the first to see the two blasted operators among the overturned tables and benches. The walls were shellacked with gore, shreds of uniforms, swatches of skin. She said, "I got two down over here." She turned to Nora. "You were saying about the décor?"

"Touché," said Nora, surveying the slaughter and destruction.

By some miracle, Haakon's abandoned mug of tea was still upright on the counter, and still steaming. He took a sip, closed his eyes, and sighed with a deep appreciation only an Englishman could muster at such a moment. He righted a bench and dropped onto it, exhausted. From there, he scrutinized the remains of the operators and said, "It's damn hard to tell if they're Russian. Everyone's red on the inside."

"Why Russian?" Blackshaw asked.

The old man said, "I was going to mention it before these chaps so rudely interrupted us. The asset's team of minders spoke English well enough. American English, I might add, if you can call it that. But during one of their telephone confabs back to their superiors, things became heated, voices were raised, and we overheard them speaking Russian."

Blackshaw was quiet for a moment. Then he said, "Ellis, do you have another one of those rebreather rigs?"

"Not on me," came the reply. "Why?"

"I know where the bastard is. We need to go home. We need to finish this."

CHAPTER 91

SPIDER WAS HEARTBROKEN. It had taken her months to screw her courage to the sticking place, and plant that kiss on Tick. Two hours after the flailing exit from the Casa aircraft, she was at Aldernay's small airfield seated next to the pilot in the aircraft's darkened cockpit. After she jumped, her track away from the plane had been easterly according to her compass, and in accordance with the plan. When she first glimpsed the ground rushing up at her, she realized her compass was off by at least ninety degrees, and she was heading due south. The instrument was supposed to be shock-proof, but it had sent her freefall screaming south out over the English Channel toward a likely death by drowning. She pulled the ripcord early in order to have time to steer back over land under the canopy. She only just made it to shore.

The mission brief was clear. If one team member landed outside the fort, the gig was still a *go* with two operators. If, for some reason, two team members blew the insertion and landed outside the fort, the mission would be aborted, with all parties having 120 minutes to regroup at the airfield before the plane departed.

After an ankle-twisting landing, and strenuous fast march over a rocky meadow, Spider was the only operator at the plane now. Barring some other casualty among her teammates, the mission had gone ahead without her. For the two hours, she had fidgeted with all the shame of the kiss, the adrenaline of the soured jump, and the undischarged nerve-lightning of a soldier suddenly withdrawn from the brink of action. She still held out hope for the mission's success, and an exfiltration of the full team from the field.

During her hike to the exit point, she had quietly rehearsed what she would say to Tick about that kiss. Some versions of her speech were full on declarations of her love couched in erotic promises. Other thoughts were shallow excuses pretending that the kiss had been nothing more than a meaningless, mischievous whim. Over the last fifteen minutes, with neither Tick nor Roach showing up at the airport, she realized that no matter what she had decided to say, no one was coming to hear it.

The pilot checked his watch and said, "That's time. We have to go."

Spider swore. She was on the verge of begging the pilot to wait for just a few minutes more when a rust bucket of a car rocking on old shock absorbers drove across the aircraft tie-down ramp to a Gulfstream 650. The jet's air-door was opening before the car skidded to a stop. Three passengers jumped out of the car. The pregnant ex-cop, the former SEAL, and the Black MACV-SOG vet. Spider was on her feet, charging toward the Casa's door and cocking her weapon before the pilot could tackle her in the cargo bay.

"No!" he growled. "It's over. Somebody else will handle them. We're done. We're gone."

"It's them! Get off me! I can finish it!" Even as she said the words, she knew the pilot was right. They had orders. There was no contingency that called for one operator to take on the three targets at a public airfield. If Tick and Roach were alive, they would have to fend for themselves. If they were killed, they carried no identification, and the mission's planners would not be compromised. If Tick was dead, a part of Spider would also have died.

Spider relaxed her body. Sensing surrender, the pilot asked, "You good?"

Spider nodded.

The pilot rolled off of her. From the dark cockpit of their plane, the pilot and Spider saw the Gulfstream's APU, engines, and lights come to life. She watched helpless as it taxied to the downwind end of the runway, turned, and roared off into the west and the night. Tears of anguish rolled down Spider's cheeks. She steeled herself, grabbed her encrypted radio. "Let's get airborne. I've got to report."

CHAPTER 92

ELLIS'S GULFSTREAM LANDED after midnight at Dulles outside Washington, D.C. The Eurocopter EC155 met them there, and whisked Ellis, Blackshaw, and LuAnna back to Smith Island. With only an hour of preparation, they were off again to the north in *Miss Dotsy*, which had been returned to Blackshaw's pier from Ocean City by his helpful neighbors, Freddie Donaway and his bride, Kathy Taylor-Donaway.

Ten hours later, *Miss Dotsy* was positioned several miles from the confluence of the beautiful Corsica and Chester Rivers on Maryland's Eastern Shore. Ellis and Blackshaw had dropped fishing lines over the side in order to look harmless. LuAnna, peering over the gunwale from time to time with high-powered binoculars, kept an eye on the brick mansion on Pioneer Point.

As Blackshaw reeled in his line for another cast, he asked LuAnna, "Everything look okay?"

"Like hell," LuAnna said. "The sentry on that pier is in BDUs, H-gear, toting an MP-5. Does that sound like somebody on a Department of State diplomatic security team to you?"

"Negafirmative," said Blackshaw.

"Looks shady. You might be right about this," said Ellis.

"Travis was killed on Dog & Bitch Island. Reckon he was trying to prevent the asset from being brought ashore from a boat that took him off Bermuda. Seems Bin Laden's only use is if he shows up alive on American soil after we crowed so loud about killing him. Then the Russians can make a true mockery of us. Between hacking elections and this, we'll look plenty stupid, like we can't handle our business. Then the jihadis open up, World War III busts out, and the big military orders for planes and ships start rolling in."

"Makes sense, their bringing him here," said Ellis. "That compound's been the Russian diplomatic retreat since the early '70s."

"But it's closed up," LuAnna said.

"And the Russians were sent packing a while ago," Ellis confirmed. "My guess, the Company spooks have likely been all over that place, top to bottom rewiring it for surveillance against the day when we forgive and forget and let the Russians take the place over again. 'Til then, it's a fine place to post up."

"Okay, but somebody high up has to know they're there, like Screed," Blackshaw said. "Who else could pull the U.S. skeleton crew watching the place off the detail, and swap in private contractors who'll turn a blind eye for the right price?"

"It's so much worse than we thought. Why do you have to take care of this, Ben?" LuAnna asked. "Can't you drop a bug in somebody's ear? Like those Feebs?"

Blackshaw said, "That's for you to do if I don't make it. We agreed. For me, it's a point of honor. We might never know how Bin Laden survived the assault. Must be a doctor, or a Company spook got turned traitor and switched in a likely looking corpse for the target. Maybe it was all Travis's fault. But I'm going to finish the mission." He checked the sun over his shoulder and said, "I'd best ready-up."

He lay on the cockpit sole out of sight from shore and pulled on his old, patched wetsuit. Then came the new rebreather unit, weight belt, mask, and fins. Ellis adjusted the flow of gases while Blackshaw strapped a compass to his wrist. A pistol lay sealed inside the watertight pouch. Finally, he was prepped and equipped much as he had been in Bermuda. This time, there was a hostile sentry keeping watch. Last of all, Ellis passed Blackshaw an old-fashioned spear gun with a reel of heavy-duty line, one end of which was attached to the barbed spear.

Despite the influx of riches to Ellis and the Blackshaws during the past year notwithstanding, the only structural modification *Miss Dotsy's* tight-fisted owner had made was adding a through-hull Bomar hatch casement in the cockpit sole that allowed a diver to enter and leave the boat unseen, instead of rolling over the side in plain view. This hatch was a much tighter fit on Blackshaw and his gear than the one in Ellis's yacht.

Blackshaw said, "Reckon it might get noisy over there before it gets quiet."

"So? Make sure you get the last shot," LuAnna said. She kissed him on the top of his head.

Blackshaw looked at Ellis, who said, "I'm not kissing you. You're going to scatter all my sweet sweet gear over the bottom of the Chesapeake. I can see it in your eyes."

Blackshaw gripped the rebreather mouthpiece in his teeth and slipped down into the Chesapeake Bay. Ellis reached down through the hatch and pulled his friend back to the surface by a rebreather strap, and said, "Good luck, you badass picaroon."

Then Ellis let go. A baffled Blackshaw sank out of sight.

When Blackshaw had dived for oysters in the past, he had breathed using a hookah rig, essentially a compressor on *Miss Dotsy* blowing air down a hose to a second stage SCUBA regulator in his mouth. And there had been the tether from his waist to the boat, and Ellis watching over all. With every stroke of his fins, he was leaving Ellis and LuAnna farther behind in the cold darkness.

LuAnna was right. Why was it his problem to solve? This swim was a far cry from the warm, clear insertion into Bermuda. No colorful fish. No playful dolphins waiting on the other end.

The Chesapeake bottom was only nine feet down, and rose gradually as he made his way toward shore with the rising tide. The overcast afternoon light kept visibility down to a few feet. Blackshaw tortured himself with recriminations—from falling out of touch with Travis, to dragging LuAnna hither and thither in search of his friend's murderer. Come to find his former teammate had died trying to prevent an international scandal that would bring dishonor down upon his country, as well as on the SEALS.

Blackshaw swam on. The bottom of the Chesapeake rose. Soon, young blue crabs side-stepped and fluttered among the subaqueous grasses swaying beneath him.

Finally, Blackshaw reached the barnacled piling of the Russian compound's pier. He dared not rise too close to the surface for a good look around. From what he could see in the waning light, the shoreline sentry was patrolling somewhere else. Time to go fishing.

CHAPTER 93

LUANNA STAYED LOW in *Miss Dotsy*'s cockpit watching the Russian compound's shoreline three hundred yards away.

Ellis cast his fishing line toward the pier, and asked, "What's your husband got against having a Plan B on sorties like this?"

"I asked him that once. He said back-up plans are like hope. They keep him from fully committing to the mission, like there's an outside force waiting in the wings to help if he screws up."

"Like God?" said Ellis.

"I wouldn't dive into that with him," LuAnna confided. "He's got himself a pretty severe crisis of faith going on at the moment."

"Some might call that a celebration of rationality," said Ellis, taking his eye off the line for a moment to watch LuAnna's response.

She kept her face still as she said, "An all-powerful god that makes innocent little children suffer is so tough for Ben to accept."

"Saying that God's ways are a mystery isn't good enough?"

"Good enough for most. Not for Ben." After a moment, LuAnna continued, "Mysteries are nothing more than unanswered questions to him, and they're certainly not a sign to pipe down and quit rocking the boat, or asking or looking or trying to figure out reasons for things he should be able to understand and grapple with face-to-face. It's why soldiering was a good fit for Ben. If Plan A shits the bed, he thinks up a new Plan A on the spot that's tuned to the circumstances of the situation at hand. Working out a Plan B ahead of when it's needed, well that's just useless dead weight in his pack."

"Do you think Ben's going to hell?"

LuAnna did not hesitate to say, "Of course not, Ellis. He's already there."

Ellis reeled in his line and cast it again. "That sentry come around yet?"

"He hits the pier every twenty-one minutes. Makes sense. Probably has a circuit that includes the whole water side of the house. Ellis, you and I know the truth."

"What's that, LuAnna?"

"We're Ben's Plan B, whether he likes it or not."

Ellis gave a low chuckle at the thought.

"Oh my blessing," said LuAnna, sitting forward with the binoculars trained toward the pier.

"What's happening?" said Ellis.

"There's been a shift change. New sentry. Ben is not going to like this. Not one bit."

CHAPTER 94

AFTER THE LONG underwater infiltration toward shore, Blackshaw gently rolled so he lay on his back in the bottom grass looking up at the surface just five feet overhead. Even at this shallow depth, the murky water would conceal him. He angled his spear gun so the wicked barbed tip just broke the water's surface, and swished it back and forth a few times. Then he lowered the spear gun completely out of sight from above.

It didn't take long. The sentry was sharp. No rent-a-cop. Blackshaw heard footsteps approaching along the pier's wooden decking. A moment later, the silhouette of the sentry leaned over the end of the pier. Blackshaw triggered the gun. The slender spear leapt out of the water, impaling the sentry in the lower abdomen, below any ballistic plate he might have worn. The harpooned guard staggered back, but Blackshaw grabbed the line attached to the spear with both hands and yanked.

The struggling sentry tumbled forward into the water on top of Blackshaw, who drew his dive knife and went to work carving the turkey. It was at this point Blackshaw realized he was killing a woman who did not wish to die.

CHAPTER 95

SPIDER WAS DROPPED at the gate at Pioneer Point by her car service. Sizing up the situation, she sent the driver away with no instructions to return to pick her up. At first it struck her as odd that the sentry box was unoccupied. When she reviewed the catastrophic last 36 hours, and the fiasco on Alderney, she changed her thinking. A lack of security here meant the wheels were coming off the operation. She entered the woods beside the road, dropped her duffle, and pulled out her trusty AK-47 and four reverse-taped banana clips. Then she headed through woods beside the lane.

Anyone else would have thought the low popping noises were old marine engines starting up far offshore. Spider knew they were suppressed gunshots. She moved the gun's selector up to full automatic. She passed Screed's SUV, and circled the big house clockwise through hedges and woods, with the tennis court on her left. The bitter boxwood scent could not cover the smell of gun smoke.

She heard a gurgling noise behind a bush, and found a privately contracted security guard stretched out on the ground with a gunshot to the face. Somehow his wide terror-filled eyes bore straight into hers, and his shattered mandible was still opening and closing, like he wanted something from her. All he got out of his mouth was a frothing spume of bloody bubbles. If he lived, which wasn't looking good, he'd be lucky if he could eat through a straw. Spider stepped around the fallen soldier, put his pistol back in his hand on the off chance he rallied and could make himself useful; again that looked doubtful. Spider moved on.

As she crept through the open door on the water side of the house, she heard three shots, and the sound of a big man slumping to the marble floor along with the tell-tail clatter of a gun. She stepped forward around a corner and saw no one.

She sensed, rather than heard, someone in the depths of a darkened doorway. She turned. A big guy in a wetsuit dating back to Cousteau had a pistol aimed at her face. He had the drop on her. She watched, waited an instant for him to tell her what to do, how to surrender. Then she realized she was not going to be anyone's prisoner today. This was it. A nanosecond later, she sensed this meathead was having trouble pulling the trigger. The poor bastard couldn't shoot a girl. *Asshole.* Spider had seen it before, and she was still alive. She kept her face neutral as she started to whip her rifle around. The flash from the pistol's muzzle was the last thing Spider ever saw.

CHAPTER 96

SCREED CHECKED HIS watch. In twelve minutes, the Internet broadcast of the century would go live. Five minutes after that, he would be driving away from Pioneer Point heading for Route 50 West, straight back to Washington, D.C., mission accomplished, with the balance of his fee wired through a sequence of cloaked accounts. He would take a well-deserved vacation, perhaps to Bali, and see what sort of offers for new and high-paying gigs rolled in after this grand slam.

Bin Laden had finally been weaned off of the Squealer drug gradually enough so that he was still compliant, but his unrelenting crying had subsided to the occasional sob; this artifact of withdrawal would not be ideal for the script, but it would not diminish the impact of the broadcast. Screed's shadow employers wanted Bin Laden to acknowledge all his crimes, and declare afresh his commitment to global Jihad. The United States would be humiliated, viewed as an impotent, passé superpower. Bin Laden's alleged killing in Afghanistan in 2011 would be regarded as a hoax. Following the broadcast, Screed was under strict orders to abandon Bin Laden unharmed at the Russian compound. Russia would receive the credit for uncovering what was to be billed as The Great American Lie, and make a show of turning the old warrior over to the U.S. where his incarceration would guarantee Gitmo would have to stay open, with all the bad press surrounding that, forever.

Screed started the camera, and hit a button on the laptop. He was eager. Let the big social media broadcast start early. Last, he turned on the teleprompter for Bin Laden to read. The script was in Arabic, but translations would be made the world over soon enough.

A husky sentry, with a voice too high for his massive build, put his head in at the door where Screed waited with his prisoner who was still strapped to his hospital bed. The sentry fluted, "Keller's not checking in."

"She's got the shore, right?" Screed was worried now. Spider had reported from somewhere over the Atlantic that her mission with Roach and Tick to stop Blackshaw and his team had failed with two likely KIA's. Not for the first time, Screed wondered if Blackshaw would have the resources to track the operation here before the broadcast.

The sentry never answered about where Keller was positioned. His face blew out into ribbons and gobbets as a bullet fired into the back of his head exited with a wet glop of teeth, eyes, and pimpled skin.

Blackshaw stepped through the door and over the sentry's corpse. He covered Screed, and said, "Bet that's your truck in the driveway with the government plates."

Screed bridled and blustered, "Do you know who I am?"

"You're a traitor. I reckon you interest me." Blackshaw turned his pistol on the man in the hospital bed and fired twice more. With that, one mission was accomplished. Another was just beginning.

CHAPTER 97

LUANNA AND ELLIS found Blackshaw inside the mansion, slouching exhausted in a straight-backed chair, his wetsuit peeled down to his waist. His gun was aimed in the general direction of an angry gagged man lying on the ground and struggling against numerous cable-ties. In a hospital bed opposite Blackshaw lay the mass murderer of innocents—all bled out to a peace he did not deserve.

LuAnna said, "Pure selfishness." When Blackshaw noticed his wife standing there, she went on. "Four sentries strewn every which-way outside, and pretty much nothing for Ellis to do except stand around and say nice things to you about a job well done."

"Bravo Zulu, Ben," said Ellis. "Strong work. I know you're not keen on shooting women. You going to be okay?"

"Sad to say, I'm working through that issue. There was Blessing, the one on the pier, and another inside. Still makes me sick."

LuAnna asked, "Remember how I said you could tell me anything?

"Yes, and I appreciate that very—"

LuAnna interrupted, "But not right now. Technically, is this place Russian soil?"

"I guess," said Blackshaw, not really sure.

"Then we better call Uber," said LuAnna. "And you should get back into your street clothes.

The bound man on the floor moaned.

Blackshaw leaned out of his chair and pistol-whipped the prisoner out cold. He said, "Ellis, could we get this fonny boy aboard *Miss Dotsy*?"

"Be happy to, Ben. Who is he?"

Blackshaw handed Ellis an FBI identification wallet.

On opening the wallet, Ellis said, "Deputy Director Bonamy Screed. That's interesting."

"That's exactly what I said. Now LuAnna, why Uber? Be honest, did something happen to the boat?"

"*Miss Dotsy*'s fine, Ben. But she's just not quick enough to get me up to the Chestertown hospital. Unless you want your child to be born a Russian citizen right here, we should get going—"

.

CHAPTER 98

BONAMY SCREED WOKE when his head struck the deck of the old boat. When the stars cleared, he saw an older Black man casting off a stern line from the Russian compound's pier. The boat's engine seemed to explode right next to his head when it started.

Screed could not speak through the gag tearing at the corners of his mouth. He sensed from the cold look in the captain's eye that there would come a time for talking, but that time was not now. It was with pure horror that Screed realized Blackshaw and his team were not going to *kill* him. They were going to *keep* him.

CHAPTER 99

FBI DIRECTOR HORNSBY joined Wilde and Lowry in Vehicle Forensics Laboratory deep in a Quantico sub-basement. Through a glass window that gave into a clean room, they watched four technicians in hooded substance isolation suits, booties, gloves, eye shields, and N95 dust masks poring over a black bureau SUV inside and out with tweezers, swabs, fingerprint kits, and small fiber vacuums.

Wilde said, "No sign of Deputy Director Screed?"

"None," said Hornsby. "And the Russians played plenty stupid, calling us to say one of our vehicles was discovered at their compound during a supervised lawn care service, and could we come get it."

"Maybe he defected?" Lowry suggested.

"Can't rule that out," Hornsby said. "Fact is, Screed was sheep-dipped at the bureau. He was NSA before hopping the fence to us, but he never cut his ties at the Old Curiosity Shop, it's plain to see. I want to think he was coerced there, or was investigating, but—"

"In person? A deputy director?" Wilde said.

"Exactly," said Hornsby. "Did you know he was an Army Ranger? A sniper. Marksmanship awards for days. Still takes trips out west to target shoot. Hangs with guys who make dialed-in long range shots like wizards. See where I'm going?"

Lowry said, "You like him for Travis Cynter's murder"

Hornsby nodded. "But it's so much worse than that,"

Hornsby pulled out his phone and motioned Wilde and Lowry to step away from the clean room window. Tapping the small screen twice, he held up a video for them to see.

In the center of the screen, a man who resembled an older, ailing Osama Bin Laden lay in a hospital bed.

"What is this?" Wilde said.

On the little screen there was at least one gunshot off camera. There were also voices off screen, close to the camera's microphone, but just out of frame.

Someone who sounded like a big man with an unusual accent said, "Bet that's your truck in the driveway with the government plates."

A second man, also out of frame, shouted, "Do you know who I am?"

"That's Screed, I believe," Hornsby interjected.

The first man, the big one with the accent answered, "You're a traitor. I reckon you interest me."

Bin Laden tried to raise his hands in a defensive gesture. His hands moved only half an inch because of leather restraints at the wrists. Bin Laden cried out. In the shadows, just outside the bright, high contrast video lighting, a man with slick black wetsuit stepped into frame, aimed a pistol at the man in the bed and fired twice. Bin Laden died. The shooter stepped out of frame. The camera microphone picked up distinct sounds of a struggle, but the picture careened sideways, presumably as the camera's tripod was bumped in the fight. The camera fell to the floor. The video ended in an explosion of static.

"It's a hoax," said Lowry.

"The time stamp was yesterday," said Wilde.

"A recent hoax," amended Lowry. "And time stamps can be faked, but maybe this is footage of Bin Laden's takedown in 2011. Where did you get that?"

"Every damn social media site on earth," said Hornsby in disgust. "Some of them have pulled it because of the violence, but Al Jazeera is still running it as a goddamn GIF."

"It's a PR nightmare," said Lowry.

Hornsby said, "Most of the comments are along the lines of what you said, that it's a hoax. For now. But we've already voice-printed the guy in the bed from when he yelped, and we ran his face through our best recognition software. It's really him. It's Bin Laden. And pretty soon, we're not going to be the only ones who know that."

Hornsby started the video again. "I want to know where the hell Screed is. I want to know who that shooter in the wetsuit is. We've got nothing on him, but he's either going to get a medal or a jolt in Gitmo. And where the hell is Bin Laden now? Or his corpse."

Wilde exchanged a quick glance with Lowry. They both recognized the shooter.

"We'll get right on it," said Lowry.

CHAPTER 100

BLACKSHAW WOKE TO a vicious cramp in his neck from dozing in the uncomfortable hospital room chair. LuAnna was looking straight at him from the bed with a fair amount of love in her tired eyes. Then she gazed down at the newborn snoring softly in her arms.

She said, "Come up with anything?"

Blackshaw said, "Your father was good man."

"True enough," said LuAnna. "But he's dead, and you're pappy's still alive—"

"So far as we know—"

"And he kills people for a living," LuAnna finished, smiling.

"That's no kind of namesake." Blackshaw rose and sat again on the bed by LuAnna. He peeked into the swaddling blanket at his boy.

He said, "*Callum Bryce Blackshaw.* Your father. Your maiden name. Our last name."

"Are you sure?" said LuAnna, with note of resignation creeping into her voice.

"You can name the next one," Blackshaw said. "Or the next two."

LuAnna gently touched the tip of her son's nose. "Hey Callum. Welcome to Earth, you little picaroon."

The baby sneezed, like the most precious thing in the world.

CHAPTER 101

BLACKSHAW SLOWED HIS rental car just enough. He was already driving the speed limit posted for the Short Pump, Virginia street near Richmond, but he wanted a better look at the physical address. It was a nice house in an affluent neighborhood with newer homes tending toward five bedrooms, and half as many bathrooms. Guessing by the rolling stock in the driveways and garages, accepting Ellis's offer to lend his Escalade would not have been such a conspicuous notion after all. But Blackshaw had turned the fancy wheels down to keep the license plate far from any prying eyes around here.

The man who Blackshaw glimpsed on the riding mower in the deep yard behind the house was interesting. Not the usual soft suburban executive drone. This guy was fit, though Blackshaw put him in his late forties. His hair was short under his baseball cap. He sat up straight on the mower, almost at attention. There were no lawn service trucks parked at the curb, no trailers bearing fuel jerry cans, weed whackers, push mowers, or high end riders steered with levers. The guy took care of his own yard.

Blackshaw rolled past the house, and pulled up just beyond a copse of trees three driveways beyond the place with the guy on the mower. He tapped out a text on his burner cell phone—something about a marketing firm offering a free trip to Las Vegas if a phone number was dialed within five minutes to talk about the virtues of investing in penny stocks. Supposedly the recipient had already won. Blackshaw knew she had already lost. The question was, how much?

Three minutes after Blackshaw sent the text, an athletic blonde woman in head-to-toe Lululemon walked her small dog down the sidewalk. By the copse of trees, she scooped up the dog, and pressed the button that retracted the leash into its handle. She slid into the front seat of Blackshaw's rental. He drove off slowly. No one noticed, because from what Blackshaw could tell, life in this neighborhood seemed to be lived in the back yards close to the pools and barbecues.

Polly Cynter said, "Can we go to Arlington? I haven't seen Travis's grave. Jim wasn't exactly cool with me going to my ex's service."

Blackshaw said, "You look good, Polly."

"You were always honest, Ben. Don't start lying now. Not today."

"Okay. We can't go to Arlington," Blackshaw said. "Not yet a while."

Blackshaw drove out of the nice neighborhood that Travis never would have been able to afford, and made his way to the Interstate.

He said, "I thought you and Travis would go the distance."

"Every best man wants to think that, Ben. Don't feel bad. My maid of honor said the same damn thing."

Blackshaw asked, "Back in 2011, when you saw Travis on leave in June, how did he seem? Was he proud?"

Polly looked hard at Blackshaw, then snuggled the little dog in an absent sort of way. She said, "Not like you'd expect. I knew where he'd been. At least I suspected. And the President was right there on the TV saying Bin Laden was dead. Even though Travis never would have let slip anything classified about a mission, DEVGRU was his team. I think the trouble between us started then. I asked him about the car that had been parked outside our place for the whole month of May—"

"What do you mean? What car?"

"It wasn't even the same car every day," said Polly. "But that month, there was a plumber's truck or cable TV truck, or one kind of car or another outside, even on Sundays. Maybe a few doors up the street—a few doors down the street. Our side. The other side. And after the President was on the TV getting his atta-boys for Bin Laden, no more cars or trucks. Or at least, they thinned out like they'd been before."

"You told Travis about what you saw."

"Sure. He asked what I'd been up to like he always did. You know we don't have kids. Wasn't ever much to tell. But I had started helping make ends meet calling numbers on this list trying to set up appointments for a pest control outfit to come check out your home. Twenty bucks for every set-up. I was good. I worked in our front room dialing and spieling, dialing and spieling, like on automatic, and I could see the street."

"And things between you and Travis got difficult?"

"He got weird about the cars and such. It was like he didn't trust me. He said I was making an excuse for a bunch of guys coming here to see me while he was away. And of course they stopped now, because now he was back home, or so he believed. I showed him my calls for the termite company. I was on that phone all day long, and well into the night when people were home. He asked how did he know which calls were work and which were me trying to hook up or phone sex other men like I was some kind of whore."

The dog licked at the tears on Polly's cheeks. Blackshaw kept driving. Traffic was light enough, but his heart was heavy with what he had to say.

"Something went down on the mission, Polly. Travis was strong-armed into doing something awful. It broke him. At the VA they call it a *moral injury*, when you have to see or say or do something that's just plain wrong. Might be just against orders. Might be worse—against being a good or decent person."

Polly shook her head. "You're wrong, Ben. Travis wouldn't take shit from anybody. I'm telling you the man had a code. Not just cash-register honest, either. It went deep with him. It's what I loved about him." Polly sobbed. "And he said I was the same way, and that's what he loved about me. I am that way. But he said I'd changed."

"You asked for the divorce?"

"I'm not one to give up, but he was crazy. He wasn't my Travis anymore. I guess you're saying he really wasn't himself, because something happened to him. But I knew it for sure when he slapped me. It was over."

Blackshaw winced at that. "Did he hit you a lot?"

"Once was enough for me," Polly said, with anger replacing the sobs. "I told him he hit like a sissy, and he must have been a weak-ass sailor. I was done with him."

Blackshaw pulled the car off the highway, and steered toward a park on the shore of the James River. There they sat in quiet for a few minutes letting the river slip past.

Blackshaw broke the silence. "Pol', the cars and trucks that May were surveillance on you. That's how the guys got Travis to do what they wanted him to do. If he balked, reckon somebody would have climbed out of the truck or the car and hurt you."

Polly's face was the picture of abject shock. After a moment, she said, "I guess they got what they wanted out of him."

"Almost," said Blackshaw. "Travis bided his time. Then he tried to make things right, but he was killed. But before that, he busted you guys up on purpose to keep you safe. If you were divorced, especially if it went down real ugly between you, they wouldn't come back after you if he got out of line. To their way of thinking, Travis wouldn't give a rat's ass what happened to you. The divorce meant you stopped being leverage."

"His lawyer was a complete idiot," said Polly. "I mean, I got everything."

"Reckon that was on purpose," said Blackshaw. "And with you safely out of the way, with the target off your back, Travis tried to set things straight."

"And got killed for it," Polly said. "So Ben, do you know who did this to us?"

"I do. There's a foreign element to the whole thing which I'm working on, but the man directly responsible for all this has been found. He's never coming back."

"Good. That's something, at least," said Polly dabbing away tears with a tissue.

Blackshaw went on, "I'm not sure you're out of the woods. What's Jim like?"

In a rush, Polly realized her marriage to her present husband was built on a sham divorce from her true love—the tears came again. "He's sweet. Quiet. He's wound kinda tight. Decent earner. I'm not calling for termite appointments—put it that way."

Blackshaw started the car, turned to and faced Polly. "Former military?"

"Navy," said Polly. "Reserves. We met after the divorce was final. I guess he was a rebound."

Blackshaw said, "Here's how things are likely to play out. In a few months, maybe a few years, he's going to start acting like Travis. You'll argue over stupid things. Maybe he'll cheat, and make it obvious that's what he's doing."

"What the hell are you talking about, Ben?" Polly looked scared.

"It'll come to a divorce," Blackshaw said. "And you'll come out okay. Don't fight it too hard, Polly. You have to let Jim move on."

"Move on where?"

"To his next assignment. Polly, I think one of the guys keeping an eye on you in the cars and trucks is still on the job. But he moved in with you. You're married to him."

Polly was poleaxed, eyes wide, her jaw working, and nothing but quiet choking sounds coming out of her mouth. When she could speak she said, "No! I can't go back to that. Can't you—do something?"

Blackshaw drove out of the park back toward the highway, eyes flicking over the rearview mirror looking for a tail. "If I do that, they'll know you're a risk, and then somebody else will come along and make sure you stay quiet. Right now, they're making sure you're not suspicious of anything that happened with Travis. Jim's probably cased your stuff, your computer, looking for any sign at all that Travis told you about what he did. If they think he told you, then they have to figure out who you might have told. This is a long-term cleanup."

"Are you going to tell me what Travis did?"

"Not a chance. Not if you want any kind of plausible deniability. You've got enough on your plate as it is. Look, Pol' if you decide you can't hack this, get a disposable phone and let me know. Don't use your regular phone. I can help you disappear. New name. New country. Money. Think about it. But if you want to stay stateside as *you*, and you think you can gut it out with Jim to the end, you have to play the game."

Polly considered. "Dad's long dead, but my mom's sick. I can't leave her alone. And Jim's being pretty decent to her. If he's bogus, he's damn good at it."

"For now. He's deep cover. It's part of his job description. I'm sorry Polly. You had to know. If you started taking flowers to Travis's grave, or mooning over him after too much wine, everything he did to protect you would be a waste. You have to lock it down where he's concerned, for the near-term anyway. Or call me. Up to you."

Polly asked, "Did Travis set things right at least? Did he fix what he messed up?"

"No. But I did."

"Even though he's dead. Wow. You boys stick together."

They drove in silence. The dog dozed off. Soon, Blackshaw pulled up at a corner in Polly's lovely neighborhood a few streets away from her home.

As Polly was about to open the car door, Blackshaw said, "Travis loved you. You two would have gone the distance."

"I think you're right, Ben. If half of what you're telling me is true, he loved me one hell of a lot."

Polly got out of the car without waking her sleeping dog. She slowly moved off toward the house where she lived with her husband who was nice to her sick mother, and who took care of his own lawn.

PARDON ME

A Blackshaw Short Story

By

Robert Blake Whitehill
With
Erin Blake

A LATE LUNCH at the Bayside Inn on Smith Island was a far better thing than no lunch at all. The Blackshaws with their infant, accompanied by Knocker Ellis, were discovering what life was like on baby time. It was even slower than island time. As a new mom, LuAnna had managed to cram half the contents of their saltbox home into the diaper bag, and that still left some additional gear for Blackshaw and Ellis to haul along in canvas totes. Their first restaurant meal as a family was a big deal, but getting out the door had taken a while.

In a quick glance at the gas dock on their way inside the restaurant, Blackshaw spied the old men of the Smith Island Council, including Reverend Mosby, sitting by the water swapping lies. A couple of these wizened seadogs were making themselves comfortable on somebody's big new fish box. The thing looked like a white plastic coffin.

When everyone was seated—baby Callum was too small yet for a high chair, but LuAnna's lap was fine—Sally Crockett stopped by and cooed at the little one. Almost by reflex, she reached into her server's apron and pulled out a beautiful Christmas tree angel she had crafted from an oyster shell, and gave it to Callum to play with. Sally had barely said, "What can I get you folks today?" before the ornament was snatched into pieces by the young man. No one, least of all Sally, minded a bit.

"Three Cs, please," replied Blackshaw.

"Crab cake and Coke it is," said Sally, jotting. "Ammonia in the Coke?"

"*Spirit* of ammonia," said Blackshaw. "I'm not cleaning the bathroom."

"When do you ever?" said LuAnna eyeing Blackshaw. Then to Sally, "And please put that precious decoration on the tab. It's just five minutes and a hot glue gun away from its original glory."

"The usual," said Ellis as he slouched comfortably in his chair.

"You love shrimp and Birch beer," Blackshaw chuckled.

Ellis sat up to say, "Don't forget my double side of tartar sauce! That completes the meal."

"Have I ever forgotten?" said Sally.

"Never," said Ellis. "And that's why I come to this joint at least twice a week when I'm on the rock. I'm like family here."

Ellis relaxed and focused his attention on LuAnna and the baby.

LuAnna said, "May I please have the cream of crab and an unsweetened iced tea?"

"Of course." Sally scribbled on her pad, and bent again to baby Callum. "Can I get anything for the newest addition?"

"Thank you for asking but he ate already," LuAnna answered adjusting her nursing bra. She ran her hands through the fuzz on top of Callum's head. Feeling his mom's touch, Callum smiled and began whacking the oyster shell on the wooden table.

"Great, I'll put your order in and be right back with your drinks." A moment of silence fell among the grownups. All eyes watched the little one bash the table.

The allure faded. LuAnna caught up the shell and said, "You're in public, young man. Let's not overdo it."

"He sure is cute." Ellis leaned in and slapped Ben's arm. "Who knew you could create something so beautiful, Ben!"

Blackshaw shot Ellis a side-eyed glance. "Cal gets his looks from his mother. You see that face, Ellis? He's the youngest Smith Islander right now."

"I'm sure he'll make your family proud," said Ellis. "In your way, you've made the Blackshaw name an island legacy."

Blackshaw's face darkened at that. "Don't start, Ellis. I wouldn't want him to pick up any bad habits this early. It's a thin line between legacy and nominy."

Blackshaw sat Cal on his knee, and bobbed him up and down to keep his baby from fussing. Callum gawked around the quaint interior of the restaurant, but suddenly was drawn to Ellis's gaze.

"Ben, let me hold him for a second." Callum calmly went into Ellis's arms and introduced himself with a gentle inspection of Ellis's face. Grabbing his nose, poking at his eyes and patting his forehead, Cal seemed to like his new friend.

"Hey buddy, I'm your Uncle Ellis. I'm gonna teach you how to drive your old man around on a boat so someday when I'm older and even more gray, I can just come along for the ride. What do you think?"

Cal bellowed, perhaps not enchanted by the job description. Ellis quickly passed the baby back to his mother.

"Way to go Uncle Ellis. You got a knack with kids," said Blackshaw.

After sniffing at the diaper, LuAnna scratched her chair back across the tile flooring and said, "He's hungry, and Smith Island isn't ready for me to whip out one of my *tig ol' bitties*."

"No bottle yet?" Ellis asked.

"Nope," LuAnna said with a grimace, "Still docking with the mother ship. And he's got a bite like a rockfish, let me tell you. If you boys'll excuse me, I'm going to try and settle him down at home."

"We can take the food out and come with you," Blackshaw said.

"No, Ben. You have business if I recall." LuAnna grabbed a diaper bag, hiked Callum up onto her shoulder, and headed out through the screen door that faced the pier.

Ellis was abashed. "Sorry Ben. I didn't know I'd upset him like that."

"It's nothing personal. He's still figuring out who's got his back. Can I talk to you about something?"

Ellis glanced at Blackshaw, whose once peaceful face was now distraught. Sitting forward in his chair to be properly attentive, Ellis said, "What's on your mind?"

Blackshaw hunched closer to Ellis and checked his six o'clock.

Ellis grew perplexed. "What's up, Ben?"

The words came out in halting dribs and drabs. "Callum's the newest Blackshaw." Ben stopped and placed his head in his hands. His fingers burrowed through his short hair. His broad hands clenched into fists. Looking up at Ellis he continued, "You've seen the crap I put LuAnna through."

Sally's arrival at the table interrupted his thoughts. Sensing tension, the canny server set down their drinks and left without asking if LuAnna's order was for packing up or cancelling.

Blackshaw went on, more measured now. "LuAnna's been through hell and back with me. I've watched time and time again her getting tangled in my messes. Reckon it's been a right merry-go-sorry for her." Fists still clenched, Blackshaw sat back in his chair. "She almost died because of me, Ellis."

Squirming with his turmoil, Blackshaw leaned over the table and grabbed his glass with both hands. "LuAnna's the love of my life. She's gifted me with a new purpose marrying me, and having Cal. I can't put that innocent kid in the line of fire. And I can't bail out on him to fend for himself like my folks did, saddling you with overwatch."

Ellis said, "Ben, I'd love to pull you out of your existential quagmire, but you need to keep it in the here and now."

Looking up, Blackshaw noticed Ellis was fixed on something out the window. Blackshaw glanced at the antique wall clock. It was long past time for the 12:30 boat from Crisfield to pull in with groceries and bed-and-breakfast guests.

Blackshaw slowly turned to look. In the distance he could make out a Black man stepping onto the pier from some type of law enforcement RHIB with a central wheelhouse. The newcomer was dressed for an afternoon of shooting in the English countryside in a lightweight tweed jacket with a wide deep pocket at the lower back for the birds. And those were some spendy looking boots.

The lost hunter was not alone. The rigid-hulled inflatable boat he arrived in was manned by a crew of two—tough looking fellows with military haircuts, and casual civilian clothing that screamed high caliber concealed-carry.

Blackshaw said, "Excuse me," to Ellis, and stood to go meet Pershing Lowry, the FBI's Executive Assistant Director for Counterterrorism and Counterintelligence.

The two men shook hands with grim forbearance, each viewing the other as infrequently useful, yet undesirable at any time.

Blackshaw asked, "Where's your sidekick?"

Lowry thought for a moment, picked his battle, and simply said, "My *wife* Molly is home on bedrest until her time to deliver. Recent events put her under a great strain. I don't have to tell you. How is LuAnna?"

Blackshaw said, "She's none too bad. Feeding Cal as we speak. Congratulations on getting hitched."

"Thanks," said Lowry. "I take it Cal is your son?"

"That he is."

"Congratulations."

"Yup," said Blackshaw. "Thanks. And no, I'm not going to show you pictures of him on my phone."

"Thank God," said Lowry.

The conversation died, and the sounds of distant engines and waterfowl around the pier were punctuated only by Orville Hurley launching a brown plug of Red Man far out into the Big Thorofare. It landed with a splash that attracted a patient pelican known to enjoy chaw in leaf form. In an instant, the bird swooped in, scooped up the plug, and flapped off.

Blackshaw retreated into his native reticence, forcing Lowry to speak first after the excruciating lull. "You have something for me?"

Blackshaw reached into his pocket and handed Lowry a little zip drive, saying, "His whole entire confession is right there."

"Bonamy Screed talked? To *you?*"

Blackshaw was slightly offended by Lowry's tone. "Of course he did. He's a smart man. He saw soon enough there weren't any percentage in clamming up."

Short of finding a laptop, Lowry had to confirm with Blackshaw what the zip drive held. "He confessed to you about killing Lieutenant Cynter."

"Yes," said Blackshaw.

"And how Bin Laden's killing in 2011 was really an abduction to use him to foment a renewed, larger terrorist threat?"

"A-firm. Though he preferred the word *capture.*"

"Was it you who shot Bin Laden in the video?"

"Can't confirm or deny," said Blackshaw staring dead into Lowry's eyes.

"Where are the remains?" Lowry asked. "Of Screed, I mean. We dealt with Bin Laden's already. Deep-sixed. Watched it myself, beginning to end."

"You first," said Blackshaw. "Did you bring what I asked?"

Lowry frowned, removing a letter-size envelope from his inside breast pocket, and said, "It wasn't easy, but this is it."

"Full pardon, or exoneration, or hold harmless for anything you and Molly think I might've done, or been involved in at any point in the past, up to and including right now," said Blackshaw.

"It sunsets tomorrow to give you some leeway," Lowry said.

"I do like me some leeway," Blackshaw admitted.

"It's worded like a deputization of sorts," Lowry explained. "Making you a special government contractor for an unspecified Other Government Agency. It also includes certain clearances that cover a multitude of sins."

"And LuAnna and Knocker Ellis too, doncha know. They were supposed to be noted in it likewise."

"I think you'll find the language suitably comprehensive where they're concerned. But Ben, from here on out, you're on your own starting midnight tomorrow."

"Signed by—"

"The President of the United States," said Lowry in a hush. "We want this business with Screed put to bed for good."

"It's not worth the paper it's written on, is it," said Blackshaw.

Lowry did not hesitate. "The whole thing can disavowed in a heartbeat. So why ask for it if you know it's practically worthless?"

Blackshaw smiled. "LuAnna scrapbooks. I figured it'd tickle her to put it in her latest."

Blackshaw put his hand out for the envelope.

Lowry pulled it back just out of reach, and said, "The remains."

"Keeping a sharp eye on those now, aren't you," said Blackshaw.

"What do you expect given what's happened?"

"Can't blame you one bit," said Blackshaw. "Now, when this whole thing started, you recall you showed me an envelope with the bullet that killed Travis."

Blackshaw removed a small opaque plastic envelope from his front pants pocket and passed it to Lowry, watching his face.

"What's this?" Lowry asked.

Blackshaw said nothing. He just kept watching Lowry until he opened the envelope's pressure seal and looked inside.

"Jesus Christ," Lowry said turning away in disgust. "Is that his—"

"Screed's trigger-finger what killed Travis," said Blackshaw. "Seemed a fitting way to wrap this up."

"Maybe," said Lowry. "Maybe not. You might not be aware, but Screed was left handed."

Blackshaw handed Lowry a second dark plastic envelope. "We weren't a hundred percent on that point ourselves, and Screed hadn't started talking yet."

Lowry tucked the two envelopes in his jacket's game pocket where bloody things belonged.

That's when Blackshaw relieved Lowry of the envelope, and said, "A pleasure doing business with you. That's a lie by the way."

Blackshaw walked back toward the Bayside Inn and his lunch.

"That's it?" asked Lowry. "What about the rest of Screed? How do I know—"

Over his shoulder Blackshaw said, "We got you the confession. We're done. We're out. That fonnyboy is your problem."

Lowry noticed the old men of the Smith Island Council filing past him leaving the pier, including the two men who had been sitting on the big white fish box that looked like a coffin.

"Blackshaw!" Lowry barely contained his frustration.

Blackshaw turned, grinned, and nodded toward the fish box. Lowry went over to it, sensing what he might find inside. To his surprise, the box moved. Lowry unlatched the lid and swung it open. Inside Lowry met the terrified eyes of a bound, gagged Bonamy Screed; his hands were heavily bandaged where his index fingers used to be.

Lowry closed the lid and latched it. Then he kneeled down next to the big fish box as if to retie a shoe, though his boots had no laces of any kind.

Lowry said, "Screed, I'm not placing you under arrest. That's actually bad news for you. Oh, I might bust you after all, maybe read you your rights, but not this minute. It's a long boat ride back to the mainland, and I'll be thinking about you and what you've done all the way. I make your odds of still being aboard when we tie up in Crisfield about 70/30 against."

The FBI man stood up from his pantomime with the nonexistent laces. At a small movement of Lowry's head, his two crewmen stepped ashore and bore the white fish box, which resembled a coffin, to their boat. The box twitched in their hands all the way, and anyone listening closely might have heard something like muffled screams; perhaps it was a distant shore bird with a lot on its mind.

Check out the first two chapters of the next Blackshaw mission:

BLAST

A Ben Blackshaw Novel: Book 6

By

Robert Blake Whitehill

PART 1
SNOW ANGEL

CHAPTER 1

THE SNOW ANGEL was dead, frozen a few inches below the surface of the locked up Chesapeake, which was more an ice field on this December afternoon than a bay. Ben Blackshaw had been out for a walk to clear his head in the frigid breeze, but the corpse was not helping at all.

He shifted to get the setting sun out of his eyes, then turned and looked back north toward Smith Island. He could see a few of his neighbors who were also out strolling on the ice and marveling at a view of their little archipelago, which was almost never possible like this, not without a deadrise workboat's deck under foot.

In the distance, Sonny and Mary Wright were whooping with delight as they whirled donuts on the ice in Wade Joyce's old golf cart. Mary, who was Wade Joyce's widow once Sonny killed him, had wed her husband's murderer in the spirit of true love, and with maybe a squidge of gratitude at being set free from the beatings the cantankerous Wade doled out. In addition to her charm and wisdom, Mary brought a beautiful deadrise to the marriage, the *Mary Todd*, as well as the golf cart.

Blackshaw crouched to examine the body as best he might under the circumstances. The snowfall on top of the ice had melted into the familiar pattern every kid loves flapping and scraping into the white stuff. On closer inspection, Blackshaw thought perhaps the shape in the snow was more like da Vinci's splayed Vitruvian Man, with narrower limbs, and less of the full outline of an angel's flowing robes. He figured the dark clothing on the corpse must have drawn in the sun's warmth to thin the snow like this.

It was damn creepy, Blackshaw admitted to himself, though as a former SEAL, he'd seen death in many forms—many of his own making. He wondered if an old grave in some sunken Chesapeake island cemetery had coughed her up to drift away until this Arctic blast said stop, hold still, make an angel of yourself, and be known again to the living. *Her.* Blackshaw noticed that's how he was thinking of the corpse.

She was face down, but her long hair fanned into an arc of dark stiff tendrils. The hair, the narrow waist, cinched in what looked to be a white apron tied at the back, the denim jeans, these weren't the signs of old burial. This was the Reaper's latest stook in his winter harvest, a harvest likely just beginning.

Blackshaw stood and turned, on the verge of giving a yell for Sonny and Mary to quit fooling, drive over, and have a look and a ponder with him. Instead he saw his friend, Knocker Ellis Hogan, slowly homing in on him across the ice in his Bugatti Veyron.

Ellis was old, without being the least elderly. He had served in Vietnam as MACV-SOG with Blackshaw's father, Dick. After narrowly escaping death from superior officers for whom they'd carried out illegal clandestine missions, Ellis and Dick Blackshaw had staggered back to Smith Island to work the Chesapeake Bay on *Miss Dotsy*, the family's deadrise. Dick Blackshaw had soon abandoned Smith Island to lead hostile assassins away from his people. Ellis had stayed on, working for Ben, culling oysters, helping with crabbing in their seasons. After fifteen years gone without a word, Dick Blackshaw made his return to Smith Island hauling hundreds of millions of dollars of government gold bullion, but with a pack of black bag operatives nipping at his heels. Bloody business followed. Ben Blackshaw gave his half of the fortune to his Smith Island neighbors.

Ellis made no such contribution. Instead, he bought the two million dollar supercar in a fit of grandiosity underwritten by the new and spectacular wealth earned with his new captain. But he'd penned up the car, a sleek snarling beast made for open roads like the Autobahn, or closed tracks like the Nürburgring, in a catawampus old shed with only thirty feet of dirt driveway leading to down to the water that surrounded the tiny hummock his house occupied. Then, in a more poetic moment tinged with boredom, he had cut the roof off the fantastic car, filled the cockpit with dirt, and planted geraniums. Ellis was *that* kind of rich.

As Ellis drew the big car to a stop on the ice next to Blackshaw, it was clear the geraniums were dead now, and the driver's seat, foot well, and pedals had been carefully excavated of topsoil. Earth strewn with old brown flower stems still buried the passenger seat. It looked like Ellis was driving a poorly tended, recently opened grave.

Ellis shut the big rumbling engine down, and the quieter sounds of distant laughter on the breeze returned while he took a gander at the woman in the ice. He turned his deep brown, care-lined face to Blackshaw and said, "I looked out my window, and thought you were out here kneeling. I told myself, *that can't be right.* I had to come out here and see."

"Hey Ellis. Merry Christmas."

"Merry Christmas. Any idea who our popsicle is?"

Blackshaw cast a glance west toward the container ships silhouetted in the channel; they too were frozen in place—at least until a thaw, an ice breaker, or both reopened Baltimore Harbor for business.

"Reckon she's not from around here, Ellis. But we're going to need some tools, some chain, and a few strong backs to bring her home."

CHAPTER 2

CHOAD LAGLEET WATCHED the black site for two weeks before he struck. NSA operatives posing as graduate students at the nearby Universidad de Cantabria in Santander, Spain, manned the rundown second floor apartment across the street from the flat where LaGleet kept his vigil. He had counted a total of six operatives on overwatch inside and out. He wondered if the dons in Spanish Intelligence, the Centro Nacional de Inteligencia, even knew a United States OGA, or Other Government Agency, was interrogating an American detainee over there at the place they'd code named Franco Station like a not-so-funny inside joke. It didn't matter to LaGleet. Faction knew what was up, and Faction was paying LaGleet's bills.

LaGleet saw one of the NSA guys, whom he called Stubby because of his disarmingly small stature and ovoid girth, shuffling down the sidewalk to Franco Station with bag from a local pharmacy in hand. LaGleet grabbed a pen, made a tick-mark on a pad beside two other slashes, and noted the time. That made three NSA operators inside, plus the target. He knew that right now, the other three spooks were actually attending classes at the university to shore up their covers.

Vickers, LaGleet's second in command who had short, dark hair, blue eyes, and a gymnast's compact yet powerful frame, stood near the apartment building finishing a cigarette; she was making sure no other operatives hit the street right away needing a tail. After a few minutes, Vickers was satisfied. She ground the cigarette butt into the sidewalk.

Less than two minutes later, she stepped through the apartment door and joined LaGleet and the four other teammates who were watching a Spanish soap opera while tearing their weapons down and reassembling them in advance the work to come.

LaGleet asked, "What was in Stubby's bag?"

"More bandages and dressings," said Vickers.

"Christ, what the hell are they doing to him?" LaGleet mused.

Vickers sat down at the little dining table in front of her wafer-thin tablet and warmed up its encryption protocols.

She added, "Also an antibiotic. It's over the counter here. Did you know that? The stuff Stubby picked up is pretty heavy duty, like Screed's got fucking MRSA. Did you know in Madrid there are two statues of the guy who discovered penicillin? Dr. Fleming. Anyway, one's right by the bull ring. Getting gored used to mean major infection."

LaGleet asked, "And the other statue—let me guess. The red light district?"

"Bingo," said Vickers.

"All kinds of ways *horny* can ruin your day," said LaGleet.

LaGleet decided to push the strike back ten minutes until Bonamy Screed's interrogators had done whatever was necessary to patch up the disgraced ex-Deputy Director of the FBI. One less thing to handle in transit. He told his team about the slight delay, and then asked, "Everybody ready to dance?"

He got casual nods and *yup*s from the crew. No steely-eyed, grim-faced *affirmative*s or *lock-and-load*s or dramatic yanking and spanking of gun parts that clacked, rattled, and snapped. The team looked like a little group of ordinary tourist moms and dads about to head out for drinks. One of his guys even went to the can for a last pee before the gig. The sheer banality of their appearance, and their utter calm before this snatch and grab job on which they might be wounded or even killed within the next thirty minutes, inspired pride and awe in LaGleet.

Vickers said, "I'm ready to send the follow-up."

"Do it," LaGleet ordered. He stood and moved next to the window peering across the way at Franco Station.

Vickers tapped the tablet once, and said, "Bombs away." Then she drew her pistol, made a quick check of its magazine, and holstered it again. She slipped the tablet into her messenger bag and looped the strap over her shoulder.

From a fake account that appeared to belong to the bursar's office at the University of Cantabria, she had just sent an email to each of the NSA operatives across the street. It said that there was a problem with their tuition payments, and if they did not show up on campus in person within the hour to address the issue (i.e. rectify their accounts), their Schengen student visa applications would be revoked, and the entire matter referred to the Ministerio de Asuntos Exteriores y de Cooperacion, whereupon deportation proceedings would be initiated. Just the kind of shit to terrify a kid on his postbac' year abroad. The wording of the email, in Vicker's excellent Spanish, made it clear that this was the third and final notification the students would receive. Though Vickers had called the email a follow-up, neither a first, nor a second email had ever been sent.

LaGleet didn't expect the entire NSA team at Franco Station to bail out like a fire drill, but if even one operative went back to campus to see what the hell was going on, it would thin the opposition ranks and make the take-down that much easier.

"Holy shit," muttered LaGleet at the window. Stubby and one more spook he'd dubbed Tybalt, because he was actor-handsome and looked like a total hothead, emerged from the apartment building and made an overly casual retreat down the street, glancing over their shoulders at odd times like rank amateurs.

LaGleet moved back to the pad, grabbed the pen, and crossed off two tick-marks. Bonamy Screed had been left in the care of just one spook. Stubby and Tybalt would be gone for thirty minutes at least, depending on whether they grabbed a taxi or walked. They'd be all assholes and elbows to get back to Franco Station once a baffled university bursar explained their tuition payments were current.

"Any phone calls to verify—anything?" asked LaGleet almost incredulously.

Vickers checked an application on her phone and looked up grinning. "Nothing."

"Emails? Cell phone? Sat-phone? Smoke signal?"

"Not even a carrier pigeon," Vickers said.

LaGleet shrugged with smug incomprehension. He said, "Shall we?"

His team, which earlier that morning had voided the flat of all personal effects, and scrubbed out all fingerprints except for a few here and there from preserved anonymous cadaver hands they had brought along for the purpose, got to their feet and headed for the door.

ABOUT ROBERT BLAKE WHITEHILL

Robert Blake Whitehill is a Maryland Eastern Shore native, and an award-winning screenwriter at the Hamptons International Film Festival, and the Hudson Valley Film Festival. In addition, he is an Alfred P. Sloan Foundation award winner for his feature script U.X.O. (Unexploded Ordnance). Whitehill is also a contributing writer to *Chesapeake Bay Magazine* and *The Audiophile Voice*.

Find out more about the author, his blog, upcoming releases, and the Chesapeake Bay at:

www.robertblakewhitehill.com

ABOUT ERIN BLAKE

In addition to creative writing, ERIN BLAKE has used her knowledge of digital development to create the free Blackshaw travel app for visiting Smith Island. Blake hails from Pompton Lakes, New Jersey.

Blackshaw Free Travel App for iOS
https://itunes.apple.com/us/app/blackshaw/id1159429726?mt=8

Blackshaw Free Travel App for Android
https://play.google.com/store/apps/details?id=com.app.swjrtgku
qrpveflmnzzipuvdiafxybkndwygscmqlbo&hl=en